A COVERT ACTION THRILLER

STONE-COLD
VENGEANCE

GW00771084

THE JAKE STONE FILES
PETER B. DUNFIELD

Stone-Cold Vengeance
Copyright © 2023 by Peter B. Dunfield

ISBN
978-0-2288-9155-0 (Hardcover)
978-0-2288-9153-6 (Paperback)
978-0-2288-9154-3 (eBook)

ALSO BY PETER B. DUNFIELD

Middle-Grade Storyline Adventure Series:
Pirates' Gold
The Magic Realm
Jack Through Time

For
Mary Berg and Tammy L. Houts.
Without your relentless positive encouragement,
this book may never have been written.

CHAPTER

1

The street—if you could call it a street—was abandoned except for a group of feral dogs packed together farther down the rutted dirt trail. As I stepped out of the air-conditioned rental car, the heat hit me in the face like a baseball bat. My shirt tightened against my body like the casing on a breakfast sausage sizzling in a frying pan. A soft breeze fluttered in my ears, but rather than bring cooling relief, it only hastened the internal cooking of my body. The acrid stench of stale urine assaulted my senses. I gagged as it infiltrated my nostrils and clung to the back of my tongue. The multiple stains running down the structure's outer walls showed this was the apparent source of the foul smell. The local clientele and stray dogs clearly used the building to relieve themselves.

A faded sign over the door indicated this was the place I was looking for—the El Patrón Taverna. Unfortunately, like the rest of this so-called town, the taverna left much to be desired. The El Patrón was a broken-down adobe shack with a red and white sign for a national brand of beer hanging at a sharp angle from a single chain on a post near the front door. The other chain had long ago rusted through, leaving the sign to swing precariously in the gentle breeze. Thermal waves rose from the old corrugated tin roof. The place looked more like a solar-powered oven than a tavern, and I wondered what I would find baking inside.

It had been a week since I last heard from my daughter, Gabby. I'll never understand what prompted her to come to this God-forsaken place for a vacation. Despite her mother and me trying to talk her out of it, there was no changing her mind. Even though I still thought of Gabby as my little girl, she is a thirty-year-old woman with my adventurous spirit and her mother's stubbornness. Once she made up her mind, there was no changing it. So, we settled on a non-negotiable pact. Gabby would call home every other night when she returned to her hotel. No exceptions. This agreement worked well on her previous escapades into other foreign hinterlands, so I had little reason to believe it wouldn't work again. She had called in faithfully for the first week to update us on her adventures.

Then several days went by with total silence and no contact. On the fourth day, without hearing from her, I tried phoning, but she didn't answer. The calls went straight to voicemail. That worried me, and of course, her mother, Gloria, wouldn't accept my attempts to explain why she hadn't called in. I told her, 'Things like this happen all the time. I'm sure she's fine and probably just forgot. We'll hear from her anytime now, and she'll tell us she's having the time of her life.' None of that worked with Gloria, who was inconsolable. The obvious solution, according to Gloria, was for me to pack a bag and get on the first flight down to Colombia to find our daughter.

Less than two hours ago, I had checked into the only hotel in town and pre-paid for three nights. The mouse-faced clerk at the front desk wasn't much help when I asked where I could find Gabby. He claimed there was no one registered at the hotel by her name, even though this was where she told us she was staying. The kid was a terrible liar and didn't hide it well. The signs were obvious, like not looking me in the eye. His constant fidgeting with his hands and shuffling his feet were also clear giveaways. I slipped him fifty bucks and asked him again. He looked around as if he was being watched and stammered that for any information in this area, I needed to talk with Don Juan Patrón. Apparently, he owned this taverna and this entire shithole excuse for a town. Mouse boy told me the man I was looking for would be here, in his namesake bar every day at this time. It was time to meet the man and find out where I could find Gabby.

I climbed the rotting wooden steps, careful not to break through into God-knows-what below, pushed the door open, and stepped inside. I'm not sure what I expected—air conditioning would have been nice—but no luck there. A solitary overhead fan squealed and complained as it tried unsuccessfully to move the thick heat around. The place looked deserted, except for a girl behind the bar. She cast me a nervous glance, then quickly looked toward the back of the room. I guess the guy I'm here to see is back there. I followed her gaze and moved in that direction. As I descended deeper into the dimly lit tavern, I couldn't help but notice the strange collection of heads mounted on the walls. It was the typical shit one might expect to see in an old, run-down, wild west-styled saloon out in the sticks. Things like rabbits with antlers, the sun-bleached skull of a longhorn steer, and other local animal heads. Either someone had a weird sense of decorating, or they just enjoyed hanging dead stuff on the walls to remind them of their hunting prowess.

Against the back wall sat a mountain of a human being in a dirty, sweat-stained straw hat slung low across his brow. The mouse-faced clerk at the hotel told me Don Juan Patrón was a big man, but big does him a disservice. This guy was massive. To call him obese would have been a gross understatement. He was at least 400 pounds, with blubber cascading from his multiple chins and jowls. It looked like he had swallowed a basketball with his protruding gut and rolling layers of lard hanging across his massive thighs. From what I could see, he was straddling a pair of chairs straining under his weight.

As I approached, he reached out with a massive pulpy paw, grabbed a handful of nachos smothered in cheese and peppers, and stuffed it into the gaping maw where a mouth should have been. A dog sprang to life, snarling and barking as I neared the table. With a sweep of his arm, he smacked the mutt across its snout, and it crawled away, whimpering back into a dark corner.

The man looked up from under the brim of his hat, tilted his head to one side, and stared at me before removing it and placing it on the table. Greasy, thin wisps of comb-over plastered against his scalp did little to hide the massive bald area. Rivulets of sweat drained down the sides of his bulbous face, soaking his stained shirt.

Other than the constant squealing complaint of the overhead fan, a deafening silence spread between us and hung in the air for a few moments as we assessed each other. The only sound was.

I took the initiative to start the conversation. "The clerk at the hotel said I was to come here and see Don Juan Patrón for information. Are you Senor Patrón?"

He scanned me closely, then responded, "I am Don Juan Patrón. What is it you want to know, Señor?"

"I was told you could provide me with information about my missing daughter, Gabby Stone."

He beckoned for me to sit at the table across from him. I didn't want to piss this guy off by appearing rude, so I pulled out the flimsy white plastic chair and sat.

"Ah, yes. You are the one who is looking for your daughter. I was told you were here in town. But what makes you think she is missing? She is a young woman on vacation in our wonderful country, is she not? Maybe she is just too busy to call you, Señor?"

"Gabby never forgets to call in when she's away on vacation, which makes me believe something has happened to her."

"I see. Information is an expensive commodity here, Señor. However, I believe I can help. For the right price, of course."

This guy was pissing me off. Not just his physical appearance but his entire attitude. "How much do you want?" I asked.

"Five hundred dollars, my friend. But first, we will have a drink together." He waved to the girl behind the bar and called for two tequilas.

The last thing I wanted to do was sit down and socialize with this guy. So I made a waving gesture with my hand and said, "I'm not thirsty. How about we get on with you telling me how I can find my daughter, shall we?"

He stared into my eyes with a dead expression. "I didn't ask you if you were thirsty, Señor. It is not polite to conduct business without sharing a drink. Don't you think?"

I knew when I was in a poor negotiating position, and he knew he was holding all the cards. The last thing I wanted to do was get on this guy's wrong side, at least until after he told me what I needed to know. So, I accepted his offer of a drink.

"Okay, just one drink," I said.

The girl cautiously approached the table with shaky hands, placed a shot glass of tequila in front of each of us, then vanished back to the bar.

Don Juan Patrón held up his shot glass and stared into my eyes. The expectation was clear. He wanted me to raise my glass, salute him, and recognize his position of authority before downing the amber fluid. So I picked up my glass as we stared each other down, held it out toward him, then placed it to my lips and swallowed the shot in one gulp. That was a bit of a mistake. Now, I enjoy a good sipping tequila from time to time, but this was horrible stuff. It tasted like kerosene and burned like a flamethrower as it went down. He downed his drink, and a hint of a smile crossed his face.

"Good, no? Would you like another one, Señor?"

My throat was burning from the fiery concoction, and I wasn't sure my vocal cords were still functioning. I shook my head and waved off his suggestion.

He continued to watch my expressions closely. "And the money, Señor?"

I had expected the need to bribe the locals. It was one constant about visiting third-world countries like this, so I had brought a sizable pile of cash with me. I pulled a wad of bills from my pocket, counted out five hundred dollars, and pushed it across the table. His massive paw whisked the cash off the table in the blink of an eye.

He looked up and said, "Have you heard of the El Presidente Resort? It is about five kilometers south of here along the beach. The resort has been abandoned for a long time, except for some enterprising young men and the occasional wild donkey."

"I can find it. Will my daughter be there? Is she safe?" I searched the vast expanse of his face for any signs of empathy or compassion. Instead, I saw only a cold emptiness in his eyes. His inscrutable features were a blank page. He was probably a killer poker player.

"I believe she will be there tonight, after dark, Señor."

"Good, then I'll be on my way. Thank you, Señor Patrón."

I pushed my chair back, preparing to stand when he coughed and motioned for me to stay seated.

"It may be dangerous for you to go there without protection, Señor." He placed a pistol on the table with a loud clunk and slid it toward me.

I nodded my head and placed my hand on the gun.

He clamped his greasy mitt on top of mine and said, "But, this will cost you another five hundred dollars, my friend."

How he got the idea we might be friends is beyond me, but I know a shakedown when I'm in one. So, I peeled off the cash and put it beside the gun. Again, my money vanished at lightning speed. I slid the gun under my belt and pulled my soggy shirt over it. With our business completed, it was time for me to get the hell out of there.

"Thank you, Señor. I appreciate the information and, of course, the other protection." I patted the gun under my shirt, stood, and walked out. I glanced up and down the dirt street and returned to my rental car before the feral dogs caught my scent.

Several questions and scenarios raced through my suspicious mind while driving back to the hotel. What will I find at the abandoned resort? Will Gabby be there, and will she be safe if she is? Will I get us out of there alive? All good questions with no clear answers. I would have to play it by ear and improvise when I went there this evening.

The only blessing on the trip back to my hotel was the cold breeze blowing from the air conditioner vents helping to lower my body temperature to slightly less than a full fever.

CHAPTER

2

I was physically and emotionally spent by the time I returned to the hotel, mainly from the oppressive heat and humidity and not so much from the tense interactions with Don Juan Patrón. As a retired field agent for a covert intelligence agency, I had dealt with assholes like him frequently enough in the past. His type is a dime a dozen throughout the third world. But the heat and humidity in this country just south of the Panama Canal really knocked me out.

I stripped out of my sweat-soaked clothing and stood over the bathroom sink with a pile of shaving cream in one hand and a razor in the other. Before spreading the lather across my cheeks and chin, I took stock of myself in the chipped and grimy mirror. At six foot, one inch tall, I still carried myself well for a guy my age. My lean, fit body had held up well for a sixty-year-old, even though the last five years of retirement had added a few unwanted pounds. My lightly flecked salt and pepper hair seemed to move more toward the salt end of the aging curve every day, but there was still a hint of ginger red in my mustache. I smiled as I remembered the many times I teased Gloria about how my genes gave our daughter, Gabby, her gorgeous light auburn hair. But, of course, Gloria believed that her natural red highlights were responsible for Gabby's hair color. She could be right about that, but I stubbornly held onto the belief that the truth lay somewhere between Gloria's view and mine.

I lathered up, scraped the three-day-old whiskers off my face, and then took a long, cool shower. I grabbed a beer out of the mini-fridge and lay naked on the bed, letting the slow-moving air from the overhead fan dry me off.

The questions I had while driving back to my hotel still rattled around in my mind. Although my confidence usually runs high in ambiguous situations like this, the current crisis involved my daughter, and that significantly raised the stakes and tension. Sipping on the ice-cold beer helped lower my internal body temperature. A soothing, cold shock shivered through my brain and down my spine as I placed the bottle on my forehead. Man, that feels good.

I rolled over and grabbed my phone off the bedside table. Time to call home. Gloria would be catatonic by now. I speed-dialed her cell, and she answered in the middle of the first ring. Jeez, was she sitting on the phone or what?

"Hello? Is that you, Jake?"

"Yeah. How are you holding up, Gloria? Are you okay?"

"Are you kidding me? You keep me in the dark all this time, and the best you can do is ask if I'm okay. You son of a—"

I gotta say, Gloria is one tough woman. As long as we've been together, we've known how to push each other's buttons in a playful, teasing way. But there are times when she is deadly serious, and I knew this was one of those times. So I had to do my best to diffuse the tension and keep things loose, so neither of us lost focus on what I was here to do.

"Whoa, whoa, whoa. Hang on a minute, Gloria. I left home less than twenty-four hours ago, and most of that time was bumping around on single-engine stubble jumpers or scrambling through remote airports. So this is the first chance I've had to call in."

"Okay, but you better keep me in the loop from now on."

I smiled as the tension in her voice dropped. "Got it. Momma's gotta stay on top of the situation. Don't worry. I'll keep you posted from now on."

"You better. So, how's Gabby?"

Even as I opened my mouth to speak, I realized I should have chosen my words better. "Well... about that. I haven't actually found her—"

It was like a bomb went off in my ear as she snapped into the phone, "Are you freaking kidding me? Where is she? What the hell have you been doing all this time?"

"Relax, Gloria. Take a deep breath... in through your nose, now release and calm down."

"Don't give me that calm down bullshit and tell me what the hell is going on and where our daughter is."

I took my own advice and inhaled deeply to calm myself before continuing. "Listen, I've been busy gathering information from some... well, let's say... interesting characters. I've got a strong lead, and I plan to meet with her tonight."

"What do you mean, interesting characters and strong lead? You either have her, or you don't. Which is it?"

"Trust me, Gloria. I've got this."

"Trust you? That's what you said in Guatemala, and look how that turned out."

"Oh, come on, not the old Guatemalan thing again. You always bring that up. You really should let that one go. After all, everything worked out fine in the end, didn't it?"

"Well, yes, but...."

"This time, I really have it under control. Things are going to be fine. I promise."

"Okay, just get our girl out of there safely. And Jake, if you let anything happen to her, I promise the authorities will never find your body when I'm done with you."

"Hey, come on. There's no need for threats—"

"That's not a threat, Jake. It's a promise. Just get her home safely, and don't mess this up."

"That's the plan. But, look, I gotta get ready to go. I'll call you when we're back at the hotel later tonight."

"Okay. And Jake, be careful out there. I love you."

"I love you too, Gloria. Talk to you later."

I hung up and stared into the blank screen on my phone. Good God, I better get a plan in place. Despite all my blustering bravado with Gloria, a couple of things were certain. If I didn't get Gabby back safely, not only would I be dead inside and never forgive myself. But I'd also have to answer to Gloria for my failure. And neither prospect was appealing.

I know all too well that when Gloria sets her mind on a course of action, she is more ruthless and cold-blooded than any enemy agent I have ever dealt with. And as a retired field agent herself, she has a unique set of skills to carry out her threats, or promises, as she calls them.

I flipped through a few screens on my phone and noted a news article about how tonight's full moon would be a total lunar eclipse. Coincidently, as luck would have it, one of the best locations to see it was right here in northern Colombia. The article explained that the lunar eclipse would reach total darkness at about midnight. I wasn't sure what to make of this, but I tucked the information away in the back of my mind. You never know when some obscure piece of data will come in handy.

Okay, time to get a plan in place. I needed to review my options with only a few hours until sundown. I unfolded a tourist map I had grabbed from the lobby and located the abandoned El Presidente Resort. So far, Don Juan Patrón has not steered me wrong. The map showed it was a quick drive from my hotel and easily accessible from the beach. I could park just north of the property and walk a short distance along the shore to the resort compound.

I took out the revolver Patrón sold me and inspected it. A solid .38 caliber Smith & Wesson with six rounds in the cylinder. That should be enough to do some damage if necessary. Or at least I could hold my own if it came to a stand-off.

I opened the cylinder and dumped the cartridges into my hand. Are you freaking kidding me? I stared in disbelief as a wave of anger washed through me. How could I make such a rookie mistake? They were blanks. That piece of shit, Patrón. A lot of protection this thing would give me. And for five hundred bucks, I at least expected a functional weapon. The only thing this would be good for is bluffing my way out of a confrontation. And that didn't give me a good feeling.

Well, it was back to square one, and the need to improvise. It occurred to me that any bad dudes I may come across won't know me, nor will they know my gun is useless. So bluffing would have to be my go-to move. I reloaded the blanks and put the gun away.

The next few hours ticked off slowly to the constant swooping rhythm of the overhead fan, marked by the periodic squeal of a bad bearing in the motor. The sun slowly set behind a grove of palm trees as dusk crept across the landscape. Finally, it was time to mount up and get going. I dressed in my darkest clothes and packed the rest of my stuff into the suitcase. Having pre-paid for three nights was incidental. There was no way I would come back this way after I found Gabby. We'll be heading straight out of town and getting as far from this place as the rental car would take us.

I tucked the revolver into my belt behind my back and folded the loose shirt over the top. Then I grabbed my bag, slipped down the back stairs, and went out to the car. I didn't want to announce my intentions by going through the lobby with my suitcase, so leaving out the back unseen was the right move.

CHAPTER

3

Sunsets in this area are spectacular light shows of blazing colors. And moments after the sun drops below the mountains, complete darkness rapidly closes in. As I drove south to the turnoff marked on the map, the natural light had already vanished, replaced by inky black skies in all directions. Nevertheless, the tourist map from the hotel lobby was pretty accurate, and I had no difficulty finding the long-abandoned El Presidente Resort. I turned north on the frontage road and slowly drove past the deserted complex. Tall palm trees rose above a solid ten-foot-high brick wall surrounding the front and sides of the dark, quiet compound. A broken-down wire fence sagged across a wide gap in the wall—probably an old access driveway into the resort.

I hoped the rear of the compound along the beach was open for easy access and not blocked by a brick wall like the front and sides. Several hundred yards north of the resort, I found the dirt lane that led to the beach and turned off the main road. As I drove toward the beach, I searched for a place to park the car where anyone going past wouldn't see it. A large grove of bougainvillea seemed like the perfect place to stash the vehicle. I figured it was unlikely anyone would come by this way at night. But, as I always say, it's better to be careful than dead. That's probably one of

Murphy's Laws. You know Murphy. He's the guy who said, "If anything can go wrong, it will." Well, tonight, I was making sure I addressed any possible glitches, so this operation would go off without a hitch. And it better go smoothly, or Gloria will kill me if the bad guys don't get me first.

I left the car parked out of sight under the flowering bushes and walked toward the beach. The gentle, raspy surf caressing the shore sounded like a giant, asthmatic beast deeply breathing as it slept. The sound of the waves covered my approach as I made my way toward the dark, brooding structures of the resort several hundred yards down the beach. The huge silvery plate of the full moon rose from behind an island off the coast. Its pale, white light cast a glistening beam across the bay's calm surface, providing enough light for me to pick my way along the rocky shore.

As I neared the back of the compound, my senses kicked into hyperdrive. With my head on a swivel, I searched the darkness in all directions, and my ears tuned in for any unnatural sounds. All was quiet. Almost too quiet for my liking. One thing was evident, though; back in its day, this place would have been an absolute gem as a destination to get away from the craziness of life.

The rocky shore gave way to a long stretch of soft white sand immediately behind the resort. About halfway across the beach, I saw signs of human life for the first time. A deep groove cut into the sand, and scuff marks suggested someone had beached a boat here not too long ago. As I inspected the scene, I noted three sets of footprints led away from the beach toward the dark compound. But oddly, only one set of footprints returned to the water's edge. That got my well-tuned senses tingling. Why are three sets of prints going in and only one coming out? And where is the boat? Something's not right about this.

The cloak of darkness folded tighter around me as I followed the footprints from the water's edge toward the rear of the resort. From somewhere within the overgrown compound, the braying of a donkey let me know I was not alone. The footprints merged onto a narrow path, passed through a hole in the fence, and veered away from the abandoned resort's broken-down, dilapidated structures. The pale light from the moon cast long, eerie shadows from the tall plants around me, making it difficult to see where I was going.

I stopped to look more closely at the surrounding vegetation. This was not a natural growth of random bushes and scrub trees. Instead, I was walking through a carefully cultivated field of well-manicured plants. This was clearly somebody's crop. The pungent smell was unmistakable—a blend of skunk and cut grass with a hint of citrus and pine brought back memories from my teenage years—marijuana. The potent odor reminded me of the dime bags of Colombian weed from the early '70s. But this well-groomed crop, laden with heavy buds, was far more powerful than what passed for pot back then. This stuff would be like drinking whiskey as compared to lite beer.

People who grow crops like this seldom leave them unguarded, whether by personnel or booby traps. That made my senses tingle even more than earlier. I turned my attention to searching for tripwires. Standing motionless, I got a better feel of my surroundings and carefully considered my next steps. I checked the path for signs of traps but found nothing, so I continued forward with more caution. Up ahead, in the darkness, a ghostly apparition drifted across my field of vision. My heart jumped into my throat, and my pulse pounded in my ears. I strained to focus on the ethereal being as it stopped, slowly turned its head, and stared at me. A shiver ran through me as the beast emitted an eerie, almost laughter-like braying sound as if mocking my presence. The albino donkey turned away and silently vanished back into the darkness from where it had appeared.

I pressed onward, following the footprints along the narrow path. The moon slowly passed behind a cloud, no longer helping my cause. Then, ahead in the darkness came another sound. I stopped and listened, my body on high alert. There it was again— faint yet demanding voices from not too far away. Careful to not make a sound, I silently crept forward. I pulled aside a couple of plants and peered into a small clearing. A terrifying scene was playing out in the yellow glow of a small, flickering fire. I knelt behind the dense vegetation and tried to make sense of the images in front of me.

Three men armed with assault rifles stood near the fire. Their forearms were inked with similar tattoos—clearly gang insignias. A young man and woman were digging shallow holes to one side. The man seemed more interested in what the armed guards were doing than shoveling. The young woman sobbed uncontrollably and begged them to let her go.

The woman had her back to me, so I couldn't see her face, but there was something familiar about her. Her long, naturally wavy, light auburn hair hung over her shoulders and covered the sides of her face. A sudden rush of recognition struck me. The woman was my daughter, Gabby. What the hell is going on here?

Surveying the scene more closely, I concluded that Gabby and her friend were being forced to dig their graves. If that were the case, then they would soon be executed. And I didn't have a moment to lose to stop this before it was too late.

A rush of thoughts raced through my mind as I processed the scene, searching for possible actions I could take. Clearly, my weapon was no match for their firepower. What hope do I have with a revolver filled with blanks against these armed thugs? But I had to do something to rescue Gabby and her friend. The only actual weapon I had was the element of surprise. My time for action came with the abrupt barking of orders from the gang's leader. The other two thugs grabbed the shovels away from the kids and forced them to their knees in the shallow graves.

I had to act, and I had to move now. But, as I rose for my surprise attack, the dynamics in the clearing changed, causing me to hesitate and hold back.

CHAPTER

4

My heart pounded against my shirt as I watched from the shadows, preparing to make my move. Gabby begged for her life as the thugs aimed their guns at her and her friend. But something didn't seem right to me. The young man with her wasn't upset or pleading for his life. He was too calm and casual about the situation. It all became clear and made more sense when he stepped out of the shallow grave and stood beside the armed men.

Gabby looked up at him in disbelief. "What are you doing, Juan Carlos? Do you know these men?"

The three gang members laughed, and one man patted him on the shoulder.

"Yes, Senorita Gabrielle. These are my men. Unfortunately, you and I will part ways here. It was fun while it lasted, but you wouldn't stop pushing me for information about my business practices."

Gabby spit at Juan Carlos. "You bastard. I trusted you and thought we had a strong connection."

"Ah, you are such a fun and spirited girl, Gabrielle. I will be sad to see you gone, but my life will continue, whereas... your life... will not. Adios, mi amiga," he said casually as his men laughed.

I'd heard enough. My hastily conceived plan was to burst into the clearing, tackle the nearest thug, and wrestle the gun away from him. Everything after that would evolve organically. As I rose in the darkness, preparing for my assault, I felt the cold, hard steel of a gun pressed against the back of my neck. I froze where I stood. Somewhere in the darkness, the albino donkey brayed in a laughing tone as it mocked my futile attempt to execute the rescue.

The gunman prodded me through the vegetation into the clearing and forced me into the shallow grave beside Gabby.

She wiped the tears from her eyes and stared at me in disbelief. "Dad? What are you doing here?" she whimpered softly.

"Isn't it obvious, Gabs? I'm here to rescue you."

She almost smiled at the futility of my statement. But, instead, as I hugged her, she sobbed into my shoulder.

"I'm so sorry, Dad."

"Don't worry, sweetie, we'll have plenty of time to discuss this later." Then I whispered. "I need you to be ready to run when I make my move."

"Ah, how touching. A family reunion. But sadly, it won't be long," Juan Carlos said.

In a quick, fluid motion, I spun around, hoping to catch them off guard, as I pulled the revolver from behind my back, and leveled it at Juan Carlos.

"Drop your weapons, or I'll shoot him!" I said with as much conviction as possible, given the circumstances.

The gunmen looked at each other and laughed. While they were enjoying themselves, a massive, dark shape emerged from the foliage on the other side of the clearing—Don Juan Patrón.

"Oh, I don't think you will have much luck with that, Senor Stone," he said, pointing at my pistol. "Juan Carlos, my son, our plan worked to perfection. Not only do we have the meddling girl, but we also have her father. Welcome, Senor Stone, to our tidy little business venture. As you can see, your daughter is alive, as I assured you she would be. But, unfortunately, neither of you will be for long."

This Patrón guy is such an enormous pile of shit. With my bluff exposed, my only hope would be the effects of the lunar eclipse. I glanced at my watch. With only five minutes left until the total lunar eclipse, I had to stall and buy some time.

"Don Juan Patrón, you're a real bastard, but you're also a father. So I beg you to give me a few last moments with my daughter to say goodbye."

"Now, there is no reason to get personal or throw insults here. We are both parents, are we not? And, of course, I am a civilized man, not a monster. So please take as long as you like to say goodbye to your daughter, Senor Stone."

Are you kidding me? Civilized man, my ass. This guy was an emotionless pig who would look good with a bullet hole in his forehead.

I held Gabby tight and whispered. "Listen closely, Gabs, and don't ask questions. Just do as I say, and we'll both be okay."

She nodded as she stared up at me through wet, bloodshot eyes.

I gently swept the hair away from her face, tucked it behind her ears, wiped the tears off her cheeks with my thumbs, then took her face in my hands and held her gaze.

"Gabby, I need you to trust me," I whispered. "When the fighting starts, run as fast as you can toward the beach, and don't look back for any reason. Do you understand?"

She nodded as the fear on her face slipped away, replaced by a look of focused resolve. She had her game face on—the look of determination she used to get as a young girl when faced with stiff competition during her youth soccer games. The look signaled the competitive spirit rising inside her to meet and overcome the challenges she faced. I love it when she has that look.

I whispered in her ear, "There's a vehicle stashed behind some bushes on a dirt road just up the beach. Get there, and I'll meet you on the street in front of the resort. But under no circumstances are you to wait for me. If I'm not there when you drive by, keep going and find your way to the consulate in Barranquilla. Understood?"

She nodded again, but a shadow of doubt and concern returned to her eyes.

I checked over my shoulder. Don Juan Patrón and his gang gathered in a tight group near the fire. No one cared enough to watch us, and their overconfidence would work in my favor. I slipped the car keys into Gabby's hand and kissed her cheek.

"I love you, Gabby."

Tears welled in her eyes again. "I love you too, Dad. Please be careful."

The lunar eclipse was progressing, slowly blocking out more and more of the moon's light. The idiots with the guns obviously hadn't noticed the surrounding area darkening as they stood in the glowing flicker of light from the small fire.

I let go of Gabby and stepped away, positioning myself as a shield between her and the gunmen. With her sheltered behind me, she had a slightly better chance of getting away when the action started.

I needed to stall until the lunar eclipse peaked and the area became darker.

"So, Don Juan Patrón, I understand Juan Carlos is your son and partner in your crime family?" I said.

"Yes, he is my right-hand man. But enough small talk, my friend. It is time to end our business. Juan Carlos, take care of these two." He handed his son a pistol and a magazine of bullets.

There he goes again with that 'my friend' bullshit. His English tutor must have forgotten to explain what the term meant.

Juan Carlos took the gun and slammed the magazine into the handle. But interestingly, he didn't cycle the slide to load a cartridge into the firing chamber. Without cycling the slide, the gun wouldn't fire.

He stepped forward and pointed the Glock semi-automatic pistol at me. "Turn around, Senor Stone." He waved the gun, directing me to turn my back to him.

I turned away from him, and he pressed the gun's muzzle against the back of my head. Juan Carlos looked over his shoulder at his friends, laughed, then said, "This will be over in a second, Senor Stone."

I looked deeply into Gabby's eyes and winked. A look of terror spread across her face. I only hoped she would follow my instructions and run when the action started.

A moment later, the gun clicked but didn't fire. That was my opening, and I wouldn't let the moment pass. As I sprung into action, everything slowed down for me. I've heard it said when you're in a traumatic situation like a car accident or other life-threatening event, time seems to slow down, and seconds seem like minutes. It probably happens when your consciousness suddenly expands, throwing all your senses into hyperdrive, which allows you to process more detailed information in a shorter period. As a result, you witness the action as if you're in a slow-motion movie. At the same time, you remain the only person operating at normal speed.

As Juan Carlos examined the gun in his hand with a confused look, I stood, spun around, and kicked him in the balls. He yelled in pain, dropped the pistol, and clutched his groin with both hands as he went down sideways, hitting the ground hard.

I grabbed the gun, cycled the slide, chambered a cartridge, and fired two rounds into his chest.

A stunned silence hung over the clearing before the unsuspecting thugs realized what had happened.

"Now, Gabby! Go and don't look back," I yelled, looking over my shoulder. She was already gone, vanishing into the bushes in full flight. At five foot, ten inches tall, the long, athletic legs that carried her to track and soccer championships in high school and college now took her to safety. A smile crossed my face. What a good kid. So much like her mother. Then I got back to business.

In the growing chaos, I fired off another two rounds, dropping the nearest gunman before he could raise his weapon. Then, as if suddenly awakened from a dream, Don Juan Patrón snapped back to reality and barked orders to his men. He stumbled backward away from the action, heading toward the front of the compound.

Good God, he moves fast for such a giant tub of lard. But you're not getting away that easily, Patrón.

I knelt on one knee, steadied the pistol with both hands, aimed, and pulled the trigger. A look of shock and disbelief swept over his massive, bulbous face as the bullet found its mark. A dark circle formed in the middle of his forehead. Patrón dropped to his knees, jiggling like so much jellied aspic salad falling from a plate on its way to a Thanksgiving dinner table.

Now, that's the perfect ending for Don Juan Patrón and an aspic salad, I thought as a smile crossed my face. But I didn't have time to relish in his demise. Bullets zipped wildly past in my direction. Time to move.

I pumped two rounds into the campfire, shattering the glowing logs. A torrent of molten ash and smoke exploded upward as the fire flared brightly, creating more chaos. It was just enough of a distraction for me to bolt across the clearing as the gunmen struggled to regain their night vision in the burst of light from the fire.

I ran past Patrón and into the bushes toward the front of the compound. Bullets snapped wildly at the foliage around me as I came to a broken-down wire fence across a gap in the perimeter wall. Headlights approached from the north along the frontage road. I clambered over the fence, hit the ground, and ran out into the street as Gabby drove past in the rental car. I pressed my tongue against my upper front teeth and whistled. The brake lights glowed as the car slowed enough for me to run up and pull open the driver's door.

"Slide over, Gabs. I'll take it from here," I said.

She slid across and buckled into the passenger seat. I jumped in, slammed the door, and hit the accelerator. Then, in the corner of my eye, a ghostly pale apparition ran beside the car on the passenger side.

"Sorry big guy, there's no room to take you with us," I said.

As we pulled away, the albino donkey brayed a melancholy tone. Apparently, the beast didn't want to be left behind with the thugs. I glanced in the rearview mirror as the pale phantom wandered back into the hotel compound and vanished into the night.

CHAPTER

5

I pressed hard on the accelerator as the dark outline of the overgrown El Presidente Resort faded into the night behind us. Gabby fidgeted with her hands and shifted in her seat beside me.

I glanced at her, then back to the road. "Are you okay, Gabs?" I said, taking her trembling hand in mine and giving it a comforting squeeze. "What happened back there was pretty disturbing. Do you want to talk about it?"

Gabby looked at me. "Yeah, I'm freaked out about that and pissed off at myself for trusting that asshole, Juan Carlos. But I'm also confused about how you knew where to find me. And those gunshots... how did you get away without being shot?"

I was afraid she might bring this up. Gloria and I agreed many years ago to shelter Gabby from our real occupations. Still, we knew the time would come when we'd have to explain everything to her.

"It's a long story, Gabs, and we'll have lots of time to talk about it on our way home. As for the gunshots, I'll say that bastard Juan Carlos won't be treating any other women the way he treated you. In the meantime, you might want to consider what you'll tell your mom. She's beside herself worrying about the mess you got into down here. But as I said, we'll have lots of time to talk about that other stuff when we get home."

I rolled to a stop at the turnoff to the main highway. A large sign with an arrow pointing to the right showed the city of Barranquilla was 250 kilometers north. I rechecked the fuel gauge. With almost a full tank, we had plenty of fuel to get us there. I turned north and gunned it.

I felt Gabby's eyes glaring at me in the glow of the dashboard lights.

She broke the awkward silence and said, "Come on, Dad. I thought we were going to die back there, and all you're going to say is, we'll talk about it when we get home. Well, that's not good enough. You might not want to talk about this, but I need some answers. And before I forget, thank you for coming to the rescue when you did."

"Anytime, sweetie. Well, maybe not anytime. Let's not make a habit of this, okay?"

Gabby chuckled nervously, unbuckled her seatbelt, and slid over beside me. I put my free arm over her shoulder and gave her a squeeze. She leaned in and laid her head against my chest the way she used to do as a little girl on long road trips. A broad smile stretched across my face as I remembered those less stressful, non-life-threatening times. But, after the last two days, they seemed like a lifetime ago.

"I love you, Dad."

"I love you too, Gabs. Try to get some sleep. We still have a long way to go before we get you home."

Gabby yawned again and softly said, "What are our next steps?"

"Our first stop will be the international airport in Barranquilla to purchase tickets on the first flight out of this hell-hole country. How does that sound?"

There was a short, uncomfortable silence as she looked up at me. "Ah... I think we have a problem with that plan. When the gang members grabbed me, they took my passport and wallet. So I don't have any identification to get out of the country."

"Not to worry, that's just a minor wrinkle. We'll deal with that at the consulate. Your mom knows a guy who works there. He'll fix you up with a replacement passport in no time."

Gabby sat up and stared at me with a questioning look. "Mom knows a guy at the consulate in Colombia? Who are you guys?"

"That's another long story that's best saved for another time. Don't worry about it now." I needed to change the subject fast. I handed her my cell phone. "Hey, why don't you call your mom and tell her you're safe?"

She put the cell phone on speaker, punched in the number, and Gloria answered immediately.

"Jake, is that you?" Gloria asked.

"Mom? It's me, Gabby."

"Are you okay?"

"Yes, I'm all right. Dad came to the rescue. And we're now going to Barranquilla. But I don't have much time to talk. We might lose the signal in the mountains. Anyway, Dad said you know a guy at the U.S. Consulate who can help me get a replacement passport."

"Yeah, his name is Billy Stevens. When you were planning your trip to Colombia, I remembered reading in my college alumni newsletter that he was working there. So tell him you're my daughter, and I'm sure he'll help you. That is if he still remembers me after all these years."

"Thanks, Mom. Bill Stevens. Got it. Look, I'll call again when we get there. I love you, Mom. Bye."

"I love you too, sweetie. Take care of your dad until you both get home safely."

I looked over at the phone and said, "Hey, I'm quite capable of taking care of myself." But Gloria had already hung up.

Gabby looked up at me and said, "Did you get that? His name is Bill Stevens."

"Got it." I glanced at Gabby and said, "There's something I want to ask you, but you don't have to tell me if it's too personal."

"What is it?"

"I've been wondering how you met Juan Carlos and got caught up with his gang members back there?"

Gabby shifted and sat up. "When I arrived in Colombia, I got bored with the tour group, so I took a side trip to scuba diving. Juan Carlos was on the dive with me, and we hit it off right away. He seemed nice and asked me out for dinner and to go dancing later that night. I hope you don't mind, but I'll stop there. After that, the rest gets kind of personal."

She was right. I didn't need to know more about what might have happened between them later that night. I could fill in the blanks myself. After all, she is an adult."

I took the conversation in a different direction. "Juan Carlos said something about how you kept pushing him about his business practices. What did he mean by that?"

"It was just the usual small talk people do on first dates. You know, the getting-to-know-each-other stuff. I asked him about what he did for a living, but he changed the subject. I thought that was odd, so I kept pressing him to tell me what he did. I probably should have been more cautious and pulled back when he was so vague and evasive with his responses. Then he invited me to join him at the old resort for a full moon party. I figured that would be fun. He told me there would be a lot of other people there, but I never imagined it was just a set-up."

I gave her shoulder a gentle squeeze. "I guess what they say about not judging a book by its cover is true. Maybe in the future, be a little more careful about who you go out with. Especially when you're out in a foreign country on your own."

"You're right. I never thought Juan Carlos would be such a slimeball and part of a drug gang."

"Anyway, I'm just glad you weren't hurt back there. Why don't you try to get some sleep, and I'll wake you when we get close to the city."

Gabby sighed deeply, relaxed against my side, and soon fell asleep. Her soft, rhythmic snoring was music to my ears. It reminded me of the contented purring sounds her kitten, Boots, used to make when she held him in her lap as a little girl.

I brought my focus back to the dark, winding road, satisfied we were both safe. As I drove into the night, my thoughts turned to our next moves once we got to Barranquilla. At least we had a contact name at the consulate who would help us get the required papers to leave the country, and that was an excellent first step.

The tension in my shoulders increased as I navigated the twisting, narrow highway through the mountains. At almost every bend in the road, another roadside shrine for someone who died there glowed in the headlights. They acted as eerie reminders of how dangerous these roads were at night. The most nerve-racking moments came when large transport trucks rushed around the many hairpin turns, their headlights heading straight for me down the middle of the road. With no shoulders to pull onto or guardrails, all I could do was clench my jaw and pray we didn't get crushed or forced over the edge of a steep mountain drop. I can see why people always say you should never drive the highways here at night. Between the crazy drivers racing headlong like they have a death wish and the feral livestock on the road, it's way too risky. But dangerous times require risky actions, and we were rushing to put those times behind us.

I checked my watch as we passed a sign showing we were 150 kilometers from Barranquilla. So far, we have made good time with no incidents or indications of being followed. At this speed, if all goes well, we should get into Barranquilla in just over two hours.

I brought the car out of a tight switchback curve and tapped the brakes. About 400 yards ahead, it looked like we were approaching a roadblock or military checkpoint. Most large cities in this country have these checkpoints to discourage drug trafficking, so I figured it wouldn't be a problem. The young military personnel usually wave tourists through without a hassle. But on the rare occasions when they become too curious, flashing some cash to signal a bribe usually expedites things. As we approached, the glow from fires in large drums highlighted several armed men dressed in paramilitary uniforms standing beside the barricade. These didn't look like the official military personnel I expected to see. I tapped harder on the brakes and slowed to a crawl about 100 yards away, wondering what to expect. Juan Carlos' pistol was still tucked into my belt, pressing against my back. If there was trouble, I wouldn't be able to win a firefight against these heavily armed men. And, of course, being caught with a firearm on me would only provoke a negative response, so I slid the gun out and put it out of sight under the seat.

Gabby sat up and rubbed her eyes. "What is it, Dad? Are we there yet?"

"Not yet. It's just a roadside checkpoint and nothing to worry about. But slide over and buckle up, just in case we have to make a run for it."

I slowly rolled up to the checkpoint, where a man stepped in front of the car, holding his hand up and signaling me to stop. As I stopped, another gunman carrying an assault rifle walked around to the passenger side, leaned over, and looked in the window at Gabby.

The man in front of the car took his time coming around to the driver's side, and with one hand on his rifle, he signaled for me to roll down my window.

As the guy looked in my window, I could have sworn I was looking at Che Guevara, the long-dead Cuban revolutionary. His face looked like those silk-screened images on the T-shirts college kids wear and the posters they hang in their dorm rooms, trying to impress their friends and increase their street cred with other students.

"Buenos Noches, Senor," the Che Guevara look-a-like said.

"Good evening, officer," I said in my most innocent and friendly tone.

"Where are you coming from, and where are you going tonight, Senor?"

"We're on our way to the U.S. Consulate in Barranquilla."

"May I see your passports, Senor?" he said, leaning over and scanning the inside of the car.

"Sure." I reached into my shirt pocket, took out my passport, and handed it to the gunman.

"And the woman's passport?" he said, nodding his head toward Gabby.

I glanced over at Gabby. She had the same look of terror in her eyes I saw back at the El Presidente Resort. I shook my head slightly, signaling her to not do or say anything.

I turned to the gunman and said, "Ah… that's a problem, officer, and it's why we are going to the consulate. Someone stole my daughter's passport a couple of days ago."

The gunman leaned into the window and again looked at Gabby. "Both of you, please step out of the car." I noticed his finger had moved onto the trigger of his rifle. This wasn't going as easy as I had hoped.

"Is this really necessary, senor?" I had my wallet out, stroking some bills, hoping he would take the hint, accept a few bucks as a bribe, and send us on our way.

Glancing at my passport, he said, "Yes, Senor… Stone, it is necessary."

He stepped back from the car as I opened the door. The gunman on the passenger side opened Gabby's door. She stepped out, and he led her to my side of the car.

"It appears we have a problem, senor. You can't leave this country without a passport," he said, tucking my passport into his jacket pocket.

My back stiffened as I straightened up. "Hey, wait a minute. That's my passport. You can't just take it from me. We've done nothing illegal. You'll hear from our Ambassador about this." I hoped my belligerent blustering would rattle the guy, and he'd rethink the bribe and let us go. But no such luck.

"Nothing illegal, Senor Stone? Do you not call the murder of several young men and a prominent businessman illegal in your country?"

Oh, oh. I was afraid of this. These were members of Don Juan Patrón's gang.

No, this wasn't going well at all. I looked at Gabby and winked. My fingers clenched into a fist as I swung at the guy's jaw. But he was quicker. The butt end of his rifle crashed into the side of my head before my arm left my side. Stars flashed across my brain as darkness closed in around me. Gabby's scream echoed in my head as I collapsed onto the pavement, and everything went black.

CHAPTER

6

The pain in my head thumped like a bass drum. Without moving, I slowly cracked open my eyes and scanned the surrounding area in the dim light. From where I lay, it looked like I was in a small hut. I tried to sit up, but my hands were tightly bound behind my back, making it difficult to balance. As my mind cleared, memories of our encounter at the check stop last night came rushing back. Then panic. Where's Gabby?

My pulse raced as I forced myself to sit up. Then I heard it. A gentle rumbling sound of snoring. Gabby lay slumped over in a tight fetal position a few feet away.

I nudged her with my foot. She stirred and struggled to sit up.

"Wh… what's wrong?" she asked as she blinked away the sleep in her eyes.

"Are you okay, Gabs? Did they hurt you?"

"No, I'm fine. But are you all right? You took quite a hard clunk to the head."

"Just a massive headache and some ringing in my ears, but I'll be okay. I'm more embarrassed that the guy caught me off guard, and I put you in danger again. Did you see where they took us?"

"It was dark, so I only saw a few glimpses from the back of the truck they brought us in. From what I could tell, they took us somewhere into the jungle."

As my eyes adjusted to the light, I confirmed we were inside a small wooden shed. A mixture of feathers and straw covering the ground suggested our prison cell was a repurposed chicken coop. Thankfully, the smell of old chicken shit wasn't too bad. A small window brought in the faint glow of morning light. Beside the window, a corrugated metal door appeared to be the only way in or out.

This didn't make sense, like so much of what's happened since I arrived in the country. Although one thing was obvious, the guys at the roadblock were Don Juan Patrón's gang members. But where they took us and why was still a mystery.

I shifted my body into a kneeling position, leaning against the wall for support, then stood. I moved to the small window. There were two men with automatic assault rifles on the far side of a large clearing in the jungle. They stood guard beside an open-walled structure with a thatched palm frond roof. Inside, several people worked at long tables. It looked like some sort of production facility. Beside the structure, a field with rows of plants stretched into the distance for as far as I could see. These weren't marijuana plants like at the El Presidente Resort, and they were definitely not tomatoes. No, these were coca plants covered in tiny red berries ready for harvesting. I shook my head gently as I contemplated our situation. Well, Stone, you really have a way of jumping out of the frying pan and straight into the fire. First marijuana and now cocaine.

Gabby joined me by the window. "Where do you think we are?"

"Geographically, we could be just about anywhere. But I'd say we're in the middle of a massive cocaine operation."

"What?" She leaned closer, looked out the window, and whistled softly. "You mean that's all cocaine out there?"

Before I could answer, a scraping sound drew my attention away from the window. As the door swung open, a rifle-toting guard in military fatigues entered and aimed his gun at me. The tall, dark-haired Che Guevara look-a-like from last night's roadblock followed behind the guard and walked toward me.

"Well done, Senor Stone. As you say, it is cocaine. You are a very observant man and obviously more than just a casual tourist to our fine country."

I stiffened and said, "Who are you, and what do you want from us? You had no reason to bring us here."

"My name is Dominguez. You are mistaken, senor. I have a very good reason for bringing you here. When you killed Don Juan Patrón, you created... how should I put it... an inconvenience for our operations. Sure, Patrón was a slob. There is no disputing that. But he was useful in his own way to the functioning of our extended business operations. And now this inconvenience you have created must be corrected and paid for."

"I don't follow you. What could we possibly do that would help your business?"

"It will start with you making a phone call to your wife, senor." Dominguez reached into his pocket, pulled out my cell phone, and waved it in my face.

"My wife? What does she have to do with any of this?"

"You will call her, and she will bring us five hundred thousand dollars. She will have exactly 48 hours from now to deliver the money."

"That's ridiculous. She can't get her hands on that kind of money in such a short time. And even if she could, there's no way she could get down here that fast."

Dominguez smiled. "Oh, but she will if she wants to see you and your lovely daughter alive again, senor."

"And if I refuse?"

Dominguez nodded to the guard, who walked to Gabby and pressed the muzzle of his rifle against her head.

Gabby remained silent, but her eyes spoke volumes as they spread wide and pleaded with me to cooperate with him.

"Senor Stone, many people come into our lovely country, but not all of them leave. In fact, some of them are never seen or heard from again. Need I say more?"

"Okay, okay. Let's make the call. Just don't hurt her."

"A wise decision, Senor Stone." Dominguez searched through my contacts, then pushed the autodial. He put the phone on speaker and held it in front of me as it rang.

Gloria answered on the first ring. "God damn it, Jake. Where have you been? I'm almost—"

I quickly cut her off. "Gloria, I need you to listen carefully. Gabby's life and mine depend on what you do next."

The phone went silent, and after a brief pause, she said, "I'm listening."

"We're being held hostage somewhere in Colombia, and they're demanding you bring them five hundred thousand dollars within 48 hours—"

Dominguez pulled the phone away and said, "Senora Stone?" as he walked out of the hut.

"Yes. I'm Gloria Stone. Who is this?"

"It does not matter who I am."

"Have you harmed my husband and daughter?"

"Not yet. I am treating them quite well... for now. But that may change depending on your response to my demands."

"What do you want?"

"You will bring me five hundred thousand dollars by ten o'clock in exactly two days from now, or both of them will die. Is that understood?"

"Yes. I understand. But how do I know you will release them after I bring the money?"

"Trust, Senora Stone. Trust. That is the only assurance you have. And remember, if you do not arrive on time, you will never see them again."

Dominguez walked farther away and out of hearing range. A few minutes later, he re-entered the hut.

"Good. I believe you have all the details needed to bring the money. Just remember to be here no later than 48 hours from now. And if you tell anyone where you are going, your husband and daughter will be the first to die. Goodbye, Senora Stone."

Gloria said, "Yes, I understand. But I want to talk to them first, so I know they are all right."

"Yes, one moment, senora."

Dominguez held the phone in front of me. "Your wife wants to say goodbye to you and your daughter."

I leaned toward the phone and said, "Gloria, will you be able to get the job done?"

"Yes, I had a nice *long* chat with your friend, and I believe I have all the information I need to deliver *the package*."

Something about how she emphasized the words *long,* and *the package* told me she had a plan.

Dominguez moved the phone in front of Gabby.

"Mom, we're okay. Just get here soon, and we'll be all right. Okay?" Gabby pleaded.

"Don't worry dear, momma's on her way."

Dominguez held the phone to his face and said, "Remember, Senora Stone, you have exactly 48 hours to deliver the five hundred thousand dollars. Or they both die." He ended the call and put my phone back into his pants pocket.

I glared at Dominguez and said, "I assume I'll get my phone back when all this business is behind us?"

"We shall see. Many things can happen between now and when your wife arrives with the money to complete our business transaction. Besides, once she is here… it may be more convenient to keep her here with you so none of you can inform the authorities of the location of our operation." He went outside, closed the door, and locked it behind him.

Oh yes, Senor Dominguez. That is something we both can agree on. Many things can happen before we have completed our business here.

CHAPTER

7

The following 48 hours passed slowly as the heat and humidity made things unbearable in the cramped quarters of our prison cell. Our only break from the heat came during the twice-a-day trip to the jungle to relieve ourselves under the watchful eye of a guard. This certainly wasn't the Ritz by any stretch of the imagination. Even the room service left a great deal to be desired. Soggy tortillas and lukewarm beans twice a day had me longing for a thick rib-eye steak fresh off the barbecue.

The one consolation was how well Gabby was holding up. She spent much of the time leaning against the wall, humming some song over and over to herself. What a trooper. Given our circumstances, she was much calmer than I had expected.

Try as I might, I couldn't see a way out of this place. Even when the guards untied our hands during mealtimes and our trips into the jungle to relieve ourselves, they kept at least two rifles pointed at us. The risk of Gabby getting caught by a stray bullet kept me from trying to wrestle a gun away from one of the guards. So, I waited and hoped for a better opportunity to escape.

Finally, the time arrived when Gloria was expected to show up with the ransom money.

"Do you think mom will get here in time?" Gabby said softly, staring off into the gloomy cell.

I nudged her with my elbow and said, "Hang in there, Gabs. If there is any way to do it, your mom will find a way."

She turned her head and looked into my eyes. "But what will happen to us if she doesn't arrive on time? Will they really kill us in cold blood?"

The fear and doubt in her eyes belied her stoic attitude. My heart sank at the futility of our situation and my inability to protect her.

I put on a brave front to give her hope and said, "Out of all the people in the world who can pull it off, your mom is that person."

I didn't answer her second question. There was no point adding even well-founded speculation to the issue. Whether Dominguez would kill us or wait longer for the ransom money was an unknown and best left out of our conversation.

I stared out the small window. By the angle of the shadows, it looked like it was about mid-morning. So unless Gloria ran into any problems, she should be here any minute. But even I had doubts whether she could pull it off in the short time she had to gather the money and get down here.

The scraping of a key pressed into the lock drew my attention to the metal door. It swung open, and Dominguez entered, followed by three armed guards. The door swung closed on its own behind them.

"Isn't it a little overkill bringing all of your guards with you, Dominguez?" I said, doing the math in my head. If all three guards were in this chicken coop with Dominguez, there was no one outside guarding the rest of the operation. This may be a big miscalculation on his part.

He checked his watch. "It is ten o'clock, and your wife has not arrived as instructed, Senor Stone. Maybe she didn't take my proposition seriously. Or maybe she decided you were not worth the expense. Either way, I am now forced to decide about the fate of you and your daughter."

I puffed out my chest in a show of bravado and stepped toward him. A guard raised his weapon and pointed it at Gabby.

I backed off two steps and said, "Now, wait a minute, Dominguez. You can't just shoot us in cold blood. Gloria said she would be here with the money. You know this isn't the easiest place to get into. So just give her a little more time."

Dominguez slowly shook his head and fingered the pistol in the holster on his belt. "I am sorry, senor, but I have already spent too much time on you. It looks as though you and your daughter will have to disappear. Then I will get on with the more important business of running our plantation."

Gabby seemed to awaken from a trance and moved to stand beside me. "Dad, what is he saying? Isn't Mom coming with the money to take us home?"

Dominguez turned to her. "I believe your mother has chosen a different path, senorita. It is most regrettable for me to do what is now necessary. But my life will go on, whereas... yours will not."

Gabby stiffened her stance and glared at him. "That's the second time someone said that to me in the last couple of days. And it didn't work out so well for him either."

God, I love this girl—guts and a brave reserve even she didn't know she had in her.

The door burst open, and a stocky person dressed in camouflage gear stepped into the doorway, silhouetted by the intense sunlight outside. The mysterious stranger raised a pump-action shotgun as Dominguez and the three guards spun around.

The shadowy stranger peered from under a wide-brimmed straw hat and announced, "Hello, boys. Momma's home."

She pumped the shotgun and pulled the trigger. CLICK—BOOM. And kept pumping and firing until she dropped all four men to the ground.

When the gunfire started, Gabby screamed. I jumped to protect her and pushed her back against the wall out of the line of fire. The first blast sent one guard flying backward, slamming into the wall with a large crimson blotch spreading across his chest.

The second blast took out another guard, who dropped to his knees and collapsed with his right shoulder missing.

Gabby continued screaming between the shotgun blasts, adding to the chaos.

The third guard turned and tried to run away. But with nowhere to go, he took a hit in the back and collapsed.

Dominguez panicked and fumbled to release his pistol from its holster. By the time he had it out and aimed, he took the full force of a blast to the face and crumpled backward.

It took less than ten seconds to take all four of them out.

As chaos gave way to silence and the gun smoke cleared, I said, "Well, it's about time you got here, Gloria. It's just like you to wait until the last second for a dramatic entrance."

Gloria kicked the guns away from the dead men and dropped her hat over what was once Dominguez's face. She then rushed over to where Gabby and I stood, pressed against the wall. "Well, Jake, it's a dirty job, but someone had to do it. Are you two okay?"

Gabby was trembling but had stopped screaming as a new calm descended in the shed. "Mom?... Is that really you?"

"Yes, dear. It's me. Did Dominguez hurt you?" Gloria said, putting her hands on Gabby's shoulders and searching her face.

She shook her head as Gloria pulled a long knife from her belt and cut our hands free.

I pulled Gloria to me and gave her a quick hug and kiss. "I knew you would handle this business in the right way."

"I'm getting used to finding solutions to the messes you keep getting into, Jake."

"That's not fair. There was only that one time in Guatemala… well… okay, maybe I have screwed up a few times. But it's not like I mess up every operation."

Gabby rubbed her wrists, looked around the small cell at the four bloodied bodies, and quickly gathered her composure. "Will someone tell me what the hell is happening in this family? Who are you, people? All this gunfire and drama?"

"Later, dear. We need to get moving before the package arrives," Gloria said, heading for the door.

"What are you talking about, Mom? What package?" Gabby said.

Gloria turned and said, "Not now, Gabs. There'll be time to talk about this later. But, right now, we need to get out of here."

I leaned over to get my phone from Dominguez. Clearly, he would not need it or any other phone ever again.

Gloria grabbed my arm and pulled me toward the door. "Leave it. The calvary is using the GPS signal on your phone to coordinate the package delivery."

Gabby stomped her foot like a petulant child and demanded, "What package? Will somebody tell me what's going on with you two?"

"Zip it, Gabby. We'll fill you in when we get home." Gloria turned and left the hut.

I followed as she marched briskly across the yard to the open structure where the cocaine processing operation stood abandoned. The last few workers ran up the access road away from the compound.

Gloria handed me a cigarette lighter and said, "Will you do the honors?"

Under the thatched roof of the structure, several long tables were covered with bins of white powdered cocaine, bags, and scales for weighing the product. On other tables, tightly wrapped packages waited to be boxed for shipment. I kicked over a barrel of solvent, letting the fluid flow across the ground under the tables. When the liquid had spread far enough, I lit a bale of dried branches and threw the lighter into the pool of solvent. Flames leaped into the air and flashed across the ground, spreading rapidly to engulf the processing area.

"We better get out of here before the rest of the barrels blow," I said, running from the structure.

My rental car was up on blocks with its wheels and doors stripped from it. Apparently, this place was also a chop shop for stolen vehicles. If nothing else, Dominguez was an enterprising individual. At least, he was until a few minutes ago.

Gloria yelled, "Damn it. I knew I shouldn't have left the keys in my car." Her rental car sped away from the compound, vanishing around a curve in the dirt road, taking the fleeing cocaine workers in it.

I headed toward a row of three rusted-out vehicles parked beside the growing inferno of the cocaine structure. I climbed into the nearest Jeep and prayed the keys were in the ignition. They were. I pumped the gas and fired up the engine.

"Hurry, get in," I yelled over the raging sound of the spreading fire as the intense heat burned my face. Every second mattered, and we didn't have time for hesitation.

Above the raging fire, a new sound was approaching from far away. The distinctive roar of aircraft rapidly closing on our position.

As Gabby and Gloria climbed into the Jeep, I slammed it into drive and stomped on the accelerator. Dirt flew from the rear wheels as the vehicle fishtailed up the dirt road. I glanced over my shoulder as two U.S. Air Force F-18 fighter bombers flew low over the coca fields, banked, and prepared for their return run to deliver the package.

This was going to be close.

The Jeep slewed sideways, spraying gravel and dust behind us as I took the winding dirt road at full speed away from the cocaine operation. The solvent barrels blew in a massive explosion sending black smoke and flames hundreds of feet above the jungle. The shock wave rocked the compound, sending a concussion wave into the forest behind us.

Gloria and Gabby ducked instinctively as the explosion's pressure wave hit us as we cut around a bend and behind the cover of thick foliage.

The jet bombers curled and rushed in for their return fly-over of the compound and dropped their payload, setting the entire area ablaze. With the coca fields and this cocaine operation destroyed, the surrounding jungle would soon reclaim the place as it should have always been.

In the rearview mirror, thick black smoke billowed skyward as we cleared the jungle and hit the highway.

I pointed the Jeep north toward Barranquilla and turned to Gloria. "Tell me how those fighters knew where to make their bombing run?"

"Remember when that idiot Dominguez had me on the phone to discuss the ransom? Well, it didn't take much to keep him on the line long enough to get a GPS fix on your coordinates. Then, after I hung up, it was easy to forward those to the right people to make a quick strike happen. And with your phone still powered up, our boys could stay locked on the GPS signal."

"But how did you know he would keep the phone turned on?"

"I told him to keep it on so I could call him if I needed instructions on how to find the place."

"Good thinking. Oh, and there's something else. We still need to go to the US consulate in Barranquilla to get replacement passports for Gabby and me. Do you think your buddy... what's his name? Will he help us out?"

"His name is Billy, and yes, as I said before, I'm sure he will help us. If he still remembers me."

Gabby sat in the back seat and listened quietly to our conversation. I glanced into the rearview mirror. She had a look of concern on her face as her sky-blue eyes stared at the back of our heads.

After the last few days, it was clear the time had come for us to have the family talk that Gloria and I had avoided for so long. There would be no glossing over what just happened. Gabby had seen both of us in action, and there would be no avoiding the conversation. Even with us having airtight non-disclosure agreements with the Agency, there would be no getting away from telling her the truth about our backgrounds. I hoped the adage, the truth will set you free, would hold true in this case. I glanced at Gloria, and she returned a concerned expression, but neither of us wanted to speak first.

CHAPTER

8

The rattling and creaking of the rusted old Jeep did little to mask the tension building inside the vehicle. A heavy silence descended on us as we fled the destruction of the cocaine fields. With each passing minute, the tension grew more intolerable. We needed something or someone to break the silence as we rolled down the highway toward Barranquilla.

Gabby continued to glare at me in the rearview mirror. She had a determined look of expectation and resolve written across her face. It was a look I had seen from both her and her mother many times before. And that look meant only one thing—we needed to talk and clear the air.

Gabby finally broke the uncomfortable silence. "Well, is anyone going to say something? Or are you going to find another way to put this off and leave me hanging in the dark about who you people are?"

I shot Gloria a look and shrugged. We both knew the time we had dreaded for many years had finally arrived. We always knew we couldn't live a life of falsehoods and deception forever. Especially not when you're raising someone as brilliant and curious as Gabby. I took a deep breath and opened my mouth while still trying to figure out where to begin. This is a typical response for me—start speaking and let my brain and thoughts catch up to my voice later.

Thankfully, Gloria jumped in before I said anything. "What do you want to know, dear?" She said, pivoting in her seat to face Gabby.

I exhaled softly, counting my luck at being let off the hook and rescued by Gloria. She has a more level-headed approach to this sort of thing than I do. It probably has to do with my tendency to speak first and think later. Whereas she is more methodical and rational in her responses to tough questions.

"Well, you could start by explaining how you found me back at the abandoned resort. Then, how did you guys learn to shoot your way out of trouble with Juan Carlos Patrón and again with Dominguez just now? Oh, and while you're at it, maybe tell me how you arranged for an air force strike on the cocaine fields? There are just too many unanswered questions about how you could do all those things."

I glanced over at Gloria and caught her attention. "Be careful what you say. You know how dangerous it will be for us if we make certain things public."

Gabby leaned forward and slapped the back of my seat. "Bullshit, Dad. Either you trust me, or you don't. Besides, if this is a secret for only our family to know, then as part of this family, I have a right to know it, too."

I cast a quick glance in the rearview mirror. Gabby's face was flushed, and her eyes glared with unwavering determination. This wasn't going well, and we hadn't even started to fill her in on our backgrounds yet.

I quickly glanced over my shoulder at her, then back to the road, and said, "Look, Gabby, whatever we tell you must remain a secret between the three of us. You can never mention any of this to anyone else. Your mom and I have signed non-disclosure agreements with the government. We're bound by Home Land Security to keep our identities and previous work secret. If word gets out that we talked about this—even with you—we could face serious jail time."

Gabby's expression hadn't changed as she leaned forward and rested her arms on the back of the front seats.

Gloria looked at me and said, "Jake, you know she's right. We have to bring her in on our family secret now. After what we have been through and what she's seen, there is no other choice. You could say the toothpaste is already out of the tube, and it's never going back in."

I burst out laughing. "Where do you get that stuff? Do you write your own material?"

Gabby's patience was running out as she slapped the back of my seat again. "Enough stalling. Just spill it, and tell me what the hell is going on with you two."

Gloria turned back to face Gabby. "I'll start at the beginning. Before your father and I retired, we worked as special agents for a federal government covert intelligence agency."

Gabby's mouth fell open. I didn't know what she was expecting to hear, but clearly, she didn't expect to hear we were government agents.

"You mean you're spies? Like James Bond or something?" she asked.

"No, not like James Bond—"

"Speak for yourself, Gloria. I always thought of myself in a Bond, James Bond, sort of way," I said and smiled.

"Oh, shut up, you old fart. No, not spies. We were more what they call field agents. We would get assigned to hotspots in various countries around the world. Our jobs changed based on the assignment. Sometimes we were required to neutralize some bad guys and help stop an insurrection in a friendly country. Or we might be required to prevent the sale of illegal arms to terrorists. On other occasions, we would observe and report on local conditions during tense intergovernmental negotiations."

"So, when you say you would neutralize some bad guys or stop an insurrection, what you really mean is you killed them," Gabby said with disgust while shaking her head.

I quickly added, "Yeah, but they were all nasty people. Sometimes it couldn't be helped. Especially if the situation left us with no other options. Like back there in the cocaine fields. We didn't have many options to work with that didn't include the use of force."

"Oh, come on. You guys taught me there are always options other than violence."

Gloria cleared her throat. "That's true, but we also taught you that sometimes a more direct approach may be appropriate when you've tried all other options and failed. For example, do you remember that big girl who kept bullying you back in Junior High?"

"Yeah, but what's that got to do with this?"

"Do you remember how you ultimately settled that situation with her?"

"I remember standing up to her and pushing back to get her to leave me alone," Gabby said.

I jumped in. "You did a little more than that. You punched her square in the face and broke her nose. I couldn't have been more proud of you at that moment." I smiled at the memory and glanced in the mirror. A slight smile turned the corners of Gabby's mouth.

"Yeah, but I also got suspended for a week for fighting."

Gloria said, "I think the point your dad is trying to make is that the girl never pushed you around again. Did she? In fact, I believe you two became quite good friends after that. So, you see, sometimes physical violence has to be an option to resolve situations when other methods haven't worked. That's what your dad and I would do with our jobs. It wasn't like we rushed in with guns blazing every time... just when necessary. Like today. If I hadn't used deadly force to neutralize those guys, you wouldn't be alive now."

"Can you stop using that term—neutralize—it kind of bothers me. It sounds like a cozy way to say, you blew a guy's head off."

Gloria continued, "As I was saying, your dad and I were career field agents, and we were good at our jobs. But, when we retired, we felt there was no need to tell you about our actual work. And certainly, when you were younger, there was too much risk if we let you know what our actual jobs were. Do you understand that, Gabby?"

Gabby's expression softened as she relaxed a little. She shook her head gently. "Jeez, and all this time, I thought you guys were in the tourism industry and just going places to scout different travel locations. But yeah, I get it. You're right. I probably would have rushed out and told my friends that my parents were secret agents. Of course, they wouldn't have believed me. After all, you both coached my youth soccer teams and made cookies for the school bake sales. I don't think any of my friends would have believed that mister and missus, normal everyday Americans were actually... stone-cold killers. Pun intended."

I laughed again. "Stone-cold killers... I like that. Do you and your mom have the same gag writers?"

Gloria swatted my arm lightheartedly. "Oh my God, Jake. You have a twisted sense of humor."

"I know, but that's why you love me." I leaned sideways and gave her a kiss.

Gabby brought us back on topic. "Okay, I get it. Some things in your past need to be kept secret. Now that your past is out in the open with me, I'll make you a promise. I won't mention this to anyone. But I need you to promise you'll keep me in the loop from now on. No more secret missions or operations or whatever you field agents call them. Do we have a deal?"

I looked Gabby in the eye through the rearview mirror. "I think we can live with that. Can't we, Gloria?"

Gloria nodded. "It's a deal. No more secrets. And that goes both ways. We'll let you know if we need to use our special agent skills, and you let us know if you're going off-grid again. Okay?"

Gabby laughed. "We've got a deal. But does that mean I can still travel to obscure locations in the future?"

I looked at Gloria, shrugged my shoulders, and said, "I don't suppose we'd be able to stop her, anyway."

"You're right about that, Dad," Gabby said.

God, I love this kid's moxie.

We continued to discuss some of our less sensitive assignments as we moved closer to Barranquilla. Gabby soon got over her initial shock of discovering our actual work histories. She was fascinated by the life and adventures Gloria and I had been involved with over the years and kept probing for more details. It was like the floodgates had opened on our past, and the rush of secrets flowed out. And as Gabby took it all in, it felt like an enormous weight was finally lifted off my shoulders.

Maybe the truth does set you free after all. As long as it doesn't get back to the government. Then the truth could get us jail time.

CHAPTER

9

It took less time than I thought for Gabby to adjust to the idea that her parents were special agents for a secret government agency. She must have suspected something all along while she was growing up. Thankfully, our cover as travel specialists in the tourism industry had worked for all those years. It had to be difficult for her when we would rush off on trips for a week or two and not take her with us. But many families balance their careers and family needs when both parents work to make ends meet. One thing was sure, the cat was now out of the bag. Or, as Gloria said, the toothpaste was now out of the tube. And so far, the fallout was not as bad as I thought it might be. As we continued to put the cocaine fields far behind us, we settled into watching the surrounding countryside.

The approach to Barranquilla took us longer than I expected. We'd been driving for over an hour and were still more than 30 kilometers away from our destination. The highway narrowed into a two-lane, undivided road. As a result, traffic crawled the closer we came to the city's outskirts. The area was typical of the poverty-stricken neighborhoods surrounding large South American cities. Rundown brick buildings, dirt sidestreets, and small shops hugged both sides of the highway. I could only describe some of the buildings as crude shelters. They certainly didn't look like sturdy houses. Their tin or thatched palm roofs and broken windows would provide minimal cover for growing young families. But in a city with over 2 million people, the socio-economic strata ranged from abject poverty to the ultra-rich. And evidently, the outer areas of Barranquilla were not where the wealthy lived or hung out.

The beaten-up Jeep's air conditioning had quit working minutes after fleeing the cocaine fields. Our drive with the windows rolled down provided some relief from the heat and humidity. But the loud thumping of the hot air blowing through the windows gave me a pounding headache. I was more than ready for a cold beer and a good meal.

Gabby sat back, fanning the sweat on her face and neck with an old map of the Colombian highway system. "How long will it be until we get to the consulate?"

Gloria rechecked the online map on her phone. "According to the directions, we should arrive in about twenty minutes. But with this traffic, I wouldn't bet on it," she said, glancing over her shoulder at Gabby.

I looked into the rearview mirror. Gabby's half-hearted smile suggested she was about to throw in the towel on this adventure.

"Hang in there, Gabs," I said, "As soon as we get sorted out with your mom's friend, we'll all get cleaned up and go out for something to eat. That'll make you feel better."

Gloria released another button on her blouse to let in more of the breeze and said, "Maybe we should stop somewhere to freshen up a bit before going to see Billy."

I quickly glanced at Gloria and then back at Gabby in the mirror. "That's a good idea. We could stop someplace to get a bite to eat and use their washroom to clean up a little before descending on lover boy's office."

Gloria slapped my arm with the back of her hand. "Oh, shut up about that. It's not like that, and you know it. You'll see. He's just a nice guy I knew way back in college." She tapped the screen on her phone. "Apparently, there's an American-style fast-food restaurant about two kilometers ahead. I've been to one of those in Costa Rica, and it was fine. With their international standards, they usually have clean facilities, and a burger and fries with a cold shake would work for me."

Gabby leaned over the seat between us. "I'm in. It's not health food, but it'll sure beat the slop they fed us back at the cocaine fields."

"Junk food it is then," I said, maneuvering into the other lane to pass an ancient pickup truck with an entire family sitting in the rear box. I pressed the peddle to the floor to accelerate hard around it and cut back into our lane to beat the oncoming traffic. Unfortunately, I didn't see the unpainted speed bump that launched us into the air. The Jeep bounced hard and bottomed out against the pavement with loud metal scraping on the asphalt. Good thing this piece of crap wasn't my vehicle, and I'd be ditching it as soon as we got to Barranquilla.

Gabby screamed and clutched her head after banging it on the roof.

"Slow down, Jake," Gloria yelled over the thrumming sound of wind gushing through the windows. "Better we get there late than not at all."

As usual, she was right. At this point, there was no real urgency to take risks on the road. We'll get there when we get there, and if that means waiting until tomorrow, then so be it. Besides, the last thing I wanted was to be pulled over by a cop for speeding. Trying to explain where we got the stolen Jeep would be impossible. So, I relaxed my foot on the gas peddle and slowed to keep pace with the other traffic.

The massive sign for the fast-food place came into view. It's kind of hard to miss the distinctly colored sign with their well-known logo towering above the other buildings in the area. I pulled into the parking lot and got out to stretch. The washroom facilities were as clean as might be expected in this part of the world. To call them adequate was a bit of an exaggeration, but they served our purpose as a place to freshen up. Relief would have to wait until we could get some new clothes and take long showers to wash off the grime and lingering stench from our incarceration over the last few days. Even though their food is consistent worldwide, the burger and fries sat like a heavy, indigestible lump in my gut. Note to self—stay away from fast-food places, and stick with local foods in the future.

After our brief rest stop, we carried on into downtown Barranquilla, following the voice commands from Gloria's phone. I parked the Jeep in a multi-level parking garage across from the U.S. Consulate building and stashed the keys under the driver's seat. I figured this was as good a place as any to ditch the stolen cartel vehicle.

"Well, we're here. Any last words before we go see lover boy?" I said teasingly as I gave Gloria a hug and a kiss. "Did I ever thank you for saving our asses back at the cocaine fields?"

Gloria's lips curled into a sly, crooked smile as she looked into my eyes, winked, and squeezed my butt. "Oh, don't worry, you'll make it up to me soon."

I love it when she thinks like that.

We entered the modern, four-story building housing the consulate. The interior air conditioning smacked me in the face like a cold, wet towel. But it felt wonderful to get out of the oppressive heat and into an air-conditioned environment for a change. On the ground floor, a bank and a coffee shop opened onto the high-ceilinged lobby. A young security officer, who looked to be in her early twenties, glanced up from her desk as we approached.

"How may I help you?" she said. Her beautiful smile lit up her tanned face, framed with long black hair flowing to her shoulders.

"How are you on this gorgeous day... Juanita?" I said, checking her name tag before Gloria muscled her way in and pushed me aside.

"We're here to see Bill Stevens at the U.S. Consulate," she said in an authoritarian tone as she glared at me.

I guess flirting with the locals wasn't a good idea—and I knew it. But I can't help the occasional harmless flirting with a beautiful woman from time to time. Of course, it would never lead to anything. Gloria is all the woman I can handle. And sometimes even she's too much for me.

Juanita looked between Gloria and me and said, "I am not familiar with someone by that name. However, the U.S. Consulate offices are on the third and fourth floors. There is a building directory beside the elevators which may help you find the person you're looking for." She turned in her chair and pointed toward the elevators in an alcove behind her.

"Thank you," Gloria said and walked away.

I leaned over and said, "Yes. Thank you, Juanita. You have been very helpful. Have a great day." Her smile was worth the beating I would get from Gloria later.

A quick scan of the sign beside the elevators showed the U.S. Consulate shared the building with other professional businesses and service companies. I noted that Bill Stevens' name did not appear in the directory. Gloria pushed the up button, and we got into the elevator. The doors opened onto the third floor, facing a wide reception desk with a pair of drooping American flags behind it. The receptionist up here was not as appealing as the one in the lobby. A buttoned-down Marine in a full formal uniform eyeballed us suspiciously as we approached.

"How may I help you?" he said, scanning our faces before lingering on Gabby.

"We're here to see Bill Stevens. Could you tell me where his office is located?" Gloria stated.

The young Marine looked at Gabby and smiled, holding her gaze for a moment, then nodded. "Do you have an appointment to see Mister Stevens?"

"No, we just arrived in town and need some help with our passports," Gloria said.

"One moment, please." He tapped on his keyboard and used the mouse to find what he was searching for. "Ah, yes. Here he is. Mister William Stevens. Please wait while I call his cubicle. Who shall I say is here to see him?"

"Gloria Stone. Oh wait, that's my married name. He may remember me as Gloria Pettigrew, a friend from college."

The Marine pointed to a row of chairs in the waiting area. "Please have a seat. This will only take a moment," he said, smiling up at Gabby, who blushed slightly and smiled back. It seemed I wasn't the only one prone to casual flirting.

As we waited for Stevens to arrive, I leaned toward Gloria and whispered, "A cubicle, not an office? Didn't you say this guy was some sort of big shot way up there with the Ambassador or something?"

Gloria whispered, "I never said he was a big shot. Only that he worked for the consulate. Besides, how would I know what his role is? The alumni newsletter only listed his location and employer, not what he does there."

I let it go. Not much point in diving into his background now. There would be plenty of time to assess the guy after I met him.

As we waited, Gloria sat quietly, probably thinking about what she would say to the guy after such a long time. Gabby and the Marine exchanged frequent, coy smiles that reaffirmed their obvious attraction. While I sat there observing all of them and wondering where we would stay for the night and how good a cold beer would be right now.

The smoked-glass doors beside the reception desk slid open, and a short, balding man with a comb-over, thick glasses, and a sizable belly emerged. I figured him to be in his late fifties, about the same age as Gloria and me. But the aging process and the bureaucratic office life had not been kind to him. We stood as the man walked toward us.

A broad smile lit up his face as he approached. "Gloria Pettigrew. Oh... My... God. How long has it been?" He held out his arms and gave Gloria a long hug—too long for my liking.

"It's Gloria Stone, now. But Billy, you look the same as you did in college," she said.

Obviously, she was trying to massage the guy's ego. If he looked like this in college, he was probably a lonely guy and didn't get many dates.

He took her hands and held her at arm's length to get a good look at her. "Nonsense. But look at you. You haven't changed a bit. Still a vision of beauty, as always. What brings you to Barranquilla?"

Okay, the guy had moved from pathetic to officially pissing me off. Not only did he not let go of Gloria's hands, he hadn't even acknowledged Gabby and me standing beside her.

I cleared my throat with a loud cough.

Gloria turned her head to me. "Oh, I'm sorry. Billy, this is my husband, Jake, and my daughter, Gabby."

The guy was gracious enough to let go of one of Gloria's hands long enough to shake ours and say, "Pleased to meet you both."

Gloria retook the lead, trying to turn the meeting to the business at hand and away from his obvious infatuation with her. "Billy, we need your help to get replacement passports for Gabby and Jake. Can you help us with that?"

"Of course. Please come with me, and we'll get the process started." He continued to hold Gloria's hand as he led us into the office area and through a maze of cubicles. He pointed to a couple of chairs beside a cubicle. "Please take a seat, and I'll be right back with the paperwork."

I looked around for signs of his actual office, but when I saw a photo of him holding a cat pinned to the partition wall, I knew this was where he worked. The poor guy never rose to anything higher than a low-level bureaucrat in an out-of-the-way part of a third-world country. Either he screwed up big time and pissed someone off along his career path, or he had low expectations and limited abilities to climb the corporate ladder. But hey, to each his own. Not everyone wants the stress and pressures of high-ranking offices. I decided to cut the guy some slack and give him a chance.

He returned with a stack of forms, put them on the desk, and immediately took Gloria's hand as he explained what the documents were for. Okay, that was enough for me. I'd given him enough slack. He was just too handsy for my liking. Maybe this was Karma paying me back for flirting with Juanita downstairs. But seriously, dude, enough is enough already.

I leaned forward over the desk and pressed between them. "Is there a conference room where we can all sit and fill these out?" I said, drawing his focus away from Gloria.

"Yes, of course. Follow me." Stevens took us across the hall to a small conference room and offered us seats around the table. As I took my chair, he made sure he sat close beside Gloria.

She looked at me and shrugged as if to say, just go with it for now.

Yeah, he was pissing me off. But I bit my lip and figured we just needed to fill out the forms so we could get the hell out of there and away from the guy.

CHAPTER

10

Filling out the paperwork for replacement passports was tedious and slightly less annoying than having Stevens hang around. As Gabby and I entered our information, he continued fawning over Gloria like a pubescent teenager at a school dance. It may have started out innocently enough as two old friends reconnecting after several decades. Still, his continued overt flirting and attention to Gloria was not only rude but irritating as hell. And his ongoing insistence on ignoring my presence, or even acknowledging me as her husband, really pissed me off. I took the high road for now and held my tongue. My goal was to get our passports replaced so we could get the hell out of this country as soon as possible. If that meant playing along with his insecurities and fragile ego, then so be it.

I looked up from my form and asked, "Bill, do you think you could get me a bottle of water?"

He broke off his attention with Gloria and said, "Of course. I'll be right back. I'll bring some for everyone."

"Thanks, Bill."

While he was out of the room, I asked Gloria, "What the hell is with this guy? He's all over you like a teenager with a crush."

Gloria shrugged and whispered, "I get it. He's way too touchy and familiar, but let's just get through this and get your passports."

Before I could reply, Stevens came into the room with three water bottles. "How's it going with the applications?" he asked as he handed me a bottle.

Gabby put her pen down. "All done here. How about you, Dad?"

I took a sip of water and said, "Yeah, I'm done, too."

Stevens took our paperwork, led us to a photo area to take some headshots for the documents, and then took us back to his cubicle.

With his full attention on Gloria, Stevens said, "The passports will take a couple of days to get all the approvals and such. Where are you staying while you're in Barranquilla, Gloria?"

What an asshole. Not even a glance my way or a polite suggestion that I may have some thoughts on the matter.

Gloria looked at me, shrugged, and said, "We haven't really thought about that yet. Do you have any suggestions?"

Stevens' face lit up light a jack-o-lantern. "I certainly do. A guy I know has a nice little hotel down near the harbor. The Hotel Costa Azul. You'll love it, and there are lots of restaurants nearby." He unfolded a map and drew a circle near the waterfront, away from the downtown core.

"Sounds lovely," Gloria said, looking at me as if silently asking for my opinion.

I was not in the mood for conversation, so I shrugged and grunted, "It could be all right for a day or two."

"It's nothing too fancy or expensive," Stevens said, looking at me like I might be short of funds. "Do you have a vehicle?"

"Not really," Gloria said, shaking her head while looking at me.

I guess she also wanted to put some distance between the stolen cartel Jeep and us. Not a bad idea.

Stevens clapped his hands together, obviously pleased with himself. I hope he wasn't expecting me to give him a high-five, a gold star, or an achievement sticker for his fridge. At this point, I was more inclined to pop him in the nose than congratulate him.

"Good, then it's settled. I'll drop you off at the hotel and pick you up when the passports are ready." He folded the map and handed it to Gloria. "In the meantime, I can show you around town and take you to some of the more exciting places in Barranquilla."

I coughed and said, "That won't be necessary, Bill. I'm sure we can get around on our own for a couple of days. We've taken up enough of your time already. Besides, I'm sure you have lots to do with your wife and family."

Gloria shot me a dirty look, and I knew I would pay for sounding rude to him. But I'd had enough of this guy and wanted to put some distance between him and us.

He looked at Gloria, then back at me. "As you wish. But I'm not married anymore. I was married briefly, but that was long ago."

Gloria was ready to move on from him, too, and said, "I'm sorry to hear that, Billy. Well, we should get going then."

Stevens dropped his personal life reveal and said, "Do you have a phone number I can reach you at when the passports are ready?" He swung his head, glancing between Gloria and me.

"You can use mine," she said and gave him the number.

"Okay then, shall we go to the hotel and get you settled in?" Stevens gathered our forms, paper-clipped our photos to them, and placed them in the outbox tray on his desk. He then led us out of the building.

On our way through the lobby, I casually glanced at the security desk. My young friend Juanita had been replaced by an old security officer with a long gray beard and a face pocked with acne scars. No flirting was required here, so I kept pace with the others as we crossed the street to the parking garage where I had abandoned the Jeep.

As we walked past our Jeep, Stevens held up the key fob and beeped the doors unlocked on a newer, high-end model Mercedes. In the States, this model would sell for over eighty thousand dollars. That shocked me a little. There seemed to be a disconnect between this guy's low-level job and the high-end vehicle he drove.

Stevens moved quickly to the passenger side and opened the door for Gloria. Obviously, Gabby and I were to sit in the back.

As we drove past the broken-down ride we came in with, I smiled and wondered how long it would stay there before someone stole it. Stevens constantly talked with Gloria, giving her a running commentary about the area as he headed north toward the waterfront along the Caribbean coast. He parked the vehicle on a narrow street alongside the Magdalena River. His description of the Hotel Costa Azul was bang on. It certainly didn't look like anything too fancy, but from the outside, it appeared clean and would probably do for a couple of days. Although the heavy iron bars on all the windows made me wonder about the neighborhood. But all in all, considering where we had been staying until today, courtesy of the drug cartel, it would be fine.

"Well, this is it. The Hotel Costa Azul. I think you'll love it. Let's see if they have a room for you." Stevens led us into the lobby and straight to the front desk like our tour guide.

An overhead fan softly squealed as the slow turning blades strained to move the thick humid air around the small lobby. The clerk jumped to his feet and came to attention when he saw Stevens approaching.

Stevens put his hands on the counter and said, "Manuel, these are my dear friends. They need a room for a few days. I'm sure you have something nice for them."

"Yes, Senor Stevens." Manuel looked at his computer screen and tapped the keyboard. "Ah yes, I have a deluxe room with two queen-sized beds, and it has its own bathroom. Very clean, very nice, and at a reasonable rate."

I'm always impressed when I hear a hotel room has its own bathroom. Maybe it's just me, but I like having private facilities to take care of my personal business.

"It sounds lovely," Gloria said as she signed the room register and slipped the clerk her credit card. She turned to Stevens. "Thank you, Billy. You've been a tremendous help."

"Anything for a dear friend." He leaned in to kiss her. It looked like he was going for her lips, but she dodged at the last second, and he grazed one off her cheek.

"I'm sure we'll be fine here for a few days. Just give me a call when we can pick up our passports." Gloria said, turning back to the clerk and collecting her credit card.

I took Stevens' hand, squeezed it tighter than would be considered polite, and shook it. I wasn't trying to crush his fingers, just letting him know I was still there and not overly happy with his behavior. This seemed to shock him out of some hypnotic trance. He turned away from Gloria and looked at me as I said, "Yes, thank you, Bill. I appreciate your help today. Take care, and we'll see you in a few days."

It wasn't like I was being rude, just letting him know our business with him had ended, and he could leave now. Some guys need a more direct hint to get the message, and he was one of those guys.

We left him standing at the front desk and walked up the stairs to our room on the second floor.

The room met my low expectations. It sure wasn't a five-star resort, nor a complete dump. And given our circumstances, it was an acceptable option for a couple of days while we waited. It came with two beds covered with worn-out bedspreads. I made a mental note to check for bedbugs and cockroaches later. The room was as advertised by Manuel. It had a small bathroom with one tiny, paper-wrapped bar of soap on the sink and another in the shower.

Gabby had said little since the consulate, but now that we were alone, she finally spoke up. "Wow, Mom, that guy Stevens is a real piece of work."

"Oh, he's not that bad. At least he's helping us get your passports, and he did find us a place to stay," Gloria said.

"Yeah, but come on. The way he was fawning over you like a lost puppy. I mean, it made me pretty uncomfortable. Sort of creepy if you ask me," Gabby said.

"Thank you," I said. "At least I'm not the only one to see that about the guy."

"Come on, you two cut Billy some slack. I realize he was a bit too focused on me, but he's probably just happy to see some ex-pats down here. Maybe he's lonely and got excited when he saw an old friend."

"I don't know, Mom. He just seemed kind of creepy to me," Gabby said as she went into the bathroom, closed the door behind her, and started the shower.

I went to the window, pulled the curtain back, and looked out at the view. We didn't have beach or ocean views from the room, but there was a nice view of the broad, muddy river across the street. As I surveyed the street below, I noticed something interesting. We had left Stevens over fifteen minutes ago, yet his car was still parked across the street.

I waved for Gloria to come over and look outside. "Oh, I think there's more to him than loneliness or being excited about seeing an old friend."

She came over, looked down at where I was pointing, and whispered, "Maybe you're right about him, Jake."

CHAPTER

11

We all finished showering and cleaning up the best we could, considering the only clothes we had were the ones on our backs. After rechecking the window, I let the curtain drop back into place. Stevens' car was still parked across the street. Over an hour had passed since we left him in the lobby, yet he was still hanging around. This guy has some serious issues. But I wanted to lighten the mood and not worry Gabby by drawing attention to our stalker out on the street in front of the hotel.

I turned the conversation to more urgent matters as I joined Gloria and Gabby sitting on the beds. "Are you guys hungry for some authentic Colombian food?"

Gabby sniffed her shirt and grimaced. "If it's all right with you guys, I'd rather find some new clothes before going anywhere to eat."

I sniffed at my armpits. Whew! That's nasty. I had to admit, I could also use a change of clothing. Only a bonfire would get the acrid stench from several days of sweat and grime out of these. It was definitely time to get into something clean.

Gloria stood and straightened her camouflage top. "I'm with you, Gabby. I need to retire these and get something less military-looking. Let's stop at a shop and pick up a few things to get us through the next day or two. Then we can get a bite to eat. A nice, relaxing evening would be a great way to unwind after what we've been through."

Before putting my shoes on, I lifted the insole of the right shoe and removed my emergency credit card. A trick I had picked up on my frequent travels. You never know when you might get held up and robbed. So whenever I travel, I always carry an emergency credit card under the insole, just in case. Fortunately, when Dominguez took my passport, wallet, and phone, he didn't check my shoes.

I slipped into my shoes and moved to the door. "Sounds like a plan. Let's head out and see what we can find around here."

We filed out onto the stairway and headed down to the lobby. I made a quick stop at the front desk. Manuel was nowhere to be found, so I grabbed a brochure from a rack beside the desk and rejoined Gloria and Gabby at the front door.

I flashed them the brochure. "What do you think about going scuba diving tomorrow? Apparently, there's some world-class diving off the reefs near here. Besides, after what we've been through, a day on the water would be a great way to unwind. You guys in?"

Gabby perked up. "I'm in for sure. I went out on a couple of dives when I first got here. And you're right, there's some spectacular diving in this area. How about you, Mom?"

"I'll think about it, but I'm leaning more toward kicking back and catching some sun. Let's get going while we still have some daylight before the shops close. We can talk about tomorrow's plans over supper."

As we hit the sidewalk, I squeezed Gloria's hand to get her attention. She looked at me, and I rolled my eyes toward Stevens' car across the street. Gloria nodded and whispered, "Yeah, I saw that before we left the room."

Stevens' Mercedes was parked in the same place since we arrived. With its tinted windows, I couldn't be sure if he was inside or not. One thing was clear, regardless of whether he was in the vehicle, he was keeping a close eye on us for some reason. I've dealt with stalkers before, but I couldn't figure out his game. And that bothered me. Yeah, he's a piece of work, all right. My gut told me to walk up to the car, tap on the window and call him out on his intrusive behavior. But my head told me to let it go and relax, at least for now. If he's still there when we come back, I'll follow my gut instinct and make contact to see what he has to say for himself. If nothing else, by confronting him directly, he'll get the message we're onto him and we don't appreciate him being around watching us all the time.

*   *   *

Our walking tour of the area turned up several tourist shops close to our hotel. They were all the same—small family-run kiosks. Nothing fancy or outrageously expensive, just the usual assortment of trinkets, woven blankets, pottery, and a few racks of clothes. We each picked out two changes of clothing and bathing suits for our dive tomorrow, then went looking for a restaurant.

Supper was a fantastic mix of grilled fish and lobster. And the cold beers were a godsend to help counteract the tropical heat. The hostess sat us on a second-floor, open-air terrace where a soft breeze off the Caribbean brought a gentle relief as the sun dropped over the horizon. The views of the Magdalena River and the ocean were breathtaking. Large yachts and sailboats dotted the inner harbor, with smaller boats tied to the piers.

Gabby and I chatted over supper about the morning scuba diving tour we would take. Gloria decided not to dive with us, but she would come along for moral support and the sunshine. With dinner finished and the thickening darkness of night closing in, it was time to head back to the hotel. Scuba diving tomorrow would start early, and I wanted to get a good night's sleep.

I settled the bill, and we headed back out onto the street.

From two blocks away, I could make out Steven's car. It was still parked across the street from our hotel. Sort of hard to miss his new high-end Mercedes. It stuck out like a sore thumb amongst the older vehicles lining the street. This time someone was standing beside it and leaning into the driver's window. I gently tugged on Gloria's hand and made a lame excuse for us to slow down and stall for a while.

We went to the front window of a shop, and I said, "I know we're not here as tourists or looking to bring back a bunch of touristy crap, but let's check this place out." Gloria followed me into the shop as I whispered, "He's still there, and now he's talking to someone else. I don't have a good feeling about this."

"Yeah, I saw that too," she whispered back.

Gabby joined us. "Hey, what are you two whispering about? You know I saw his car, too? Sort of hard to not see the creep lurking outside our hotel all this time. What do you think he's doing there?"

I put my arm around her waist. "You never cease to amaze me, Gabs. We didn't want to alarm you by saying anything before, but since you already saw him—"

"Oh, come on, Dad. I'm not blind or naïve. I spotted his car when we left the hotel. So, what do you think he's doing?"

"I don't know. But we better keep our heads up from now on. And by the looks of things, he may have an accomplice with him now. So let's act cool and not look at him as we return to the hotel."

Gabby smiled, leaned into me, and whispered, "I'm kind of enjoying this undercover agent stuff. Very exciting and cool."

I gave her a squeeze. "Not so fast, Mata Hari. You're a long way from being a trained agent."

"Who's Mata Hari?"

"Are you serious, Gabs? She's probably one of the most infamous and well-known female spies from the First World War. I'll explain later. Let's head back to the hotel and not draw any attention to us or give Stevens and his friend the idea that we're on to them."

We left the shop without purchasing anything, much to the anguished pleading of the clerk. As we approached the hotel, I noticed the Mercedes was gone. However, a rusty, old pale blue Ford Econoline van was parked in its place across the street from our hotel.

* * *

Morning came early, and we headed out before sunrise to catch the dive boats before they left the harbor at the crack of dawn. The dive shop was about three or four blocks from the hotel, so we had no time to waste.

As we left the hotel, Gabby said, "I see the blue van is still there. Do you think the guy is working with Stevens to keep an eye on us?"

Gloria said, "It's too soon to tell for sure. But I'd guess he's one of Stevens' men."

Gabby's question was answered less than an hour later as we left the dive shop with the boat captain, who would take us out on the water. The blue van had moved to a position just up the street from the dive shop.

We helped load the scuba gear into the small panga boat at the marina and hopped aboard. Our captain, Raphael, guided the boat away from the dock toward open water. I looked back at a solitary figure standing on the dock, holding his hands to his forehead to shield his eyes from the sun's glare. Whoever he was, he wasn't being very subtle about watching us. As we cleared the harbor, Raphael kicked the twin 150-Horse Mercs into high speed. According to the divemaster back at the shop, our destination was a shallow reef about fifteen kilometers offshore and down the coast from Barranquilla.

I turned away from the harbor and let my concerns about Stevens go for the time being. There would be plenty of time to deal with him and his friend later. Today was a day for family bonding and some fun. Gabby and I sat in the stern of the small open boat while Gloria sat in the bow, clutching her wide-brimmed straw hat so it wouldn't blow away. A broad smile crossed my face as a warm feeling grew inside me. The boat bounced off every ocean swell, and each bounce sent a delightful jiggle through Gloria's well-toned, voluptuous body. The edges of her shoulder-length, blonde hair with natural highlights of silver and copper blew across her face. What a woman. Still the sexiest gal I've ever known.

Gabby poked me in the arm with her elbow. "What's so funny, Dad?"

I leaned closer and yelled over the roar of the engines. "Funny? Nothing really, just enjoying the view."

She followed my line of sight and laughed. "Oh, you two. Get a room."

"Well, we would, but we can't seem to shake a certain pesky guest sharing the room with us." I put my arm around her and gave her a hug.

Gabby turned the conversation to the more serious matter of diving safety. "When was the last time you went scuba diving?"

Many years ago, before my agency career, I trained as a Navy SEAL to handle weapons and think tactically and as a proficient scuba diver. I had kept my skills honed during my career, with frequent vacation dives with Gloria and Gabby as she grew up. But after I retired, I let my diving lapse.

"At least five years ago. Maybe more. You said you had been out recently? That's good, so I shouldn't have to keep a close eye on you while we're down there."

"You keep an eye on me? I'll likely have to keep a close eye on you. Especially if you haven't been out diving in five years. Scuba diving isn't like riding a bicycle. You need to refresh the skills often and at least before every dive."

"Yeah, I get that. Why don't we review the equipment features and hand signals before we arrive at the reef?"

I took another long look at Gloria in her bathing suit, jiggling away at the front of the boat. The goofy smile returned to my face once more.

Gabby elbowed me in the ribs. "Stop that. We need to focus on getting ready to dive. There'll be plenty of time to be with Mom when we are back on the boat. And later tonight, if need be, I'll go out for a drink or two, and you can put a sock on the door handle or something, so I'll know when it's safe to return."

"Okay. You have my undivided attention. What's this called again?" I said and laughed as I held up a mask.

Gabby and I reviewed all the hardware and equipment to refresh what they were for and how to use them. The most important being the buoyancy control vest and breathing equipment. We practiced the essential hand signals we would use to communicate underwater and talked through our entry technique, descent, and hold times when coming back to the surface.

The time went by fast as Gabby took me to school. It's surprising how much you forget about diving when you haven't done it for several years. After the shore vanished below the horizon, Raphael slowed the engines, stopped, and dropped the anchor.

The reef lay sixty feet below the surface. Time to suit up and take the plunge.

We planned to make two 30-minute dives with a light lunch break in between.

But plans have a way of changing when you least expect it. You know the saying that God laughs while we make plans? Well, he or she must be laughing hysterically right about now.

CHAPTER

12

I inspected Gabby's buckles and hoses to ensure they were all fastened and in the correct places. Check! She returned the favor and checked all my equipment was properly fitting and in working order. Finally, we were ready to go. Rivulets of sweat ran down the inside of my skin-tight neoprene wetsuit. Working under the unforgiving sun was unbearably hot. I couldn't wait to feel the cooling effects of the water.

Gloria came to the back of the boat and gave me a kiss. "Have fun, but remember what I said about keeping an eye on our girl while you're down there. The same rules apply underwater as they do on land."

I laughed and said, "It's more likely she'll be watching out for me."

Gabby put her mouthpiece in, gave me the okay-to-go signal, and did a backward roll over the side of the boat into the sapphire blue sea. I waited for her to resurface and adjust her buoyancy. As she settled on the surface, she gave me the OKAY signal. Time for me to take the plunge. I bit down on the hard rubber mouthpiece, closed my lips around it, and tested the airflow. I shuffled to the edge of the boat, held the mask and regulator against my face, and rolled backward into the water. Tumbling upside down and backward into the open ocean always disorients me, but the cold snap of seawater soaking through the wetsuit brought me to full attention. Effervescent bubbles bloomed all around me as I rolled into an upright position. A quick pulse on the buoyancy vest inflation tube brought me back to the surface. I paddled my arms and legs to rotate until I found Gabby bobbing in the swells, waiting for me to give her the OKAY signal. Everything felt good. The weightlessness and joy of scuba diving rushed back to me as I remembered how much I loved diving.

We were ready to continue our dive. I signaled I was okay and ready to go. She responded with the hand signal to start our descent. I dog-paddled over to the anchor line and held on. Our dive plan had us following the anchor line down, then adjusting our buoyancy to float just above the bottom so we wouldn't damage the delicate coral. Gabby went first, and I followed her down. Every few feet, I popped my ears to equalize the pressure. I let out more air from the buoyancy vest to help my descent. Essentially, the buoyancy vest is like a balloon. The more air in it, the more you rise in the water. Even with hundreds of dives, I always found it challenging to find the right balance of air pressure, lead weights, and inhalation levels. And this dive proved to be more difficult than I remembered from my previous experiences.

At the bottom, I adjusted my buoyancy vest, letting more air in or out until I stabilized a few feet above the reef. Gabby seemed to be enjoying my struggles to find neutral buoyancy. I think I saw her laughing as I took turns sinking rapidly, shooting upward, then descending again. She eventually took pity on me and came over to help. Once I found the right balance needed for stability, we headed out to explore the reef and its inhabitants.

Multi-colored coral of all shapes and sizes spread out across the ocean floor. Large fan-shaped coral, mixed with tall, elkhorn species and massive ball corals that looked like brains, clung to the rocky bottom and swayed in the gentle current. I stopped and pointed at a giant moray eel sticking its jagged-tooth face out of a hole in the rocks. Gabby pointed to a large school of striped sergeant major fish off to one side. I looked at the surface shimmering high above us, with diffused sunlight streaming into the water. Overhead, a shark casually swam past, showing no interest in the pair of strange creatures on the bottom who had entered its domain. I decided to keep an eye on it in case it changed its mind, got curious, or came closer to check us out.

As we explored this alien yet beautiful new world, our time below quickly passed. I checked my watch and tank air pressure. With just over half a tank remaining, it was time to head back to the boat before we ran out of air. I waved to Gabby to catch her attention, pointed to my watch, and signaled it was time to return to the surface.

As we turned our dive to head back, a distant roaring sound echoed through the water. It sounded like a boat motor. I looked up to the surface but saw nothing but sparkling sunshine. Our boat was still out of view and quite a distance from our location. I figured the sound must be from Raphael starting the engines. But determining where a sound is coming from underwater can be deceiving. We took our time returning while making steady progress back to where we started our dive. I looked up as I waited for Gabby to join me at the anchor line. A second boat floated beside ours, silhouetted against the sparkling surface.

Suddenly, three loud booms thumped above us. Something wasn't right about this, but sixty feet below the surface, there was nothing I could do but wait. I signaled for Gabby to stop before starting our ascent.

The second boat sped away from ours. It took a couple of moments to realize something horrible was happening on the surface. I looked across at Gabby and gave her the danger signal. Then I signaled for her to come closer to me. That turned out to be exactly the wrong thing to do.

We came together under the boat and held onto the anchor line as we slowly ascended to the thirty-foot level. We needed to maintain our position there for several minutes to clear any excess nitrogen from our blood. The last thing we needed was to get the bends without access to a decompression chamber aboard our boat. As we held our position and waited, the anchor line suddenly went slack in our hands.

A shadow swept across us, causing me to look up. But it was too late. I watched in horror as our boat slipped lengthwise below the surface and rapidly sank. Gabby followed my line of sight and looked up. She only had time to raise her arm to protect herself before the hull of the sinking boat slammed into her. The impact sent her tumbling downward as our boat slid between us on its way to the bottom. As it passed, I saw two massive holes in the hull. Then I saw Raphael lashed to the steering wheel, his eyes wide open in a death stare, with a steady stream of blood flowing out of a gaping chest wound.

Gabby floated across from me, limp and unresponsive. I finned hard to get to her. Her eyes were closed, but thankfully her mouthpiece was still in, and she was breathing normally. I held onto her and continued our ascent, pulling her to the surface and adjusting our buoyancy to keep us floating high in the water.

I spat out my mouthpiece and yelled, "Gabby, can you hear me?"

She opened her eyes, spit out her mouthpiece, coughed out a mouthful of water, rubbed her head, and moaned, "What happened?"

"The boat hit you as it sank. Do you remember that?"

"What boat? All I remember is we were going up, and I heard some loud thumps. Where are we?"

Her lack of memory concerned me. I was worried she might have a concussion or internal injuries. So my priority was keeping us safe and afloat until a rescue boat came for us.

"Can you tell me if anything else hurts?" I said, running my hands over her arms and shoulders.

She cried out when I touched her right arm. "I think my arm is broken, and my head hurts like hell, but everything else feels okay."

"You took a pretty hard hit to the head and arm. I think you probably have a concussion. You'll need to stay awake. Can you do that for me, Gabs?"

She closed her eyes and slowly opened them. "I'll try. Where's mom? And where's the boat?"

This is bad. Gabby's head injury was causing a lot of disorientation and short-term memory loss. She needed urgent medical attention to check if she had a cracked skull or internal bleeding and get the broken arm set in a cast. At least I couldn't see any open wounds or external bleeding.

I worked with her to ensure she was stable and floating effortlessly on the surface. I figured we could stay afloat with the residual air in our tanks and vests for quite a while. But for how long? I put my face under the water and looked for our sunken boat. I briefly considered going down to retrieve extra air tanks, but that thought immediately vanished when I couldn't see any sign of the boat. Besides, there was no way I would leave Gabby alone on the surface with her injuries.

Instead, I turned my attention back to our immediate need—survival. I called for Gloria, hoping she dove overboard when our boat was attacked and was still in the area. But there was no answer. The only sign of her was her straw hat floating nearby.

I filled Gabby in on our situation the best I could, but there were too many unanswered questions. Where was Gloria? Who killed our captain and sank the boat, and why? And, of course, when will we be rescued?

All good questions with no clear answers.

CHAPTER
13

Late afternoon approached as the sun slowly moved closer to the horizon. The punishing heat under the full glare of the sun was unrelenting. Even with my wetsuit soaking up seawater, I felt like I was being steamed alive. I dreaded the thought of being lost at sea, especially with nighttime rapidly approaching. But I also longed for the darkness to bring cooler temperatures. To make things worse, we hadn't seen or heard any boats since ours sank. Our chance of being rescued was fading faster than the dying sunlight. With a growing sense of futility, I had quit blowing the emergency whistle tied to my vest hours ago. My hope for a positive outcome for our situation diminished with every passing hour.

Beside me, Gabby floated on her back. Our buoyancy vests were serving us well—so far. Then, I rechecked our air supplies. Both tank gauges showed we were almost out of air, and any residual wouldn't last much longer. My only hope for survival was that the remaining air would keep our vests filled so we would stay afloat long enough to be rescued.

My mind constantly drifted between checking on Gabby and wondering what had happened to Gloria. I was confident that her training would keep her alive and safe wherever she was. However, my priority had to be with us being rescued soon. So I brought my attention back to the present moment.

I held Gabby close with my arm looped through her left arm. Trying to immobilize the broken right arm was a challenge as we bobbed and swayed in the swells of the open ocean. Eventually, I found a way to stabilize her injured arm by securing it against her chest with a strap from her vest. She seemed to be resting easier now and in less pain. Every hour or so, I examined her eyes. The pupils remained equal, and she reported no problems with her vision. She showed no outward signs of a severe inner head injury or brain swelling, which brought me some solace. But of course, I'm not a doctor, just a concerned parent trying everything I could to keep her alive.

"How are you holding up, Gabs?"

She rolled her head to look at me through her mask and spit out her snorkel. "My arm still hurts, but I can manage if I don't move it or tighten the muscles. But a couple of Advil or Tylenol would really help. And the headache is still there, but not as bad as earlier. It only really hurts when I laugh. So no jokes, Dad."

She flashed that beautiful, carefree smile she always seemed to have. Even in the worst imaginable situation, she still found a way to lighten the mood.

I smiled reassuringly at her and said, "I promise, no jokes."

"How are you doing, Dad? Are you still okay?"

Do I lie to her about my concerns about not being rescued or tell her the unvarnished truth? I went with a combination of both.

"I'm okay. My vest is taking most of the strain out of staying afloat. So I don't have to spend too much energy on that. But with night approaching, I'm concerned about not being rescued before darkness sets in."

"I guess we just have to make do with the hands we've been dealt and pray someone comes along and spots us floating out here," she said.

I didn't have the heart to tell her I wasn't confident about our odds of being rescued, especially in the dark. "You're right about that, and there's no bluffing or folding on this hand. My biggest concern right now is keeping you awake through the night. I always heard you're not supposed to let a person with a concussion fall asleep in case of internal injuries. So, how are you feeling about staying awake for me?"

"I'd like to tell you, I'm okay with that, but I'm exhausted. I've been fighting to keep my eyes open for some time."

"We're just going to have to do whatever we can. How about we sing a song together when you get groggy and feel like sleeping?"

"Sounds like a plan. Got anything in mind?"

Only two songs came to mind, and one didn't seem appropriate, given our circumstances. "I can only think of a couple of songs at the moment. How about, *Row Your Boat*?"

"*Row Your Boat*? Seriously? Is that the best you can do? There has to be something else. What's the other song?"

"Well, to be honest, I didn't think the theme song from the movie *Titanic* was appropriate."

"Good call on that one. Then *Row Your Boat* it is. We'll just pretend we're sitting around a campfire."

There was her smile again and a soft giggle.

I pulled her close and rechecked my arm interlocked with her good arm. I put our snorkels in our mouths as she laid back with her head resting on my shoulder. As we drifted, daylight faded as the sun edged closer to the horizon. Out in the middle of the ocean, darkness falls almost immediately after sunset. Once the sun dropped below the water's edge, night would be on us.

From time to time, I poked Gabby in her good arm and started a round of *Row Your Boat*, muffled through my snorkel, and she would quietly join in. It sure wasn't an opera night at Carnegie Hall. But after a couple of rounds to make sure we were both still awake, we would settle back into our relaxed, floating position.

As the sky's dome darkened, a heavy blanket of stars emerged and spread across the heavens. The Milky Way is amazing when there are no stray lights from civilization to diffuse its delicate brilliance. Unfortunately, the moon was waning after the lunar eclipse several nights earlier. But it still provided enough light to clearly see Gabby next to me.

The hours passed slowly, marked by the moon's transit across the starry sky. My eyes were getting heavier and heavier as exhaustion took a deeper hold of me. My legs and arms were numb from the inactivity of just floating and holding Gabby tight to my side.

I started singing another round, "Row, row, row your boat, gently down the stream…."

Gabby joined in, but her voice grew weaker with each chorus. "Row… row… row—"

I poked her arm again. "Hang in there, Gabs, and try not to fall asleep."

"Okay," she slurred through the snorkel.

This was going to be the challenge of my life. Keeping her awake and not falling asleep myself was draining every ounce of energy I had remaining in me.

I restarted the chorus. "Merrily, merrily, merrily, merrily…."

"Life is but a… dream." Gabby's voice continued to weaken.

Yeah right. Some dream. This was a frigging nightmare.

I don't know when it happened, but darkness and exhaustion took both of us, and everything changed forever.

CHAPTER

14

A gentle yet persistent nudge shook me out of deep sleep into the transitional realm between semi-consciousness and fully awake. The warmth of the morning sun caressed my face as I lay motionless in a dream-like state. My arms and legs hung from my body like sacks of meat—numb and lifeless. There it was again. Gloria bumped my side more urgently and friskier this time as she moved in for a morning snuggle. Mm... good morning, gorgeous. I ran my hand over her cold, rough side. Wait, what?

I rolled my head to the side and opened my eyes as a massive shark bumped my side again. The triangular dorsal fin sliced through the water, and its pointed tail splashed as it turned and swam away. My dream-like state shattered instantly as a jolt of adrenaline rushed through me. I came fully awake as something dragged me under the surface, gasping for air and thrashing my arms and legs the best I could. Through the bubbles and confusion, I stared into the face of another shark biting into one of my fins. I kicked the beast in the snout with my other foot. It let go and turned away. I sputtered and coughed out salt water as I struggled back to the surface.

Now at full attention, I realized, to my horror, that Gabby wasn't beside me.

Where was she? How could I have let myself fall asleep?

A mixture of adrenalin, fear, and guilt washed through me as I lifted my leg and inspected my fin. A long tear split the fin where the shark had taken a bite to see if I was food.

"Gabby," I called out as loud as I could. But only a stifled, croaking sound came out of my parched throat.

No answer.

I turned around and repeatedly called her name. Again, no answer.

I fumbled for the emergency whistle hanging from the side of my buoyancy vest and blew several blasts. I strained to hear her response, but it never came. As the feeling and circulation returned to my limbs, I mustered all my strength and paddled my legs hard. My effort lifted me as high in the water as possible, which wasn't much. I looked over the swells before sinking back to the surface. I repeated the process in the other directions. But again, no signs of Gabby.

Damn it, how could I let this happen?

I knew berating myself for being human and exhausted would not get her back. But that didn't calm me or help me feel less responsible for losing her sometime in the night as we slept.

Panic set in as long-forgotten memories flashed me back to a time when I lost her as a little girl. The fear that gripped me all those years ago had returned. We had gone to the crowded county fair, and I was distracted at a carnival game trying to win her a giant stuffed panda bear. When I turned around to give her the prize, she was nowhere to be seen. She had vanished into the thick, anonymous mass of humanity. I ran through the crowded fairgrounds, desperately searching for my 5-year-old girl. I eventually found her playing with a small puppy near a ride. As panicked and stressed as I was, Gabby was the opposite. In fact, she was calm and didn't even realize she was missing. Ah, the naivety of youth. But that experience was forever stamped into my memory. It reminded me of the great responsibility of protecting my little girl from all dangers, even imaginary ones. And our current situation was very real. Somehow, I had lost her again. This time, out in the open ocean, and she had severe injuries.

My frantic search for Gabby took a back seat when another heavy bump shook me. The shark had returned and was pushing me sideways across the surface of the water with its snout. And this time, the massive beast thought I was food. I put my snorkel in my mouth and ducked my face under the surface. A broad, flat head pushed against my vest while its stone-cold predator eyes stared at me. I punched it in the eye with every ounce of strength I had, and it sharply turned away.

The next attack would not be as playful. The shark knew it was dealing with live bait and would come back more aggressively next time. And where was the other shark? I fumbled for the knife sheathed on my right leg and pulled out the six-inch blade. It wasn't much, but it was all I had to fight off the beasts.

I swiveled my head back and forth, watching for the dorsal fin and tail. It could come at me from any direction, and I had to be ready for the next strike. Off to my right, about twenty yards away, a dorsal fin and tail circled and swam past. I put my face in the water and followed it as it went by. The tiger shark was at least twelve feet long with a bulging belly. This beast was well-fed and obviously a voracious killer.

The shark turned to make another attack, and this time I was ready for it, or at least as prepared as possible. I calmed my breathing and steadied my resolve as the massive predator cautiously moved closer. This would be a life-and-death fight, and I knew what side of the equation I wanted to be on. It suddenly changed speed and lunged forward to attack with its mouth opened wide, exposing several rows of jagged, razor-sharp teeth. I waited until the last second as the shark made its final thrust toward me. I stabbed upward with the knife driving the blade deep into the flesh under its jaw, slicing a long gash into it as the beast's forward momentum carried it into me. The force of the attack knocked me rolling over onto my side. I regained my balance and looked under the surface as the wounded beast bolted downward away from me, trailing a stream of blood behind it. Thank God the blood was his and not mine. I had given it a serious wound that would have it thinking twice about returning. Two smaller sharks in the area curled and followed the wounded shark deeper and out of view. With any luck, they had found their breakfast, and it wasn't me.

My triumphant jubilation didn't last long as my buoyancy vest rapidly deflated. The bastard's teeth had punched a hole in it, and I was losing air fast. At this rate, I would lose all assisted buoyancy in seconds. I slowly sank as the final bubbles hissed from the gash into the water.

Seawater rose around me while I struggled to stay on the surface. I had to shed any extra weight. I flopped around, trying to unbuckle the useless vest and empty air tank, which were now dead weight. The deflated buoyancy vest and air tank fell away and sank into the depths. With less weight pulling me down, I received some lift from the neoprene wetsuit, but not much. I laid on my back and took slow, deep breaths, using my lungs as floatation bladders to help me stay on the surface.

Instinctively, my hand reached for the emergency whistle. But then I realized it was at the bottom of the ocean, attached to the vest. So from now on, I would have to stay awake and use what little voice I had left to call for help if I heard any boats.

Fortunately, the sharks didn't return. But they were only part of my problem. You know that saying, 'Water, water everywhere, but not a drop to drink?' Well, dehydration was hitting me pretty hard. Lost at sea under the full sun without fresh water was taking its toll. The sun was unmerciful as it rose toward midday. I felt like a sausage grilling on a barbecue with no shade and only the wetsuit for protection.

"Help! Gabby, are you out there? Help!" I croaked through parched lips and dry throat. I had to keep trying to get someone's attention, even if the odds were against me. One thing is for sure, no one could call me a quitter. Giving up was not in my DNA.

Without floatation help, I had to work at staying afloat. By mid-afternoon, my strength was gone. My legs had quit working hours ago, and my arms were increasingly useless for keeping me afloat. Despite my efforts, my eyes rolled back as I succumbed to the elements and lost consciousness. From somewhere in my subconscious, the broken sounds of, 'row, row, row your boat,' accompanied by a soft groaning hum entered my mind. All sense of time vanished and took with it any fragment of hope I had remaining.

With the foggy recurring drone of *Row Your Boat* playing over and over in my head, a new sound entered from somewhere. A low growling buzz all around me. Then something grabbed me by the collar of my wetsuit. But I couldn't fight anymore. If the sharks had returned, I would have been helpless to fight back this time. All my strength was gone. I was at the mercy of the sea.

I felt weightless as something lifted me high in the air. Then slammed me down on a hard surface. From a faraway place, through the fog of unconsciousness, I heard a familiar voice cutting through the echoing tune of *Row Your Boat* pulsing in my head.

Something or someone was rubbing my face and hands.

"Dad, Dad. Thank God we found you. Are you all right?"

I tried to make my mouth move and form the words, but my lips were stuck together. I mumbled as best I could. "Gabby?"

"Dad, wake up."

A sharp slap across my face caused me to open my eyes. A beautiful angel stared down at me. As my eyes gained focus, Gabby came into view.

"I thought I lost you," she said as tears dripped onto my cheeks as she crushed me in a one-armed hug.

She pressed a bottle to my lips, and I gulped, choked, and coughed out a mouthful of cold, fresh water. Then I continued swallowing mouthful after mouthful.

I gazed into her heavenly sky-blue eyes. "Gabs, is that you? Where am I?"

"Thank God we found you. We've been going around in circles for hours."

I gathered as much strength as I could and rose on my elbows. I was lying on the bottom of a small fishing panga boat. Gabby was hovering over me, and a scruffy older man stood beside her. Maybe this is Heaven, and he's God. Gabby hugged me again.

My senses returned after guzzling two bottles of water and a handful of crackers. It turned out that Pablo, a local fisherman out of Cartagena, had rescued Gabby just after dawn. Apparently, the ocean currents had carried us several kilometers southwest of the reef where our boat sank. Pablo spoke excellent English and said there had been no reports of lost boats or missing divers in the previous 24 hours. Curiously, no one had reported us missing or started a search and rescue operation to find us.

I looked around the small boat and had to ask, "Did you see any signs of your mom?"

She just shook her head and frowned.

Gabby and I settled onto the padded bench at the stern of the boat. Pablo gunned his engines, taking us toward the Cartagena harbor. With Gabby and me back together, it was time to get some answers. Like, where the hell was Gloria, and was she okay? Why would someone take her, kill our captain, Raphael, and leave Gabby and me to drown out in the middle of the ocean? But first, we needed to have Gabby's injuries checked out and treated by a doctor.

CHAPTER

15

Pablo navigated his small fishing boat into the Cartagena harbor and brought us to a gentle stop along an aging pier. I couldn't help noticing the differences between the boats at Pablo's dock and the others lining the harbor. Massive sailboats and luxury yachts looking like small cruise liners were securely locked behind fenced-off docks. These pristine yachts stood in stark contrast to the tiny, blue and white fishing boats bobbing on the gentle swells of the inner harbor. Here the local fishermen eked out a living, taking tourists out on the water for a few hours of deep-sea fishing. And if tourism was down, they went out to catch fish to feed their families.

Pablo nudged his boat against the dock and jumped out. He looped the stern and bow ropes around the dock cleats and cinched them tight. I struggled to gain my balance and fell over, barely catching myself on the side of the boat.

Pablo ran over and said, "Please, senor, you have been in the water too long to walk on your own. Let me help." He reached into the boat, took my elbow, and helped me onto the dock.

I can't say he was wrong. After almost two days in the open water, it was as if my legs had forgotten how to walk.

I happily accepted his help. "Thank you, Pablo."

He then helped Gabby onto the dock and stepped between us, taking each by the arm, and slow-walked us up to the parking area. Gabby also struggled to get her legs under her after our plight at sea.

Pablo led us toward a rusty old, dark blue Toyota pickup.

"This is my truck, senor. Where may I take you?" Pablo said, unlocking the passenger door.

I shook his hand. "Pablo, thank you for everything you have done for Gabby and me. I don't know how we can ever repay you for your kindness. I hate to even think about what would have happened if you hadn't rescued us."

A brilliant, gap-toothed grin spread across Pablo's tanned face, causing deep wrinkles to form at the edges of his eyes. "It was nothing, senor. Any of my buddies would have done the same thing. The sea can be a dangerous place for even the most experienced person. All of us fishermen take pride in helping those in need whenever we can. Now, where can I take you?"

I looked at Gabby, who shrugged, then I turned back to Pablo. "You have done too much already. I don't want to inconvenience you anymore. But if you could call a taxi to take us to the nearest hospital, that would be a great help. Gabby needs to have her injuries looked at before we head back to Barranquilla."

Pablo opened the passenger door. "It is no inconvenience at all. Please let me take you there. The hospital is on my way home. So it will not be a bother at all."

Gabby moaned as she climbed into the truck and said, "Come on, Dad… the adventure continues." She was clearly still in a lot of pain despite her good-natured bravado.

The hospital was a short drive from the harbor. Pablo parked near the Emergency entrance and rushed around to help us get out.

"Once again, Pablo, I'm in your debt. Thank you, Senor." I shook his hand vigorously and patted him on the shoulder.

Even after the hell I'd been through in the last 48 hours, his broad smile gave me hope and optimism. His positivity and selfless help reassured me of the inherent good nature of mankind. And I needed that reassurance after the trials we had been through over the last week.

The hospital entrance doors slid closed behind us as the welcomed relief of chilled air-conditioned air swept over me. The neoprene wetsuit had dried and tightened around my body, making movement uncomfortable. In the ocean, the black rubbery suits are a godsend for protection. On dry land, not so much. In the tropical heat, they are restricting and uncomfortable. However, with my change of clothes somewhere on the bottom of the Caribbean, I was stuck wearing what I had available. At least the tight-fitting suit helped keep Gabby's broken arm immobilized. After what we had just been through, I counted the smallest blessings as they came.

Pablo spoke rapidly in Spanish to the admitting nurse, who kept glancing between Gabby and me as she took notes. She asked Pablo several questions, then led us into a curtained cubicle, leaving Pablo standing in the lobby by the desk.

"Please wait here, Senor and Senorita. A doctor will be with you in a moment." The nurse pointed toward two gurneys for us to sit on.

A few minutes later, a young doctor entered our cubicle and said in perfect English, "I understand you had a rough experience while scuba diving. How may I help you?"

I took charge and said, "Someone scuttled our boat, and as it went down, it struck Gabby in the head and arm. I think she may have a concussion and a broken arm."

The news that someone deliberately sank our boat didn't seem to phase him. As an emergency room doctor, I imagine he had heard some pretty wild stories.

He calmly asked, "And you, sir? How are you feeling? Were you injured?"

"I'll be all right. Just dehydrated and tired. It's Gabby I'm worried about."

He turned his attention to Gabby. "And Gabby, how are you feeling?"

"I'm fine. Just a few aches and pains. Don't believe a word my dad says. Sharks attacked him and left him floating in the full sun for two days. He'll need to be checked out, too."

The doctor smiled. "Yes, I will look at both of you. But first, I'll have you drink some electrolytes to balance your blood work. One moment please."

He stepped out into the hall and returned with four bottles of fluids.

He handed us two bottles each and said, "I want both of you to sip on these. Take your time to rehydrate while I do some tests and make sure you're both okay to go home."

After a thorough examination and the bottles of electrolyte drinks, the doctor summarized his diagnosis. In his opinion, Gabby had experienced a concussion. Although he found no signs of internal damage or bleeding, he recommended she get a thorough neurological workup of her head when we returned to the States. He set her arm in a cast from her fingers up over her elbow and secured it in a sling. As for me, he said a few days rest with lots of fluids, and I would be fine.

"Well, that wasn't as bad as I thought it would be," Gabby said as we walked out through the sliding doors and back into the heat and humidity of the late afternoon.

"Just how bad did you think it was going to be?" I said, looking her in the eyes.

She quickly changed the subject. "Hey, isn't that Pablo over there?"

Pablo puffed on a large cigar while leaning against the side of his truck. Then, he looked up, waved, and walked across the parking area to join us.

"Pablo, what are you still doing here?" I said.

"How could I leave such nice people stranded in Cartagena with nothing to wear but those," he said, pointing to our wetsuits.

"Come, I'll take you to my home, and we'll get something more comfortable for you to wear. Then you'll have a good home-cooked meal, and tomorrow I will drive you back to Barranquilla."

I shook my head vigorously. "No, Pablo, that's too much. I can't ask you to do that. You've already been incredibly helpful and done more than I could have hoped for."

Pablo laughed and waved me off as he opened the truck door. "Senor, you have asked me for nothing. It is my pleasure to assist you and your daughter. Cartagena can be more treacherous than the open water, especially for those unfamiliar with the city. How could I possibly cast you adrift into the wilds of the city, dressed like this and hungry? No, it will be my family's honor if you come for dinner and stay until the morning."

Gabby shrugged her shoulders. "And the adventure continues. Let's go."

It was clear we had few options in this strange city without money. Besides, the thought of spending the rest of the night in this tight rubber suit did little to encourage me.

"Thank you, Pablo. We would love to join you and your family this evening."

"Good. Then it's settled," Pablo said as he got behind the steering wheel and started the engine.

*   *   *

Pablo and his wife Maria lived with their five children in a tiny cement block house on the northern edge of town. The family members didn't seem surprised when we showed up with Pablo. Maria smiled and instructed the children to put out two more places for supper. Next, Pablo led us into his bedroom, where he rummaged through a closet and handed me a change of clothes. He then asked his oldest daughter, Sofia, who was about Gabby's size, to find something suitable for her to wear. Even though the clothes were a little big on me, the freedom from being out of the wetsuit felt wonderful. And the loose fit allowed room for air movement, which helped me feel more comfortable and relaxed than I had in days.

Maria and her daughters served a delicious meal of grilled sea bass, stuffed peppers, rice, and beans. After supper, Pablo offered me a cold beer and a cigar. Gabby shot me a dirty look. I guess she thought it was too soon after the incident at sea to indulge in alcohol.

I shrugged, accepted the cold beverage, and said, "Hey, beer is a good electrolyte replacement drink, and the doctor ordered us to stay hydrated. So, I'm just following the doctor's orders." I'm not sure she bought my rationale, but so be it.

As the evening progressed, I kept nodding off as the family sang traditional folk songs, and their five-year-old girl, Dolores, danced to entertain us. The last couple of days had finally taken their toll, and I slept like a log for most of the night. I was startled awake in the middle of the night by a dream about Gloria being lost and scared. I shook it off and resolved to do everything possible to find her and get her home as soon as I returned to Barranquilla. But first, I needed to get Gabby on her way home to the States for more medical assessment.

*   *   *

In the morning, Gabby said she had slept well through the night. She was noticeably more comfortable after having her arm set in the cast. Although, I suspect the pain meds helped as well.

Maria fed us a hearty meal of eggs and beans, then sent us on our way. I hugged her, thanked her, and promised to repay her for her gracious hospitality. She giggled and modestly held her hand over her mouth to hide her broad smile. But nothing could conceal the joyful glow and twinkle in her eyes.

The drive from Cartagena to Barranquilla took us over three hours. We headed directly to the dive shop near our hotel. Pablo would not hear of me paying him for his troubles or giving him some money for gas. We said our goodbyes and watched as he turned his truck around and headed back toward the highway and home. I couldn't help thinking that if you pay attention, you'll find angels are all around us. All we need to do is look. And for us, Pablo and his family were true angels.

The dive shop was quiet, with only one young clerk behind the counter. All the other employees were out on scuba diving tours. It took quite a while for me to explain what happened to our scuba diving equipment. Apparently, it's not every day that scuba divers return with a tale of their captain getting murdered, their boat sunk, and losing all their rental equipment. Eventually, I agreed to pay the hefty bill for the missing equipment before the kid returned my credit card. I guess that's why they hold your cards as security when they rent you the gear. The guy at the counter didn't ask about the boat or our captain. Even when I told him about the incident and the murder, he shrugged and said, "Many unusual things happen on the ocean, senor."

That wasn't the response I had expected. But then again, much of what had happened to us so far in Colombia was unexpected. We left the dive shop and walked back to our hotel. The pale blue van and Stevens' Mercedes were nowhere in sight. I knew it was a long shot to hope I would find Gloria sipping a beer and lounging in the tiny bar off the lobby. Or, at the very least, surrounded by a cluster of local police with notepads. After the murder of our dive captain, the deliberate sinking of the boat, and the kidnapping of Gloria, I knew that was unlikely. But I had to cling to even the tiniest elements of hope that she was still alive and out there somewhere. One thing was clear: I needed to get to the bottom of what was happening and find Gloria at all costs.

CHAPTER

16

The hotel lobby was empty, and so was the small lobby bar. The faint hope that I would find Gloria safe and relaxing with a cold beer vanished. Manuel sat slumped in his chair behind the front desk and hadn't seen us enter. He jumped to his feet when I slapped my hands on the counter. An expression I could only describe as shock rushed across his face when he recognized us. He stepped back from the counter as if he'd seen a ghost.

I wasn't in the mood for socializing with this guy, so I got right to the point. "I've misplaced my room key. Can you give me another one?"

Manuel's eyes shifted rapidly between Gabby and me. His hand shook as he handed me a key. "Yes... Yes. Welcome back, Senor Stone.... How was your... scuba diving trip?"

Welcome back? Are you friggin' kidding me?

I was angry, tired, and suspicious of everyone not named Gabby or Pablo. I felt like kicking ass and taking names later. And if this guy kept talking, he would do just fine to vent my rage.

I ignored his questions and took the key. Gabby followed me upstairs. I can't say it surprised me to see the condition of the room, but I still felt some shock at the mess. Before leaving for the scuba diving trip, we ensured the room was neat, and the few clothes we had purchased were neatly piled on the beds. Now, our clothes were strewn all over the room. The place had been ransacked.

"Oh my God, we've been robbed," Gabby said, putting her hand to her mouth in shock.

I held her arm to keep her from entering the room. I wanted to preserve the scene until I looked things over and assessed what had happened.

"Wait here for a minute, Gabs. I want to check this out and look for clues about who or why this was done." My eyes swept the scene for details as I stepped into the room.

"I'll go and tell the hotel manager that someone broke into our room," Gabby said.

"No, not yet. I don't like the look of that guy. He seemed too surprised to see us return from the diving trip. And remember, he's Stevens' buddy, and if they're working together, he may have done this or know who did."

The room didn't appear booby-trapped, so I waved Gabby in.

"It's okay to come in. Close and lock the door behind you. I want you to look through all the clothes and stuff for anything that stands out to you."

Gabby picked the clothes up off the floor, folded them, and put them on the bed. "This is strange. All your clothes are here, but mine and Mom's are gone. Do you think she returned and took her clothes to another room?"

"I don't think so, Gabs. That's not something she would do. It's pretty clear to me that whoever took her off the boat came here and took her clothes as well. And that's a good sign."

"How can that be a good sign? Mom's been kidnapped, and her clothes taken from our room…. Oh, I get it. Why take her clothes unless she's still alive and being held somewhere?"

Gabby was starting to think like an agent. There's hope for her yet.

"Right, and I need to find her soon," I said as I pulled the curtain aside and looked down onto the street.

"What do you mean, *you* have to find her? Don't you mean *we* have to find her?"

"No, Gabs. The doctor was right about your injuries. You need to get back to the States and have further tests done to make sure there aren't any internal damages in that head of yours."

"So, what's your plan?"

I had to admit that I didn't have a plan at the moment. With all the bits of seemingly unrelated information floating around in my head, I needed time to bring it all together. And time was a critical commodity. As each hour passed, the chances of getting Gloria back alive became less likely. Especially since I couldn't see a trail to go after her yet.

"The only option we have is to get in touch with Stevens. He's definitely not my favorite person, but he is the guy getting us our passports."

I searched the room for his business card and found it under a chair by the window. I picked up the room phone and punched in the number for his direct line. It rang three times before he answered.

"Good afternoon. You have reached the United States Consulate in Barranquilla, Colombia. This is William Stevens. How may I help you?"

What a pompous asshole. All cheerful and business as usual, as if nothing had happened.

"Bill, this is Jake Stone. We have a problem. Our room was broken into."

The line went quiet as the weight of hearing my voice sunk in. Stevens obviously wasn't expecting to hear from me again.

After a long, awkward pause, I said, "Bill, are you there?"

Stevens cleared his throat. "Ah… yes, yes. I'm here. Did you say your room was broken into? Are you all right, Jake? Was anyone hurt?"

This guy is just too slick, trying to sound innocent and concerned.

"I'm fine. But Gabby was injured during our scuba diving trip. So I need to get her back to the States as soon as possible for some follow-up tests."

"Yes, of course. I understand. Your passports are ready, and I'll arrange for tickets home for both of you."

Both of you? Why wasn't he referring to the three of us? Was he already discounting Gloria not being with us? But how would he know that?

I didn't mention that Gloria was missing. If he had anything to do with her disappearance, then I wanted to play along for a while and see where it took me.

"I appreciate that, Bill. But I don't think it's safe for us to stay at this hotel. Whoever broke into our room could come back."

"Right. Look, why don't I come over and get you two? I'll arrange for you to stay overnight in a safe house we use from time to time to protect government officials. Then you and your daughter can fly out tomorrow. Let me make the arrangements, and I'll be there in less than an hour."

"Sounds good. And Bill, thank you. I really appreciate your help." I hung up the phone.

Not one mention of Gloria. That son of a bitch knows where she is. I was sure of it.

Gabby went to the window and looked outside. "What did he say?"

"Stevens will be here soon to take us somewhere safe for the night. Then you'll fly out tomorrow. Let's get the clothes into the plastic laundry bags and get ready to leave."

That son-of-a-bitch, Stevens. If he's harmed Gloria in any way, I'll make sure he experiences pain he never knew existed. It's one thing to come after me. But when you come after my family, then you're messing with the wrong guy. The rage inside was building to a full boil, and someone was going to pay for harming Gabby and kidnapping Gloria. But I needed to keep a cool head and approach things methodically. I took a deep breath, put my arm over Gabby's shoulder, and stared at the Magdalena River across the street.

CHAPTER

17

Less than an hour after I had spoken with Stevens, he pulled up and parked his car across the street. I watched from our hotel window as he stepped out and walked toward the lobby.

"Okay, Gabs, our ride is here. Now, remember to let me do the talking about what happened on our diving trip. I don't want him to think we suspect him of being involved with your mom's disappearance."

"I get it, but if he's—"

I took her elbow and turned her to me. "I know how upset you are about your mom, but it's critical that you keep your wits about yourself and not let anything slip. If he thinks we suspect him, he could harm your mom. Clear?"

Gabby looked into my eyes with a serious expression. "Clear. I won't say anything."

"Good. Then let's go."

She grabbed the plastic laundry bag with my clothes and headed for the door.

Stevens and Manuel were having a heated discussion at the front desk as we exited the stairwell. Manuel saw me coming, lowered his gaze, and nodded toward us. Their conversation abruptly stopped. Stevens turned and stepped forward with a dumb smile on his face. I walked past him without saying a word or acknowledging his existence. My insides were seething with anger and suspicions about this pathetic excuse for a human. My gut told me he had a role in Gloria's disappearance and the attempt on our lives. But of course, I couldn't prove it—yet. The last thing I needed was to let it slip that I was onto him as my prime suspect.

"I'll settle the bill now if you don't mind," I said, slapping my credit card on the counter and staring at Manuel with steely eyes.

Stevens moved beside me as if he hadn't noticed me ignoring him. "Don't worry about that, Jake. I've taken care of the bill for you. Courtesy of the U.S. government. It's the least I could do after the break-in."

My brain desperately wanted me to scream, 'The least you could do? How about dying a slow, painful death, you smug, worthless piece of shit?'

But I held my tongue and calmly said, "Thanks, Bill."

"By the way, where's Gloria?"

"That's a good question, *Bill.*" I put extra emphasis on his name. "Someone murdered our dive captain and took her off our boat while we were scuba diving. They then sank the boat and left Gabby and me to die at sea. We need to go to the police station, report what happened, and get them on the case to find Gloria."

Stevens stopped at the hotel door and said, "Oh no. What do you mean she was taken?"

His reaction was too casual to be genuine. He expressed no shock or concern, which I expected, given how he fawned over Gloria a couple of days ago. So I kept my responses measured and filled him in on the details as we drove back into the downtown area.

Stevens glanced over at me as he drove through traffic. "Oh my God, Jake. That's terrible. But you know, Colombia can be a dangerous place, especially for tourists. Let's get you settled into the safe house, then I'll contact the police and make out a missing person report. That way, you won't have to worry about it. Oh, and here are your passports. I think they did a pretty decent job for such a quick turnaround. The tickets for your flight out tomorrow afternoon are in the folder on the seat beside you."

I took the passports from him, picked up the ticket envelope, and put them in my shirt pocket. It seemed like the only thing I had going for me was that Stevens completely underestimated who he was dealing with. As long as he thought I was an inexperienced tourist on vacation, I would have a chance to take him by surprise and wring the truth out of him. All I needed was time and opportunity. I could also use some professional help. What I was about to embark on was always best done with a well-trained partner to assist. But first things first. I had to get Gabby out of the country and back home, where she would get the medical attention she needed. Once she was safely on her way, I would focus on finding Gloria and permanently take out all those responsible for her disappearance.

Stevens stopped in front of an older, two-story condo building with a sturdy white brick facade.

"Well, here we are. We use this condo from time to time to house high-ranking dignitaries in emergency situations. So you'll be safe here. But to be sure, I would advise you to stay close to the condo and not leave the room for too long. Let's have a look inside, shall we?"

What a dip-shit. Who does he think he's kidding?

Stevens led us into the building and up the stairs to the second floor. He held out a set of keys. "This key is for the main front door of the building, and this one is for the condo. I think you'll find it's well equipped with everything you'll need. You can order food and have it delivered, or there are a few restaurants in the area that are pretty good. But as I said, it would be best to go out only for short periods. At least until we know there are no new threats, and you're safely on the plane tomorrow."

I took the keys, unlocked the door, and stepped inside.

When Gabby realized I wasn't about to say anything, she said, "Thanks, Mister Stevens. We really appreciate your help."

Hearing Gabby's comment made me realize how cold and dismissive I was to the guy. And that wouldn't help my cause.

I turned and said, "Yeah, thanks, Bill. This is very generous of you. Let me drop off our things, and we'll go with you to the police station to put in our report."

"Oh, it's my pleasure. Anything to help fellow ex-pats in need. Just get settled in and relax, and I'll file the report with the police on your behalf. Look, I'll leave you two now and come back tomorrow to take you to the airport. I'll pick you up at noon. Okay?"

The guy was trying too hard to be cool and probably felt good playing the role of the big-shot bureaucrat he thought he was. But he wasn't a good actor, and his every move and comment reeked of deception.

I closed the door behind him as he left the room. Gabby stretched out across the bed and yawned. Her injuries and our ordeal were taking their toll on her. As for me? I was riding an adrenalin rush brought on by the prospects of dealing with Stevens and getting Gloria back. My mind raced as the early stages of a plan fell into place.

"Why don't you take a short nap, Gabs? And I'll go out and find a nice place for us to have supper later?"

"Sounds good. But remember what Mister Stevens said, it can be dangerous out there if you're not careful. So, keep your guard up, and don't get into any trouble without me there to back you up."

What a kid. Even though her mom and I told her what we had done for a living, she still didn't fully understand my capabilities for dealing with dangerous situations.

"Don't worry, Gabs. I'll keep my head up and eyes wide open. Besides, what could possibly happen in broad daylight?"

I locked the door behind me and went down the back stairs and out the side door of the building. If Stevens was still lingering in the area, I didn't want him to see me leaving or follow me. I peered around the corner of the building and noted his car wasn't there, nor was the pale blue van. My first stop would be the small electronics shop I saw as we drove up to the condo building. I walked to the shop, and fortunately, it was still open. Large posters in the window advertised cell phones and pre-paid data plans. Exactly what I needed to put my plan into motion.

The girl behind the counter spoke a bit of English, and I spoke a bit of Spanish. Unfortunately, neither of us sufficiently grasped the other's primary language to carry out an intelligent conversation. Not the best way to conduct business, but somehow our lack of language skills worked, and we communicated enough for me to convey what I needed. With a mixture of hand signals and disjointed Spanglish, I told her I needed a pre-paid smartphone. Nothing too fancy. Just a basic phone. But it needed the capability of loading some apps and, of course, lots of minutes and data.

She laid several models on the counter. Who knew burner phones were such a hot item in Colombia? I looked them over, selected a phone I was familiar with, and made my purchase.

I placed my first call to my most trusted friend and confidant. We call him Uncle Eddie, and he is always hanging around our house back home for barbecues, celebrations, and parties. He's also Gabby's godfather, so she's known him all her life. But Uncle Eddie is more than a family friend. He's also a fellow agent with unique skills and abilities. His specialties include wiretapping, surveillance techniques, and background checks. And he has deep connections with multiple agencies. In fact, Gloria told me it was Eddie who called in the airstrike on the cocaine fields by locking the jets onto my phone's GPS signal. So yeah, Eddie is a talented guy and someone you want to know and have close to you when you need help.

I dialed Eddie's number, and he picked up on the second ring.

"Hello. Who is this?" he said, obviously noting the unlisted number of my burner phone.

"Eddie, it's me, Jake. I need your help."

"Of course. What do you need? But where are you guys? The last thing I knew, Gloria was heading to Colombia to rescue you and Gabby."

He listened as I brought him up to speed with what had happened since Gloria arrived.

"Oh, my God. Are you guys all right?"

"I'm fine, but as I said, Gabby has a head injury and a broken arm."

"What can I do to help?"

"I'll stay here on the ground until I get Gloria back. But Gabby will fly home tomorrow to have some follow-up medical tests. I need you to get her a new smartphone and use your special magic to set it up so I can have ears on her day and night. I want to make sure she's safe until we clear up everything going on down here. I suspect there's more to Gloria's disappearance than meets the eye. But I still don't know how big this is."

"Got it. What time is Gabby scheduled to arrive?"

"Her flight will arrive at Dulles airport at 22:35 tomorrow night."

"Good, I'll be there to pick her up. Don't worry, I've got it at this end. How can I reach you if I need to?"

"I think I'll stay dark here. No incoming calls. I'll track Gabby's movements and interactions from here and call you if I need you to get involved. How's that sound?"

"Sounds good to me. I'll stay close to her until you and Gloria get home. And Jake? Make sure you get that lovely bride of yours back here safely."

"That's the plan, Eddie. Thanks again for doing this for me. Talk to you soon."

"Anytime, buddy. Bye for now."

The line went dead. My shoulders relaxed as I felt a weight lift, knowing that Gabby would be safe with Eddie back home. Although there was still the overhanging dread of not having a fully baked plan in place. Things would have to develop organically on the fly as the situation unfolded. Right now, I needed to find a good restaurant for us to eat at, then head back to the condo. One thing I knew from my years in the field is that even the most detailed plan is only good until it's put into motion. After that, things usually change rapidly. Being alert to reading the play as it unfolds and responding quickly to changes would mean the difference between life and death.

CHAPTER

18

With Eddie on board and in the loop, my stress level subsided—but only a little. There was still the matter of getting Gabby safely out of the country without Stevens knowing I stayed behind. Somehow, I needed to find a way to give Stevens the slip at the airport. There was no way I was getting on that plane and leaving the country with Gloria still out there somewhere. And the last thing I needed was to tip my hand to Stevens and let him know I was still in the country. I wanted him to think I wasn't around, which should give him a sense of comfort. And that's usually when guys like him will let their guard down. All I needed was a small opening for him to make a mistake, and I would be there to take him out.

As I walked the neighborhood back to the safe house, I checked several restaurants featuring regional food choices on the menus posted by their doors. Any of these would be a terrific place for supper tonight. My next stop was a bank. Cash is the most flexible way of paying for stuff and the least likely to leave a trail. I used my credit card to take out some cash at an ATM. I knew the exchange rate was pretty steep, but it shocked me as the machine spit out one million Colombian pesos for my request of three hundred bucks.

Thank God for the large denomination bills. At least I didn't have to carry the cash around in a suitcase or duffle bag.

As I approached the safe house, the aroma of food wafted over me, triggering a deep hunger. A street vendor on the corner was hawking freshly fried empanadas with various fillings. I had the old guy bag a couple for me to take back to the condo.

Gabby stirred, stretched, and yawned when I entered the room. "How did it go finding a restaurant?"

"Great, and not a mugger or thug anywhere in sight," I said and smiled.

"Sure, joke about it all you want, Dad. But don't forget what's happened to us since we arrived in Colombia. This place isn't very safe."

"You're right, Gabs. I wasn't making light of it. Just trying to lower the stress for both of us. I find it's always best to stay calm while keeping a keen awareness of what's happening around you, so you don't get surprised. Living under constant stress and paranoia is a sure way to burn out early. But you're right. Colombia has given us enough reasons to stay focused and vigilant."

Gabby sat up on the bed and sniffed the air. "What's that delicious smell?"

"I thought you might like a quick bite to eat before we go for dinner. So, I picked up a couple of empanadas from a local food vendor on the corner. Chicken or beef?"

"Chicken sounds good, thanks. Do I have time to shower and freshen up before we head out?"

"Of course, there's no rush. We've got all night."

Gabby must have been as hungry as I was. Her empanada vanished in a couple of bites. I almost felt bad eating mine as she licked her fingers clean. But not bad enough to give her mine. She headed to the shower and closed the bathroom door behind her.

As reassured as I felt with Eddie up to speed and working with me, I wasn't about to let my guard down until this whole mess was over. Despite what I had told Gabby, this was still a hostile environment, and I needed to stay ready for any eventuality. Something was bothering me, and I couldn't quite figure it out. And my tingling senses didn't disappoint me. When I heard the shower flowing, I crossed to the window, pulled back the curtains, and looked down onto the street. The rusted, pale blue Ford van was back and parked a short distance up the road. Stevens' guy had returned to keep an eye on us.

I decided to not let Gabby know our stalker was back. No need to worry her about that. With her broken arm and head injury, she had enough to worry about.

We left the condo at close to seven o'clock to go to one of the local restaurants I had scouted earlier. Before leaving, I slipped a small piece of paper into the hinge side of the door.

"What are you doing?" Gabby asked.

"This is a little trick I picked up to let me know if someone goes into our room while we're away."

"Do you think Stevens or his guys will try to get into the condo?"

"I don't know. I guess we'll find out when we get back. But as you said, after everything that's happened to us lately, it's always better to be suspicious and take extra precautions."

"I'm glad to hear you say that. I thought you were being too casual about the risks down here."

I put my arm over her shoulder and gave her a hug.

As we hit the sidewalk, I noted the blue van through the corner of my eye. We turned in the other direction and walked away from the condo. I stopped outside the *Caribbean Seafood Kitchen* to scan the menu beside the door. Posters on the restaurant windows advertised they made the best authentic local cuisine in the city.

"How does this place look, Gabs?"

"The menu looks fabulous. Let's try it."

The posters didn't disappoint. The food was amazing. We shared the mixed seafood platter of grilled lobster, garlic prawns, coconut prawns, red snapper, and sides of coconut rice and beans. The chef and his wife, who owned the place, were delightful. They looked like twins—short, rotund, and well-fed. I figured they were in their late sixties. They attended to our every need, and the pride they took in their restaurant oozed from them. I paid with my credit card and left them a generous cash tip. Just a way for them to not have to declare the tip for tax purposes. I figured every bit helps, so why not?

As we left the restaurant, the evening air felt noticeably cooler. The thick humidity and heat from the day were being pushed aside by a gentle, cooling breeze off the Caribbean. The street was quiet for just after nine o'clock. And that helped me stay focused on my surroundings without too many distractions. We took our time strolling along the street, checking the shop windows. I thought of Gloria and how she would love it here under different circumstances. Lots of little shops lit up inside with arts and crafts on display. It seemed like every second shop was a silver jewelry dealer. And they had some pretty spectacular emerald settings that really popped and grabbed my attention. But obviously, I wasn't in the market for trinkets or jewelry, so we kept moving toward the condo.

As we entered the condo building, the pale blue van was still parked up the street. I led the way up the stairs to the second floor.

I took Gabby's arm as we approached our door and slowed her down. "Wait here for a second."

"What is it? Is something wrong?"

"Just stay back over there against the wall," I said, staring at the small piece of paper on the floor beside the door.

Someone had been in the condo. But who and what were they looking for? It seemed pretty clear that the who in this equation was the guy in the blue van.

"You're scaring me. Tell me what's going on," Gabby said.

This was no time for long explanations, but after everything we had been through together, I owed her the truth. At least that way, she would be better prepared if anything happened to me.

I pointed to the slip of paper on the floor. "I think someone went into our room while we were out."

"But why? We have nothing worth stealing."

"Good question and I don't have the answer to that. So, I need you to step back down the hall a little and stay flat against the wall."

"What are you going to do?"

"I'm going to open the door and check it out before we head in. But I need you to be as quiet as possible, so I can listen for any telltale sounds. Got it?"

"I got it. Just be careful."

Gabby stepped back down the hall and pressed her body against the brick wall. I nodded when I thought she was a safe distance away. I unlocked the door and carefully turned the handle. So far, so good. The door moved open easily, but I heard a quiet but distinct click at the midpoint—a triggering device. With only a millisecond to respond, I threw myself out of the doorway and dove to the floor.

CHAPTER

19

The blast rocked the building. I crawled through the smoke and debris toward Gabby. The force of the explosion knocked her to the floor. From what I could see, she appeared shaken but not injured. I looked back to the smoldering door of the condo, shattered and hanging from a single hinge. Fortunately, the door opened inward, and its heavy wooden construction slammed shut in the blast, which kept the worst of the explosion away from me and probably saved my life. The sturdy brick walls of the hallway buckled but held and blocked most of the blast from causing more damage to where Gabby had been standing.

"Gabby, are you hurt?" I knew I was talking but couldn't hear my own words. Instead, all I heard was a high-pitched ringing in my ears.

Gabby's lips moved, but all I got was ringing.

I lifted her to her feet and led her along the hallway and down the emergency exit stairwell. We stepped into the night air at the side of the building as other residents rapidly rushed out of the building and joined us. Inching our way through the crowd of confused and frightened people, I led Gabby toward the front of the building. Before entering the street, I stopped and looked for the blue van. If the guy was still there, I didn't want him to see us. It would work in our favor if he thought we had died in the blast.

The van wasn't parked where it had been after supper, so I stepped onto the sidewalk. Flames and smoke billowed out of the shattered windows of our condo. Broken glass and debris littered the street. The faint sound of fire alarms, shouting, and crying people around me pushed back the ringing in my ears as my hearing slowly returned.

"Can you hear me? Are you hurt?" I yelled into Gabby's face.

She was staring down the street and pointing. I followed her gaze. Turning the corner at the end of the block was the pale blue van leaving the scene before the fire trucks and police arrived.

"That's the guy who's been watching us for Stevens, isn't it?" she said.

"Yes. Now we know who broke into our room. And I suspect he's the same person responsible for murdering our captain and sinking the boat while we were scuba diving."

I forced my way through the crowd, leading Gabby away from the building.

"I'm more convinced than ever that Stevens is at the bottom of all this, and he's behind your mom's kidnapping. After all, he's the only person who knows where we're staying."

"I never liked that guy. Such a creep and so weird." Gabby put her hands to her head and groaned.

"You're hurt, aren't you?" I stopped and ran my hands over her head but didn't find any blood or signs of injury. "Let's go to the hospital and get you checked out."

"No, I'm fine. It's just a nasty headache, probably from the concussion and the blast. I'll take a couple of pain meds, and I'll be fine. But what do we do now?"

What a trouper. I would never have dreamed she'd be this tough and resilient in the face of danger. But here she was, rising to the challenges as they continued to hit her.

"Okay, but I need to make a phone call. I want to get you out of here tonight. There's no way we're calling Stevens about this. If he's behind the attacks on our lives, I want him to think we're dead."

I dialed Eddie's number. The high-pitched ringing in my ears had backed off enough that I could hear his voice when he answered on the second ring.

"Eddie, the situation just changed down here. We need help to get Gabby out of the country tonight."

"What happened?"

"I can't talk now. I'll fill you in later. The main thing we need is an emergency airlift back to the States for Gabby. Is that something you can leverage with your connections in the air force?"

"Absolutely. Call back in ten minutes, and I'll have some details for you."

The phone line went silent.

I led Gabby through the crowded street farther away from the condo. There was no way I wanted any of the residents to point us out to the police as the two strangers they had seen in the building earlier that day. That could lead to too many questions I wasn't prepared to answer.

We entered a bar on the corner. Thankfully, it was almost empty as most of the patrons were outside watching the chaos as police and emergency vehicles arrived to fight the fire and check for any casualties. I ordered a beer for myself and a bottle of water for Gabby. We sat in a booth at the back of the room where we could remain invisible to the crowd when they grew tired of rubbernecking and came back in.

Gabby slid into the booth across from me. "What are you going to do now?"

"First, we'll get you on your way home. Then I'm going after Stevens and getting your mom back."

Gabby cracked her water open and downed two pain meds. "Sounds like you have a plan."

"Not yet. I need some time to think things through once I know you're safely out of the country. Fortunately, Stevens will think we both died in the explosion, so he won't be expecting me to be coming for him."

I checked my watch. Time to call Eddie back. I dialed his number, and he picked up right away.

"What do you have for me, Eddie?"

"Good news. There's a U.S. Air Force base on the south side of Barranquilla. It's attached to the main international airport. Can you get a ride out there?"

"Shouldn't be a problem getting a cab at this time of night."

"Tell the driver you must get to the Ernesto Cortissoz International Airport by 23:00. A Marine will meet you outside the international departure area. And Jake, it's wheels up at midnight, so you better get going."

"Got it. Thanks, Eddie, you're a lifesaver. And will you meet Gabby when she arrives stateside?"

"Absolutely. I'll be there with her new phone. Have you got a pen handy?"

I turned to Gabby and said, "Hey, Gabs, can you grab me a pen and a piece of paper from the bartender? Thanks."

While Gabby was at the bar, Eddie told me about the bugging device he installed on her new phone. The phone would transmit a signal via an internet site secured with the latest encryption. All I needed was to log in and download an app. Gabby returned and handed me the pen and paper. I quickly noted the relevant details for the surveillance app and tucked the paper into my pocket.

"Thanks, Eddie. I'll talk with you soon. What's that? Oh sure, just a second." I handed Gabby the phone. "He wants to say hi."

Gabby and Eddie chatted for a few minutes, then she hung up and handed me the phone. She smiled and said, "Uncle Eddie said we better get going right away. The transport won't wait for us if we're late."

That was a nice touch for Eddie to talk with her. I hoped the brief connection with home and family would go a long way to relaxing her and easing any worries. It also let her know we weren't alone in this. We walked a few blocks to make sure we were well away from the emergency crews and crowd before I flagged down a cab.

The ride from downtown Barranquilla to the airport took less than an hour. The guy put the boots to it when I showed him a handful of cash and said there was a big tip for him if he got us there before eleven o'clock.

A young Marine named Private Amelia Lopez was waiting for us at the curb outside the departure terminal. She led us over to the U.S. Air Force section of the airport.

I watched with mixed emotions as the troop transport took off. On the one hand, Gabby was now safe and would soon be home where Eddie could keep an eye on her. But, on the other hand, I was really going to miss her. I shook off my melancholy and turned my attention to my new mission. But first, I would need to get some help. This was going to be more than a one-person operation.

CHAPTER

20

With Gabby on the flight home and out of danger, it was time to go after the bastards that took Gloria. One thought had crystallized in my mind over the last few days. Whoever tried to kill us and took Gloria was in for a world of hurt when I caught up with them. Trying to kill me was one thing. But when they went after my family, they crossed a line and took things to another level. And I was going to make them pay. To do that, I would need some expert help. Joint missions with unknown assets were never the best tactical solution. But in a foreign country, against murderers who have expertise with explosives, I didn't have much choice. I needed help, and I would take what I could get. A phone call to my former employer would be my first move.

It had been several years since I had contacted the agency. But the phone number was permanently burned into my memory. If anybody could connect me to a local agency asset, they would be the ones to do it.

I punched in the number and waited while it rang.

After the third ring, a female voice came on the line. "How may I help you?"

No corporate identification was given or cheery welcome. Just a flat, mono-toned, almost robotic voice—all business.

"This is Jake Stone. I'm in Colombia and need to contact an agency asset here."

"Please hold."

Instead of putting me on mute with elevator music in the background, I heard the clicking of a keyboard.

The robotic voice returned a few seconds later. "I have no record of a Jake Stone. Goodbye."

The phone clicked and went dead.

Are you frigging kidding me? Is this what the agency has become since I retired? I stared into the phone, hoping whoever had been on the other end could feel the daggers I was sending her.

I looked around the arrival area and moved away from the crowd. Too many people could overhear me, and my next call might get heated and loud. So I found a bench outside where I could be alone for a few minutes. This time I would try begging and see how far that got me.

I redialed. The phone rang, and the mechanical female voice answered again on the third ring. "How may I help you?"

"This is Jake Stone again. Please don't hang up. I need you to hear me out for a second." I waited for some acknowledgment, but all I got was silence from the other end.

Okay, I better make this good. "I'm a retired agent, and I need the Agency to connect me with a field agent here in Colombia. It's a matter of national security."

Okay, so I exaggerated a little.

More keyboard clicking.

"Code name?"

Code name? Oh, right, how could I have forgotten? We never used our real names when on assignment. Instead, the Agency assigned every agent an alpha-numeric call sign and a code name. It was a critical agency rule that we remain anonymous to protect ourselves and our family members.

"MP-3, the Music Man," I said, as a smile crossed my face. I always loved that name. It was a little on the nose, but I liked it all the same.

More clicking from the other end.

"Please hold while I put you through."

The next voice I heard was a familiar one. "Music Man, how the hell are you? I haven't heard from you in ages. How long has it been? Five years? Man, time sure flies by." It was my old handler, MS-6, code-named, Mastermind.

It was good to hear her voice, especially now. I figured if anyone could help me, it would be her. She had never let me down in the past.

"Not so great at the moment. I'm down in Colombia and need help with a touchy situation."

"Right... I thought you were retired and kicking back, relaxing, weaving baskets or something?"

"I am. Well, not exactly weaving baskets. But something has come up that's dragged me back into the field. And I could really use your help to connect with an agency asset here in Barranquilla."

"You know I'm not supposed to release assets to help former agents."

"I know, but I'm at my wit's end. Someone has taken Gloria and tried to kill my daughter and me several times in the last few days. I think it's got something to do with a drug cartel."

The phone was quiet for a few seconds. Then more keyboard clicks. If this didn't work, I would be on my own to get Gloria back. But, at least I still had Eddie on my side, so there was some hope.

"You say this is about a drug cartel, and they have BCP-6?"

I always loved Gloria's call sign and code name. BCP-6, Buttercup, was the perfect cover for the focused and ruthlessly efficient manner she approached every mission.

"That's right. I think one of the guys working at the U.S. Consulate in Barranquilla is involved, but I don't have any firm evidence to prove it."

"Give me a minute, Music Man." The phone went silent as she put me on hold.

It seemed like I was waiting for an eternity, and the dopey background music didn't help. While I waited, a steady stream of humanity flowed out of the arrivals doors, dragging their luggage behind them. Some headed to the parking area, while others went straight to the curb and climbed into buses or cabs.

Several minutes passed before Mastermind came back on. "Okay, I have authorization for you to meet with one of our deep-cover agents. His code name is Deep Dive, and his call sign is DP-5."

"Got it. Deep Dive. Where and when can we meet?"

"I'll have our asset meet with you in Sharky's Bar near the docks tomorrow night at twenty-one hundred hours. Your security password for the meet is scuba dive. Is there anything else you require at the moment?"

I considered what else I might need. "I suppose an arsenal of high-powered weapons would be out of the question?"

There was not even a hint of humor from the other end of the line. "If that's all, then good luck MP-3. Goodbye."

The phone clicked off, and I was left silently staring at the continuous flow of humanity streaming from the airport terminal.

Well, that's a start. At least I'll have access to a field agent, and once I make contact, I'll see how things develop from there. But first, I needed more cash. The cabbie who got us to the airport took most of what I had as his reward for getting us here on time. The ATM inside the terminal provided me with another sizable wad of bills.

I hailed the first taxi in the line and climbed in. This time, I told the driver there was no rush and to take me to a hotel near Sharky's Bar.

I leaned back into the rear seat and closed my eyes. Images of Gloria and Gabby alternated in my mind. One was safe, and the other somewhere unknown.

CHAPTER

21

I must have nodded off to the rhythmic rumble of the tires over the pavement. The next thing I knew, the sudden absence of movement and a pulsing red glow brought me back to attention. The driver parked his cab in front of a hotel with a flashing neon sign. I stared at the sign, then looked to the driver, who assured me this was a nice hotel close to Sharky's Bar, as I had requested. I scanned the facade of the building and had doubts about his judgment. It looked more like a red-light district pay-by-the-hour place than a respectable hotel. But, under the current circumstances, I didn't have many options. My priority was to stay off the grid and invisible, so Stevens would think I died in the explosion. I thanked the driver, paid the fare, and slipped him a tip for his efforts.

I checked into the hotel using a false name and paid with cash. In this type of pay-by-the-hour place, it was common for clients to not leave a paper or credit card trail. I gave the desk clerk a healthy tip so he would look the other way and not ask questions or require proof of my identity.

As I expected, the place was a dump. But, it would serve my needs for the night. I lay on top of the sunken mattress and stared at the ceiling fan, slowly rotating overhead. In a place like this, I wasn't going to risk bedbugs by climbing under the sheets. Besides, the heat and humidity had only backed off a little since sunset. Eventually, I drifted off with the flashing sign outside pulsing behind my eyelids.

* * *

Morning arrived right on cue. After a restless night with loud grunting and groaning sounds from nearby rooms, I couldn't have been happier to see daylight again. I got off the bed as the first golden rays of sunlight leaked through gaps in the worn-out curtains. So far, the worst part of this operation was the waiting and not knowing what had happened to Gloria. All night, my mind raced with unanswered questions and uncomfortable dreams.

I tried to silence the voices in my head. But they kept coming back. Where was she? Who had taken her, and why? Was she injured, or was she okay? If Stevens was behind all this, I had to believe killing her was not beyond his capability. He clearly had a murderous side. Especially if he was responsible for the scuba diving incident and the explosion at the safe house. And it was also apparent that he has connections with the guy in the blue van who blew up the safe house. Besides, Stevens put us in the condo for safety in the first place, and only he knew we were there. How else would the guy in the blue van know where to find us? Yes, I had lots of questions, and at this point, most of the answers pointed toward Stevens.

It would be a long day of sitting around waiting for my scheduled meeting with Deep Dive, so I called Eddie to check in on Gabby.

He picked up on the second ring. "Hello?"

"Hey, Eddie. It's Jake. How did it go with Gabby last night?"

"Great. She arrived right on time at Andrews Air Force base, and I took her straight home. I'm picking her up later today to take her to the hospital for some follow-up tests. But she seems pretty good to me."

"I really appreciate this, Eddie. You're a great friend… hell, you're family."

"Hey man, you know I'd do anything for my goddaughter and you and Gloria. She's got the phone, and it's all set up. Have you downloaded the *Earz* spy app yet?"

"Not yet. I'll do that as soon as we're finished here."

"Good. Remember, the app and listening device are invisible to her, so she won't know you're keeping tabs on her. Now, tell me, what's going on down there? Any more information about Gloria and where she is?"

"Nothing yet. I've made arrangements to meet with an agency asset in the area. That'll go down tonight, and then I'll see where I go from there. You know what it's like dealing with unknown agents. It's always a bit of a crapshoot, but it may be my only option. I'll check the person out, and if they look like a good fit, we'll work on a plan together."

"Just be careful and remember, you were decommissioned five years ago. In this game, that's a long time to be inactive. So don't rush into anything. Especially since this is personal. I know you don't need to hear this, but I'll say it anyway. Make sure you leave your emotions out of this, or you could mess up big time and get yourself and Gloria killed."

Eddie was right. The worst thing I could do was let my emotions guide my actions. That was a sure way to overlook important details, get caught off guard, or screw things up. I needed to maintain a level-headed, analytical approach.

"I hear you, Eddie, but this got personal as soon as they tried to kill Gabby and me, then took Gloria. And regardless of the old saying, getting back into the game isn't like riding a bike. However, the longer I'm in the field, the more muscle memory comes back to me, and my response time catches up with the action. So yeah, I'll be careful. Give Gabby a hug for me and tell her I'll call in when

I have more information. But most importantly, let her know I've arranged for some help down here, so she shouldn't worry about me. Make it clear to her that I'm safe and in good hands. Okay?"

"You got it, Jake. Talk to you in a while."

The phone went dead, and I was left alone with my thoughts as my concerns magnified again. I needed to get active to take my mind off the situation until later this evening. A walk along the docks and waterfront should help me relax.

A quick look out the window confirmed the pale blue van or Stevens' Mercedes was not in the area. I knew it was unlikely they would be out there, but I needed to make sure before heading outside.

I left the hotel and blended in with the tourist traffic as I made my way down to the waterfront.

Small mom-and-pop tourist shops lined the street in front of the main pier. I ducked into one and negotiated a price reduction on a Panama straw hat, oversized sunglasses, and a T-shirt. The shirt had broad yellow, red, and blue stripes—the colors of the Colombian flag—and *Colombia is for Lovers* stenciled across the front in bold lettering. I figured since I wanted to stay invisible, I should get stuff to blend in with the other tourists in the area. But when I looked in the mirror, I realized the colorful shirt might not have been the most inconspicuous. At least I blended in with the hordes of locals in their national soccer teams' colors and the tourists down here on vacation.

The day seemed to drag on forever. There wasn't much I could do except wait until this evening when I would meet Deep Dive at Sharky's Bar. The hours slowly ticked past while I kept a low profile, trying to stay cool in the oppressive heat.

Even at low tide, I love the smell of the ocean. The area around the waterfront had an intense aroma of salt water, seaweed, algae, and barnacle encrustations coating the wooden pylons supporting the pier. A light lunch of grilled fish and a salad with a tall lemonade helped keep my internal temperature down during the onslaught of the midday sun.

Relief finally came as the sun moved toward the horizon, and evening brought a cooling breeze off the water. Before heading to Sharky's, I grabbed a couple of empanadas from a street vendor on the pier and a bottle of water. I didn't know how the rest of the night would play out, so grabbing a quick bite to eat would tide me over until after the meeting with Deep Dive.

Sharky's Bar had the vibe of a poor man's sports bar. A small television mounted high on the wall behind the bar was tuned to a soccer match. Given the loud cheers and groans every time a player in yellow, red, and blue got control of the ball, it was pretty clear Sharky's was a regular haunt for locals.

I took a stool at the end of the bar. From there, I had a clear view of anyone entering.

The bartender came over with a soggy towel over his shoulder. "What can I get you, senor?"

I scanned the bottles on the wall behind the bar. "What's your best tequila?"

"The only tequila we have is *Patrón Reposado*, senor."

I just about choked. "Ah... I think I've had about enough Patrón for a while, thanks. How about a beer?"

The guy obviously wouldn't understand my hesitance about drinking Patrón tequila, but that didn't phase him in the least. He shrugged and pulled on a spigot, pouring me a foaming pint of beer. I scanned the room to see if my contact was already in the bar. Of course, I had no idea what Deep Dive looked like. But it's always good to keep a close eye on everyone around you, just in case. I checked my watch. I was early by about fifteen minutes. So I turned back to watching the game while nursing my beer.

The Colombian team dominated play for most of the game. The players on both sides moved the ball back and forth on the field, and when the home team scored, the crowd in the bar roared their approval. As the place exploded with cheers, I felt a tap on my shoulder. I turned and looked into the face of a thirty-something man with piercing, sky-blue eyes and thick, blonde hair tied back in a ponytail. His deeply tanned and weathered face suggested he spent a lot of time in the sun. I figured he was maybe a fisherman or laborer looking for a handout.

"Can I help you?" I said.

The guy quickly glanced around us and said, "Could I interest you in a scuba dive?"

Was this the asset I was here to meet? He had used the security password. I took another look at him and said, "I did a scuba dive the other day and didn't enjoy it too much."

He nodded his head sideways, indicating for me to follow him toward the back of the bar, away from the rest of the crowd. I grabbed my beer and followed him. He took a booth where we could talk without being overheard. Given the rowdiness of the customers watching the game, I sat beside him. That way, we wouldn't have to yell at each other, and we could see if anyone approached.

He leaned over. "You must be the Music Man."

"And you're Deep Dive?"

"You got it. I understand you're looking for some help to get your wife back?"

Mastermind had apparently filled him in with at least some details.

"Yeah, it's a long story, and I don't think we should go into much detail here. Is there somewhere more private we can go to talk?"

He nodded, gulped down his beer, wiped his mouth on his sleeve, and said, "I'll meet you around the corner in a few minutes. I'll be in the old seafood panel van. Just knock on the back door when no one is looking."

A van? Do all the spooks down here drive vans? Oh well, you know what they say about beggars not being choosers. I waited a few minutes, finished my beer, and left the bar. The van was a short distance up the side street from Sharky's. It was just as he described it. An old seafood van. And I mean, it was ancient. It was covered with faded and peeling images of prawns, lobsters, and fish, with *Mariscos Frescos,* painted across the sides in sun-bleached lettering.

I looked up and down the side street, and not seeing anyone in the area, I rapped on the back door. The door opened to a glowing array of computer monitors and high-tech equipment. This was getting interesting. Deep Dive was obviously some sort of tech wiz-kid, and those skills could come in handy. Given my limited technical abilities, maybe he could help me set up the surveillance app on my phone to monitor Gabby's activities back home.

The man I knew only as Deep Dive waved me into the van.

CHAPTER

22

I stepped inside the van and pulled the door closed behind me. He folded down a small jump seat on the wall and gestured for me to sit beside him under the dim glow of an array of computer monitors. With his dark-tanned complexion, he looked more like a fisherman than a field agent. I guess it takes all kinds in our business.

I reached out my hand to shake his. "I think we should start again. As you know, I'm a former field agent with the agency, and I go by the call sign MP-3 with the code name Music Man. Unfortunately, I find that a little cumbersome and cold, so if you don't mind, you can call me Jake. I'll keep my last name out of it to preserve my anonymity for now."

He leaned forward, took my hand in a firm grip, and gave it a good business-like shake. "I get the whole anonymity thing. It's critical in our line of work. And for me, in deep cover, it could mean the difference between life and death. But you can call me Jimmy."

With the basic introductions out of the way, I figured we should explore our backgrounds. That way, we would better understand each other's capabilities if we got into any action together. Mostly, I wanted to know more about the skills and abilities he brings to the table.

"Are you okay if we talk about each other's experience and skill sets?" I asked.

Jimmy pulled the toothpick out of his mouth and crossed his legs. "Sure, why not? Mastermind didn't go into much detail about you. Just that you used to be an agent. So, I figure it's okay to talk about this stuff."

I kicked things off by reviewing what I did during my career before I retired. It didn't take long to go over the basics, my skill set, and a broad overview of previous operations. I avoided going into the details of my missions because of the non-disclosure agreement I signed before retiring. However, I also told him about Gloria's role as an agent.

Jimmy nodded as he listened. He seemed impressed with my training and background. "Wow, you've really been around, Jake. And I don't mean that in a, you're an old man, sort of way."

"Thanks. I'll take that as a compliment. It takes a lot of skill, training, and luck to survive long enough to reach retirement age and be alive to enjoy it."

"From Navy SEAL to a covert agent. That's a pretty big career shift. Do you mind me asking what prompted the move to the agency?"

"Not at all. After a few tours as a SEAL, I figured a less hazardous job might be better for me. Also, I wanted to meet someone and have a family. The agency was always searching for new recruits back then, and they made me an offer. In fact, that's how I met my wife, Gloria. We met during basic training at the agency. Unfortunately, she didn't like me at first. She thought I was too cocky. But I eventually won her over during our first joint mission. The agency assigned us to go undercover as a married couple on vacation in Guatemala, and... well... I guess I grew on her. How about you, Jimmy? How long have you been in the game?"

He quickly scanned the video monitors as if expecting some relevant information to pop up, then returned his attention to me. "Obviously, I don't have your scope of experience, but I'm well on the way. The agency recruited me ten years ago out of M.I.T., where I graduated with a Master's in Information Technology. This is my third big assignment. Previous to this, they posted me in Nicaragua and Argentina. So I guess I either impressed the brass, or I pissed someone off, and they wanted me out of the way." He flashed a set of brilliant white teeth as a broad smile swept across his face.

I laughed, then said, "Sometimes it's hard to tell what they're thinking. Isn't it?"

"Yeah, but seriously, I've been embedded here in Colombia for over a year. It seems I'm getting type-cast. So far, all my assignments are about drug cartels in Latin America. The agency sent me down here because they suspect someone inside the consulate is working with the cartels to facilitate drug smuggling into the States. They've got me in so deep that I've basically blended in as a local. You don't want to stand out like a tourist, right?" he said and smiled as he nodded toward my colorful T-shirt.

I looked down at my *Colombia is for lovers* shirt and laughed. "Hey, a lot has happened in the last few days, and I needed something to wear."

Jimmy held up both palms in a surrender pose. "Hey, I'm not judging. Look at me. I'm not exactly a fashionista myself. Besides, it worked for you back there in the bar. You blended in like a local soccer fan."

I turned the conversation away from my clothes and back to his situation and assignment. "You've been undercover on your own for over a year? Man, that's got to be tough."

"Yeah, it can wear on you at times. But, on the other hand, since I have to blend in and mix with the locals, I've made some pretty close friends along the way. Although, there is never anyone to talk shop with or dump on after a tough day at the office. If you know what I mean?"

"I hear that. It's one of the many benefits of being married to another agent. You get to debrief and let off steam with someone you trust who's also familiar with the job pressures."

I turned toward the monitors and pointed with a wag of my chin. "Seems like one of your skills is surveillance?"

"As I said, my background is in information technology. And when you're in deep cover, you pretty well have to be self-sufficient in a lot of skills. Surveillance is a big one for me. But I'm also trained to use a full range of weapons. In fact, while in training, I picked up top marks for sharpshooting. I can snipe a cricket at a hundred yards. I'm also pretty good with explosives, and as you can see, I still have all my fingers and toes." He flashed that smile again and wiggled his fingers.

I was starting to like this guy. We had done enough small talk for me to know that Jimmy was a capable agent with a broad mix of valuable skills. I hoped those skills would carry over into action when we needed them the most. Time to get down to my mission and see if and how he could help.

"I don't know how much you were told about my situation. I feel like I'm running against a tight timeline and need to act fast to get my wife back alive."

"Mastermind filled me in with the basics. Seems you've had a pretty eventful time down here. As I understand it, someone grabbed your wife off a boat while you were scuba diving, leaving you stranded out in the open ocean. Then the place where you're staying gets bombed. And before that, you had a couple of run-ins with cartel members. Does that sound about right? So, how can I help?"

Apparently, Deep Dive received a pretty thorough update from Mastermind, which was good to hear. I didn't feel like going into the whole story since there were more urgent actions to set in motion.

I took the burner phone out of my pocket. "First off, I could use some help to set up a surveillance app on my phone. A buddy of mine up in D.C. put a listening device in my daughter's phone—"

He held up his hands and cut me off. "Whoa. That's not cool, man. Bugging your daughter's phone is definitely not cool."

"No, it's not like that. She was down here with me, and the cartel tried to kill her on four separate occasions. So I only need to keep tabs on her remotely while I'm looking for my wife. Gabby's back home in D.C., and I have to put a plan in place to keep her safe until this cartel situation is over."

"Wow. I didn't know they were targeting her as well. Okay, what app do you need to have installed?"

I pulled the slip of paper out of my pocket and handed it to him. "Those are the specs and the name of the app."

Jimmy scanned the note. "Oh yeah. That's a pretty useful little app. Can I have your phone for a minute? This shouldn't take long to install and get running."

I handed him my burner phone.

Jimmy tapped on the phone and maneuvered through several screens. "It's a pretty basic but solid app and invisible on the phone you're monitoring. Your buddy's a pretty sharp guy. Maybe he should be a spook, too."

I let that drop. There was no need to tell him about Eddie and his background. At least not yet.

The entire operation took only a few minutes. All the while, Jimmy hummed a familiar tune. But I couldn't quite place it. All I could remember was the song had been a massive hit several years ago.

He handed the phone back to me and said, "There you go. You're all set to spy on your kid."

I looked at the screen and shrugged. "Sounds easy for you. But which app is it, and how do I use it?"

He laughed, then leaned forward. I guess he sensed my limited skills with technology. He patiently took me on a guided tour of the app and showed me how it worked and how to connect with Gabby's phone.

When he was done, he said, "Okay, you're all set. Double-tap on the app to start the program, hold it to your ear, and listen. When you're done, click the CLOSE icon, and it will turn off. Then, double-click on the app when you want to listen in again, and you're good to go."

I double-tapped on the app, held the phone to my ear, and heard Gabby's voice. Over some soft background music, Eddie's voice came through as he spoke to her. I listened for a couple of minutes and realized they were at the hospital. They were probably waiting to see a specialist for some tests for her head injury. Wow, this is pretty cool. Sure, it was an invasion of her privacy, but under the circumstances, a temporary but necessary intrusion. I'd have Eddie remove the app once all this was behind us.

"Thanks, Jimmy. This is terrific."

"No problem, man." He opened a drawer and pulled out a small box. "Put this in your ear. It will connect automatically to your phone with Bluetooth, so you don't have to hold the phone to your ear. There's also a microphone in the earpiece so we can communicate with each other in the field."

I pushed the tiny device into my ear and winced. The volume was way too high. I quickly lowered the volume button on my phone and smiled.

"And she won't know I'm eavesdropping on her?"

"Correct. The app turns on the microphone and is invisible to the target phone's owner. It only sends a signal one way—from her phone to yours. So, she can't hear you on the other end. It's a pretty slick but scary piece of technology if it's in the wrong hands. You never know when Big Brother is watching. Or, in this case, when papa is listening."

I tapped the CLOSE icon, and the earpiece went silent.

This was going to work great. At least until I got home.

CHAPTER

23

I pulled the earpiece out. "You said the agency believes someone in the consulate is working with the cartels. Have you got any idea who that is?"

Jimmy looked a little sheepish at the question. His forehead furrowed, pulling his eyes into a squint. "Sadly, we haven't picked up any noise to move the needle one way or the other. Sure, there have been a few suggestions about who it might be. But so far, every lead has hit a wall. Our focus has been on the top-level guys in the consulate. We think the senior staff would have the right connections back in the States and down here to facilitate their smuggling operations. But like I said, up until now, we haven't got anything clear to go on."

"I think I have an idea who it might be. Have you heard of a guy named William Stevens? He's a low-level bureaucrat who thinks he's a big shot."

"Yeah, I took a look at him recently." Jimmy opened a binder and flipped to a tab. "Apparently, Stevens is a career bureaucrat. He's been stationed at the consulate for over ten years. But so far, we don't have any evidence to tie him into the cartel activity at this point in our investigation. From what we can tell, he's kept his nose clean and out of trouble."

"I'm pretty sure he's the guy who ordered the attacks on my daughter and me. And I believe he's the person most likely behind my wife's kidnapping."

"What makes you think that?" Jimmy said, jotting a note in the binder.

"Of course, all I have are suspicions at this point and nothing concrete, but I think he's someone of interest. A lot of his recent activities point to him as my prime suspect. Like from the moment I met him, he's been all over my wife. He doesn't try to hide his obsessive infatuation with her. He's just one hell of a sleazeball."

Jimmy looked up from the binder. "He sounds like a real piece of work. Being a sleazeball is one thing, but it's quite a leap to think he's also a key member of a drug cartel. Have you got anything else that points to him as a person of interest?"

Jimmy was right. Just because the guy was a tactless shithead and clearly obsessed with Gloria doesn't make him a drug smuggler.

"You're right. But he's also been hanging around outside our hotel, monitoring our every move. He then assigned another guy in an old, pale blue van to monitor our activities. After the condo safe house explosion, we saw his guy driving away. To me, that's more than a coincidence. It was the second attempt on our lives since we met Stevens and noticed his guy in the van watching us. So there's a lot that points to him. Especially if he's hired a hitman to take us out. After all, only Stevens knew we were staying at the safe house."

Jimmy made a few more notes in the binder as I talked, then looked up. "From what you're saying, there's at least circumstantial evidence to link Stevens to the bombing. I suppose we better get some ears on the guy to gather more information. All my listening devices at the consulate are installed in the fourth-floor offices where the higher-level bureaucrats work. Apparently, Stevens has a desk on the third floor. So it should be pretty easy to get a bug on his phone."

"But how do you plan to get in there? There's no way I want to show up and let him know I'm still alive. I want the bastard to think he killed my daughter and me in the bombing. That way, he's more prone to let his guard down and lead me to Gloria."

"I hear you, man. Don't sweat it. As I said earlier, one of my key skills is surveillance. I also use aliases to blend in when I have to. They know me at the consulate as an occasional cleaning crew member. The security group has screened and vetted me so I can access the building whenever needed. That's how I got into the fourth-floor offices to plant the other bugs." He looked at his watch, a battered old analog Timex. "We'll get on that tomorrow night. It's too late for me to get onto tonight's cleaning crew. Hey, you got a place to stay in the meantime?"

I considered the pay-by-the-hour, no-tell-hotel I stayed in last night. "Not really. I guess I could go back to the dump I was in last night, but—"

Thankfully, he cut me off right away. "No problem. You can crash at my place. It's nothing fancy, but you can have the pull-out couch for a few days. Besides, that way, we can work on the tactical logistics for our next steps in our spare time."

"Thanks, Jimmy. I really appreciate that."

Jimmy clicked a switch, and the monitors shut down, casting the van's interior in darkness. He turned on a flashlight app on his phone, slid a panel in front of the monitors, and locked it in place. Then, he closed the laptop and put it and the binder in a backpack. The desktop collapsed flat against the wall under the hidden monitors and locked into place. In a few quick moves, the high-tech mobile office vanished and looked like nothing more than the inside of an old fish van. Amazingly, with the equipment hidden and the jump seats snapped back against the wall, there were no visible signs the van was used for covert surveillance activities.

He climbed through to the driver's seat and started the engine. I climbed into the passenger seat and instinctively grabbed for the seatbelt. No luck there. This vehicle predated mandatory seatbelts, so I had to rely on trust and prayer. Trusting that Jimmy was a good driver and praying we made it to his place in one piece.

*   *   *

Jimmy was right about his place. It wasn't much. But I didn't need much. All I needed was a clean place to sleep. His apartment was tidy, and the pull-out couch was surprisingly comfortable, especially after the sagging mattress at the no-tell-hotel the night before. The next morning came early. I was eager to get going and start planning our next steps, and the smell of coffee brought me to consciousness. I rolled off the hide-a-bed and pushed it back into its sofa formation.

Jimmy was sitting at the kitchen table in front of his laptop. "Good morning, Jake. Help yourself to some coffee. The cups are beside the coffee maker."

"I'd love one. Have you been up for a while?"

"Yeah, about an hour or so. I'm a light sleeper. I kept thinking about what you said about Stevens and how I could access his desk. When I came out to put the coffee on, I heard you snoring and decided not to wake you."

I poured myself a cup of thick, black coffee. The steamy brew smelled wonderful, and the expected caffeine jolt would kick-start my day. I pulled out a chair and sat across the table from him. "Did you come up with a plan for accessing Stevens' office?"

"I've sent a text to the housekeeping company the consulate uses. It's a high-turnover, low-paying gig. So people frequently quit or call in sick. As a result, they almost always need extra help. Since I'm already cleared by security, they call me whenever I let them know I'm available for a shift. With any luck, there will be an opening for tonight. I should hear from them by noon at the latest. The gal who does the scheduling and staffing likes to get the night crews set up early so she can head home and kick back with her family."

"So what's the plan, and how can I help?"

"The plan is for me to go in and plant a bug in Stevens' phone. There's a multi-level parking garage across from the consulate where you can wait for me."

"I know where it is. I dumped a cartel vehicle there a couple of days ago when we escaped from the cocaine fields."

"Good. Now, all we need is the notification from the cleaning company that I'm on the roster for the night shift."

*   *   *

As I've said, in this racket, waiting is the most challenging part. But you can't force things, or you can put yourself and the mission at risk, so I was used to waiting for the right moment to present itself. But given this operation's personal nature, the waiting was more intense this time. Time felt like it slowed to a crawl or stopped altogether. I needed a distraction to get my mind off the nightmarish thoughts about what was happening with Gloria.

I put in a call to Gabby, and she answered right away.

"Hello, who is this?"

Who is this? That stung a little until I realized there was no way for her to know it was me calling from the burner phone. Instead, my phone would be displayed as an unlisted number on her screen.

"It's Dad. How are you, Gabs?"

"Oh, Dad, thank God, it's you. I've been worried sick since I got home. Did you find Mom and get her back yet? Are you okay? When are you coming home?"

"Whoa, whoa, slow down. First of all, I'm fine. I've connected with another agent here to help me find your mom. And no, I haven't found her yet. We're making plans to go after that little prick, Stevens. I figure he's our most likely suspect. But enough about that. Did you go to the hospital yet?" I didn't want to blow my surveillance of her phone, so I made it seem like I didn't know she was there last night.

"Yeah, Uncle Eddie took me. He's been great since I got back. He even got me a new phone. What a guy. Anyway, the specialist ran an MRI and said everything looked fine in my head. No screws loose or parts rattling around in there." She giggled quietly.

I could almost see her beautiful smile in my mind, and it warmed my heart to hear she was safe and not seriously injured.

"That's great news. But I think they should take another look to check for those loose parts again. I'm pretty sure they may have overlooked something," I said, joining her laughter.

She ignored my joke and said, "The doctor gave me a prescription for some pretty strong pain meds because I'm still having occasional headaches. He says it's a mild concussion, and I'll be fine in a week or two. Oh, and the arm feels better too. Uncle Eddie insisted they do an x-ray to make sure all the bones were set properly. So, I'm good to go with a new and improved cast."

"Wow, that's great news. I'm going to ask Uncle Eddie to keep a close eye on you for a few days to make sure you're okay. If you need anything, just call him, all right?"

"Got it. But don't worry about me. I'm fine. Just focus on getting mom back and returning home safely."

"That's the plan. I love you, Gabs. Take care, and I'll call in a while with an update."

"I love you too, Dad."

I hung up and dialed Eddie, who answered right away.

"Eddie, how's it going up there? I just got off the phone with Gabby, and she sounds great."

"Yeah, she's doing well. Everything checked out with the doctors. How are things progressing down there?"

"Nothing new to report yet. But thanks for taking Gabs to the hospital last night. By the way, that listening device is amazing. Thanks for that, too."

"No problem, buddy."

"I told Gabby to take it easy for the next few days and that you would keep a close eye on her. Are you okay with that?"

"Are you kidding me? I'd sleep outside the house if necessary."

"Well, let's hope it doesn't come to that. Look, I gotta go. The agency hooked me up with an agent here, and we're putting together a plan to go after the guys I think took Gloria. I'll keep in touch. Talk to you soon."

"Okay, bye for now."

I hung up and went for another cup of coffee. The extra shot of caffeine would rev up my engine and get me focused. As I poured the pungent brew, Jimmy's phone pinged.

He looked at the screen. "It's the cleaning company. I'm in for the night shift. We're good to go tonight at 18:00."

And the waiting game continued, but at least things were moving forward.

CHAPTER

24

At 17:45, Jimmy parked the fish van around the corner from the consulate building, and we walked into the parking garage. The cartel Jeep was still where I had left it on the second floor facing the consulate. From its parking stall, we had an unobstructed view of the main entrance, where we could monitor anyone coming or going to the building across the street.

I checked under the driver's side floor mat for the keys. "Ah, here they are," I said, holding them up. "I have to say, I'm a bit surprised the vehicle is still here. Back in the States, if I left a vehicle abandoned like this with the keys in it, the thing would have been stolen by now."

Jimmy laughed as he slid into the passenger seat. "Yeah, same thing down here if you left it on the street. But parked up here, the thief would have to pay the parking fees to get it out. And by the look of this... piece of shit, it's probably not worth the pesos to liberate it."

"You've got a good point, but for a piece of shit, it drives all right and will help us if we need to follow anybody. I mean no disrespect or anything, but the fish van is a little hard to miss if we're tailing somebody."

"No offense taken. You're right, and with my monitoring gear in the van, we'll need to rely on both vehicles from now on." He checked his watch and looked at a small group gathering in the courtyard in front of the consulate. "Time to go. Put your earpiece in so we can stay in touch while I'm inside."

I pressed the tiny earpiece into my ear, and it all but vanished. It always blew me away that something this small and virtually undetectable could be so useful for communicating with each other.

Jimmy inserted his earpiece and said, "Testing. Can you hear me?"

"Loud and clear," I said, giving him the thumbs-up.

He returned the thumbs-up signal and clipped a photo I.D. card to his shirt. A few moments after he left the vehicle, he emerged from the garage, crossed the street, and joined the group of janitorial workers. He was whistling that tune again. The same one he was humming last night in the van. What the hell is the name of that song? I still couldn't quite place it. All I could remember was that back in the '80s, it was a massive hit on the radio.

Jimmy's voice came through in my earpiece. "Hola, Carlita."

A short, rotund, middle-aged woman with dark, shoulder-length hair turned and waved to him. "Hola, mi amigo. It is good to have you join our crew tonight."

Jimmy blended into the group and listened while Carlita—apparently the supervisor—gave out the instructions for the crew. Finally, she turned to Jimmy and said, "Logan, I want you to work on the third floor."

Logan? Who the hell is that?

It didn't take long for me to figure it out when Jimmy responded, "Yes, no problem, senora."

"Logan? So now you're Logan?" I said into his earpiece.

He glanced up toward me and shrugged his shoulders.

I guessed Jimmy used Logan for at least one of his aliases in his deep cover roll. This guy was full of surprises.

As I waited in the Jeep, the late afternoon turned to dusk, and the reds and purples of sunset morphed into a deep indigo sky as night fell on the downtown core. Jimmy... I mean, Logan had vanished into the consulate an hour ago. At this time of night, the parking area was empty and quiet. I suppose it was used mainly by people working in the consulate building during the day. The occasional casual chatter between him and other cleaning crew members came through my earpiece. He was definitely playing it cool, waiting for the right moment to plant the bug in Stevens' phone.

When the only sound I could hear was of him whistling that song, I figured he must be alone. I said, "How's it going, Logan? Have you found Stevens' cubicle yet?"

"Yeah, I've found his desk," he whispered into my earpiece. "Not much of a work area for a self-proclaimed big-shot, is it?"

"No, the guy is just a low-level grunt with an oversized sense of self-importance. I guess it's his way of compensating—"

Jimmy abruptly cut me off. "Hang on, security is coming toward me."

The next thing I heard was the distant voice of a security guard. "Hola, senor, are you almost finished in this area?"

"Ah, good evening, senor. I'm just about finished here. Is there something you need from me?" Jimmy asked.

"I spilled my coffee in the reception area. Could you come and mop it up before it stains the floor?" the guard said.

"Right away, senor. Just give me two minutes to finish here, and I will be right out."

"Mucho gracias. I appreciate this. I'll wait for you at the front desk."

"I'll see you soon." A few seconds passed, then Jimmy whispered, "That was close. I was about to work on his phone."

Then he started whistling that familiar song again as he planted the bug in Stevens's phone.

What is that song? God, now it was stuck in my head and would bother me until I could remember what it was. Then it suddenly hit me. It was a hit from the 1980s about stalking and spying on an ex-lover. Weird how most people thought it was a love song.

"Are you kidding me, Jimmy? Seriously, *Every Breath You Take* by the Police? Really? That's too funny," I said.

Jimmy stopped whistling. "It's my theme song for this sort of operation. Pretty spot on, don't you think? But what's life all about if you can't have fun in this game?"

"You're a funny guy, Jimmy. Now just finish up and get the hell out of there before someone figures out what you're up to."

"All set. Give me a few minutes with the guard, and I'll make up some excuse to leave early."

Another half-hour passed with lots of light chatter between Jimmy and the guard. Apparently, the guard had no clue what he'd done at Stevens' desk. Their light banter stopped when Carlita approached.

"How is everything going, Senor Logan?"

"Actually, I feel like I'm going to be sick, which would leave a real mess, Senora. Maybe I should go home early. I hope you don't mind. I've finished cleaning the office spaces in there."

"Don't you dare get sick on the clean floors. Go home and call me when you can work a full shift without being sick."

"Gracias, Carlita. I'm sure it's something I ate, and I'll be fine in the morning."

A few minutes later, Jimmy emerged from the front of the building, and a security guard locked the door behind him. He shot me a subtle thumbs-up as he crossed the street and headed in my direction. The entire operation took less than two hours.

My only hope was the bug would work when we needed it to. Unfortunately, to find out, I would have to wait until tomorrow when Stevens was back at his desk.

CHAPTER

25

Jimmy climbed into the Jeep. "Can you drop me off at the van, and I'll drive it back to my place? Then join me inside the van, and I'll walk you through how the system works."

"No problem. It sounded like everything went smoothly in there. Although, I freaked a little when the guard approached you at Stevens' desk."

"Yeah. I thought he busted me for sure. But it's all good, and everything should be online after I set up the program."

I paid the parking fee and pulled the Jeep out onto the street. The fish van was still where we had left it earlier. If thieves had a choice, they wouldn't be looking at that old thing, especially if other newer options were available.

Jimmy hopped out and leaned through the window. "I'll see you back at my place in a few minutes. I'll be in the back of the van. Just knock when you arrive and climb in."

I followed him back to his place and parked behind him. A quick look up and down the street showed we were alone, so I rapped on the door and stepped inside. The computer monitors were lit up, and Jimmy was already at the laptop tapping in code.

He glanced quickly at me as I folded a jump seat down from the wall and sat beside him. "I'm setting up the program for the surveillance bug. Hang on a couple of seconds, and I'll show you how it all works," he said.

He went back to tapping on the keyboard.

I hoped the bug would work as expected so I could eavesdrop on Stevens and hopefully pick up the information to help me find Gloria. Unfortunately, both of those conditions were still unknown, and I don't like ambiguity. I told myself that with Stevens' over-inflated sense of self-importance, he just might be bold enough to take cartel-related calls in the office. On the other hand, he could be innocent and not involved with the cartel or Gloria's disappearance at all. However, my gut told me there was something there, and I would find out one way or another soon enough.

Jimmy finished tapping on the keyboard and leaned back in his seat. "Okay, we're all set. Lean in, and I'll walk you through the program and how it works."

I sat on the edge of the seat and stared at the screens. "What am I looking at?"

"I've loaded the specs for the bug on Stevens' phone into the computer. Every bug has its own frequency, so each operates independently of the others. The one on Steven's bug is the band across the top of the screen." He pointed to a broad, greenish band with grid lines on it that stretched across the entire width of the screen. Stevens' name was entered beside the green band in the left column.

I nodded as he continued, "I've set the program to run whenever his phone activates for outgoing or incoming calls, even if he doesn't pick up. When the bug activates, a file is automatically created and records the voices on both ends of the call."

I was impressed with how far spy technology had come in the few short years since my retirement. Of course, in the information age we're living in, I should have known the current systems would be light years ahead of what I used back in the day. But technology was never my thing. Younger people, Gabby and Jimmy's age, are more comfortable with this stuff. They grew up with it. Living with and using information technology is second nature to their generation. Me? Not so much. Computers and high-tech stuff took on a more prominent role near the end of my career. By then, I had my hands full, just tracking down and taking out the bad guys. I always left the techie stuff to the younger agents and analysts. My level of technical abilities begins and ends with the ON/OFF button. Anything beyond that was best left to the experts.

"When Stevens gets a call, the program starts and begins recording, even if we're not here monitoring the system," Jimmy said

I pointed to the other three horizontal bands below the one designated for Stevens' phone. "What are those for?"

"The next two bars are for the other bugs I previously installed on the fourth floor. Even though they have provided no useful intelligence, I don't have the authority to take them down."

I rubbed my chin and said, "So, let me see if I get this right. If the program records the calls, we can play them back later and not have to sit in here waiting for something to happen?"

Jimmy crossed his arms over his chest and leaned back. "That's the beauty of this program. When a call comes in, or if a call is started from the target phone, the program pings my cellphone, notifying me the bug is activated. So, wherever I am, I'll know to check the files later. I've set up Stevens' line to ping your phone as well. That way, even if we get separated, the program will notify both of us when his phone becomes active. And with the program loaded on the laptop, I can take this system anywhere as long as there's WIFI service available. I've set up a mobile WIFI link through my cell phone, so we don't have to bake in the back of the van all day waiting for something to happen."

"That's probably the best news I've heard about this system. It gets damn hot and stuffy in here." I had to admit even with my marginal tech skills, his system impressed me.

I pointed to the fourth band at the bottom of the screen. "And this line? Who is that monitoring?"

"No one yet. If you like, I can set it up to monitor your daughter's phone in the same way as Stevens' phone."

I shook my head in disbelief at the technical capabilities available in the back of a seriously old, worn-out fish van on the side streets of Colombia. "That would be terrific. Can you set it up to ping just my phone and not yours?"

"Of course. Do you still have that piece of paper with the app information and your daughter's phone number?"

I handed Jimmy the paper. It took him a few minutes to download and set up the app within his surveillance program. "Done. Now you can open the app on your phone to listen live through her microphone, as I showed you before. And you'll also receive a notification when she uses her phone for an incoming or outgoing call. That way, you can either listen live or check the recordings later."

I pulled my phone from my pocket. "How about a little live demonstration?"

"It's ready anytime you are."

I dialed Gabby's number. The bar with her name beside it lit up on the first ring, and my phone pinged as the program sent the automatic notification to me. Then, on the third ring, Gabby's voice came through the phone, and with it, a thin line spiked into the graph bar, measuring her voice. "Hello? Who is this?"

"It's me, Dad. I just wanted to check to make sure you're still okay."

"I'm fine, Dad. You don't need to call me every few hours. I haven't had a headache all day, and that's a great sign that I'm on the mend. Unless you count the headaches, you and Uncle Eddie are giving me with all the frequent check-ins."

I love hearing her laugh so effortlessly. It was a far cry from the harrowing experiences we went through down here only a couple of days ago. "I hear you, Gabs, but I'm executing my parental right to be overly protective of the ones I love."

"I'm just teasing you. I get it. I really do. But you need to focus more on finding Mom and getting her back. Any update on that?"

I looked at the computer screen as the jagged lines of our voices scratched up and down in the graph area, then looked at Jimmy. He gave me a thumbs up, indicating the program was functioning perfectly.

"There's nothing new today, but I'm hoping we'll hear some chatter now that we've got a bug on Stevens' phone. Don't worry about anything down here. Just rest and get your life back to normal. As things move along, I'll keep you updated. Listen, I gotta go. I love you, sweetie. Just go easy on Uncle Eddie. He's only looking after the ones he loves, too."

"I will, Dad. I love you. Stay safe, and get Mom back. Bye for now."

The line went dead, and I put the phone in my pocket. Jimmy tapped a few keys and hit the ENTER button. A replay of my conversation with Gabby started.

This technology was pretty incredible stuff. And as Jimmy had said, it was scary to think who could be monitoring our every move without us knowing it.

CHAPTER

26

We got our first promising hit at noon the next day. Jimmy and I hung out in his kitchen, monitoring Stevens' phone line on the laptop. Up to that point, the activity on his office phone was the usual bullshit of tourists looking for help finding a dentist, a doctor, or getting replacement passports. All that changed with a phone call just after twelve noon.

My phone pinged as the bug in Stevens' phone activated. I listened through my earpiece as he picked up.

He answered with his standard bureaucratic spiel. "Good afternoon. You have reached the United States Consulate in Barranquilla, Colombia. This is William Stevens. How may I help you?"

"Senor Stevens, we need to talk about your guest. She is… very mean and violent toward my men and me," said a male voice with a thick Spanish accent. The man's agitated tone suggested he was under a great deal of stress.

"What's the matter, Martinez? I told you not to call me on this number unless it's an emergency." Stevens' tone shifted from friendly to annoyed when he heard the caller's voice.

"But, senor, this is an emergency. The woman keeps hitting the men when they take her food and water."

"And what do you want me to do about it? I'm paying you to keep her safe and comfortable. So, do that," Stevens snapped back at the caller.

The man named Martinez paused, breathing heavily into the receiver. "But Senor Stevens, she is insulting and violent. I had to stop one of the men from hitting her this morning. They don't want to go near her anymore."

"She better not be hurt, Martinez. I told you no harm is to come to her. I will hold you accountable if she's injured. Do you understand?"

"Yes, senor. When will you come to take the woman somewhere else? If she keeps treating the men this way, I don't know how long I can keep them from hurting her."

"My plan is to move her in a few days. But if you and your men cannot carry out even this simple task, then I will make other arrangements tonight after I get off work."

"Gracias, Senor Stevens. I will make sure the men do not harm the woman until you arrive."

"You better. Or there will be hell to pay."

The phone went dead.

Despite my training, my excitement rose, and my heart raced. Gloria was alive. At least, I hoped it was her they were talking about.

The graph lines on the laptop returned to flatline, and the screen went quiet.

"So, we have our first hit," Jimmy said, leaning back in his chair. "Do you think they were talking about your wife?"

"Yeah, there's no doubt. It would be like Gloria to give them a hard time and cause them as much grief as possible. Nobody messes with her and gets away with it. But I'm concerned about where he's keeping her captive and how well-guarded is she?"

"I'd guess he's got her stashed somewhere off the grid and not at his house."

"Which means I'll have to follow him to where he's keeping her when he gets off work. At least now I have evidence that Stevens has her and that she's still alive."

"From what that guy Martinez said, he's got several men guarding her. They're probably armed and ready for a firefight. So we'll need to be prepared." Jimmy stood and said, "I think it's time to show you the arsenal."

He led me down to the street and climbed into the back of the fish van. I looked up and down the road and, seeing no one giving us a second thought, climbed in and closed the door behind me.

Jimmy lifted a panel on the floorboards where the spare wheel was stowed. "Give me a hand with this, would you?" he said, lifting the wheel jack out of the way.

I got on my knees and helped him lift the spare wheel out of the depression on the floor. He loosened a nut and raised another cover. Underneath was a neatly ordered array of weapons. Four Glock 9 mm pistols were laid out in form-fitting indentations, complete with several high-capacity ammunition magazines. Beside them were the parts for a sniper's rifle with a scope and sound suppressor. Included in the stash was an assortment of flash-bang percussion grenades, regular grenades, two sets of night-vision goggles, and a small handheld parabolic listening device with headphones. Jimmy was loaded for war or at least a minor insurrection.

"Well, well, Jimmy. You pack enough heat to bring down a small army," I said with admiration.

"As I said before, in long-term deep cover, I have to be ready for any situation. And I always like to have various options available if needed. It sounds like we may be going into battle tonight, so pick out what you prefer to use."

I picked up a Glock pistol, pulled the slide back, and inserted a high-capacity magazine clip into the handle. The gun's weight felt comfortable in my hand as the muscle memory from years of use returned to me.

"This will do quite well. It was my standard issue weapon back in the day, so I'm very familiar with it," I said. Then I unloaded the gun and returned the magazine and pistol to their place under the floorboards.

Jimmy stopped me. "No, you better hang on to that. I suspect we'll need them soon. The conditions are rapidly changing, from monitoring to engaging. And the guys holding your wife are likely heavily armed and ready to fight."

I picked up the pistol, reinserted the magazine, then locked the safety. "Thanks. What's your weapon of choice?"

Jimmy lifted the parts of the rifle out of the floor. As he assembled the gun, he said, "I prefer the sniper rifle. But I'm also very comfortable with the Glocks for close-range action." He finished assembling the rifle. "All set to go. Now all I need is a target. Oh, and these might come in handy as well." He handed me some night-vision goggles and lifted the parabolic listening device out.

I helped him return the cover over the rest of the stash of weapons. With the floorboards back in place, the inside of the van looked like any other old fish van again. And no one would ever suspect that under the floorboards lay a sizable arsenal of high-powered weapons.

Jimmy broke down the rifle and put the parts in a duffle bag along with the goggles and listening device.

Now we just had to wait for Stevens to leave his office.

I drove the Jeep to the garage and parked on the second level in a position overlooking the consulate. Where I had a clear line of sight to the front entrance. Stevens' Mercedes was parked at the far end on the same level as us. Following him should be easy enough. Even though he had no reason to suspect I was in the vehicle tailing him, I still needed to take extra precautions so he wouldn't see me. And that might be difficult.

We didn't have to wait long for him to leave the office for the day. Apparently, Stevens was shutting down and leaving work early.

It was time to make him pay for messing with my family and me.

CHAPTER

27

Stevens exited the consulate and rushed toward the garage. He kept glancing over his shoulder as if someone might be watching him.

"There he is," I said. "And he looks paranoid."

Jimmy and I slid low in our seats so Stevens wouldn't see us. I caught a glimpse of him in the side mirrors as he rushed by on the way to his car.

He beeped open the door locks on the Mercedes and climbed in.

I waited for the sound of his car engine to fire up, but it didn't come as expected. After a long pause, I poked my head up and looked out the window. Instead of leaving right away, he was just sitting in the driver's seat, holding his head in his hands.

I slid back down and whispered, "What's he doing? He's just sitting there like he's in a coma or something."

"My guess is that call from his man, Martinez, rattled him, and he's trying to figure out his next move."

Jimmy put on the headphones and pointed the parabolic listening device toward the Mercedes. I took another look. It appeared like Stevens was waiting for something or someone. But then he leaned sideways over the passenger seat and vanished for a second. When he sat up straight again, he rubbed his nose and shook his head. Stevens repeated this movement several times.

Every time he sat upright, he shook his head and wiped his nose again.

"What the hell is he doing?" I whispered.

The Mercedes' engine suddenly roared to life. We both ducked out of sight below the windows as he slowly drove past us and down to the exit. I turned the ignition key, and... nothing happened. The engine kept turning over but not firing.

"Oh, come on. You lousy piece of shit." I pumped the gas pedal and turned the key again. The engine sputtered and coughed a dark cloud of smoke from the rear.

Stevens' silver Mercedes turned right on the street below us and merged into the traffic. I jammed the Jeep into gear and took off after him. The squeals of our tires echoed as I wound down the ramp to the exit. Jimmy handed me some coins for the parking toll. I almost took out the gate when it took its time rising out of the way. I pulled into the light traffic and raced up the street. We caught up to Stevens two blocks from the garage, and I slowed my pursuit to not draw attention to us following him.

I glanced at Jimmy. "What the hell was he doing back there?"

"It sounded like a lot of sniffing going on."

"Do you think he was snorting cocaine? It sure looked like it, the way he kept rubbing his nose every time he sat up," I said, maneuvering the Jeep through the slower vehicles to keep pace with the Mercedes.

"Good observation. If he's doing coke regularly, it might explain some of his behavior and why he looked paranoid as he left the consulate."

Stevens worked his way through the late afternoon traffic and out of the city. From what I could tell, he was heading up into the hills on the other side of the Rio Magdalena. We followed him over the bridge spanning the wide, muddy river. The highway narrowed into a winding, two-lane road a short distance from the river. Traffic thinned the farther we got from the city limits. I slowed the Jeep to keep us well behind him but still in sight. Eventually, he turned off the highway and took a narrow dirt road through the jungle.

I took the dirt road and followed the cloud of dust his vehicle left in its wake. About three kilometers off the highway, a narrow driveway appeared on the left side. I slowed the Jeep to a crawl. The Mercedes was parked at the end of the driveway in front of a small cabin. I drove a short distance past the driveway, turned the vehicle around, and pulled off the road as far as I could. The last thing I needed was for the Jeep to block the road and have someone honk their horn for me to move it. From where I parked, I had a clear line of sight to the driveway entrance but not the cabin.

"This must be where he's holding Gloria," I said, stepping out of the Jeep.

I pulled the Glock from my belt, released the safety, snapped the slide back, and loaded a round into the chamber.

Jimmy assembled his rifle and stepped out on the other side. He loaded a round in his Glock and tucked it behind his back. "I'm not sure I'll be able to get a clear shot with the rifle in this foliage, but I'm good to go. This is your ops, boss. What's our move?"

To be honest, I hadn't thought that far ahead yet. All I had thought about was staying undetected while tailing Stevens to where he was holding Gloria hostage. But I knew from my earlier experience at the El Presidente Resort that I needed a plan. And that plan had to include watching my back.

"I figure he won't hurt Gloria, and he's probably here to check on her. So, let's take up perimeter positions where we can keep an eye on the cabin. Then, after he leaves, we'll make our move and get her back," I said, brimming with confidence.

Jimmy reached into the Jeep and pulled out the night-vision goggles and the parabolic listening device. "And now we'll have eyes and ears on the situation." A wide smile swept across his face. I could tell he was enjoying this opportunity to get into some action for a change.

As dusk fell on the forest, the light in the area was fading fast. The reduced light would help conceal us. As the shadows covered our movements, we snuck back along the edge of the road just inside the thick jungle undergrowth. I silently signaled to Jimmy that I would move off to the right side of the driveway and position myself in the trees at the edge of the small clearing in front of the cabin. Jimmy pointed to the opposite side of the driveway, where he would set up. From our positions, we could triangulate on the cabin's front door and the Mercedes.

Jimmy moved with the stealth of a panther into his position and lay on his belly. He pointed the parabolic antenna at the cabin to listen in on what was happening inside. I thought I was being extra cautious and silent as I shifted through the trees. But suddenly, all hell broke loose. Gunshots echoed through the forest. I dove to the ground, aiming my pistol toward the cabin door, and prepared to return fire. I was expecting a shower of bullets to come zipping in my direction. But, instead, everything went eerily quiet. Then a few moments later, the front door burst open, and Stevens ran out, leading Gloria by her arm behind him.

I leveled the pistol and aimed, but I couldn't fire. Gloria was too close to Stevens to get a clean shot off without the chance of hitting her. Stevens stopped beside the car and hugged Gloria tightly, then pushed her into the car. He jumped in and fired up the engine. Before I could react, the car raced up the driveway and swerved onto the dirt road. Within seconds the red tail lights of the Mercedes vanished around a bend, and they were gone.

I raced back to the Jeep and climbed in as Jimmy opened the passenger door.

"What the hell happened back there?" I said, turning the ignition key.

Nothing happened. The engine groaned as it turned over without firing. I pumped the gas pedal and kept trying. The smell of gasoline told me the engine was flooded. We weren't going anywhere soon.

"Son of a bitch. How could I let that bastard take her again?" I said, slamming my hand on the steering wheel.

CHAPTER

28

My phone pinged as I sat behind the steering wheel of the dead Jeep, stunned by my complete failure to rescue Gloria. In a red haze of anger and frustration, I pulled the phone from my pocket and tapped the surveillance app. Either Gabby was calling someone, or she was receiving a call. I hoped it was Eddie, the only other person I could trust to take care of my girl back home. And with things heating up down here in Colombia, I felt helpless to protect her.

As I listened, an unfamiliar voice came through the earpiece.

"Hello, Marcos Rodriguez here. How may I help you?" a well-spoken voice said without a hint of an accent.

Who the hell is Marcos Rodriguez?

"Marcos, it's me, Gabrielle. How are you doing, my old friend?"

As Gabby spoke, a vague memory came back to me of some guy she knew several years ago. She had known Marcos since their college days. If I remember correctly, she had a huge crush on him back then. But their relationship never became anything more than friends.

A long pause held the space on the phones before Marcos asked, "Who is this?"

"Oh, come on, Marcos, your memory can't be that bad. It's me, Gabby Stone. Don't you remember me from school?"

Another brief pause, as if he was trying to recall her voice and the person associated with it. "Oh, Gabrielle. How are you? This is a pleasant surprise. What are you up to these days?"

"Please call me Gabby. I just got back from Colombia, and boy, that was a scary trip."

"Colombia? Wow, I hear that can be a pretty dangerous place at times."

"For sure, and believe me, I've had my fill of danger for a lifetime. There's way too much to tell you over the phone. How about you buy me lunch tomorrow, and I'll fill you in on all the details?"

"Tomorrow? Let me check my schedule." Marcos paused for a few seconds. "Yeah, tomorrow looks good for me?"

"Perfect. I'll pop over to your office, and we can go somewhere local so you can get right back to work afterward."

"How about we meet at Gino's Italian Restaurant instead? It's only a block down the street from my office. Hang on a second while I get you the address."

"No, it's okay. I can find the restaurant. I've been doing a little spying on you, so I already have your office address." Gabby said and laughed innocently.

"Ah… all right. I look forward to seeing you again and catching up. See you at noon tomorrow. Bye, Gabby."

The phone went silent as they hung up. In the background, I could still hear Gabby whistling cheerfully. I assumed she was feeling good about the prospect of having a date and getting her life back to normal. And I was relieved that the bugging device Eddie set up on her phone was working so well.

I considered calling her to check in but thought she might get suspicious if I phoned her after every call she made. So I dialed Eddie instead.

Eddie's familiar voice answered on the second ring. "Hello?"

"Eddie, just wondering how it's going up there?"

"Oh, hi, Jake. Everything's good up here. How's your mission going? Did you locate Gloria?

Even though my rage was calming after hearing Gabby's voice, I was still hot about my failure to stop Stevens from getting away with Gloria. "Yeah, we found her. But that son-of-a-bitch Stevens got away from us. He took her before we could close in on him. Then this piece-of-shit vehicle wouldn't start, so we lost them. At least now I know Stevens definitely has her. When I catch up with him, he's gonna wish he'd never been born."

"Hey Jake, remember your training. It never helps to let your emotions get in the way during an operation. I know what you're going to say. How can you not get emotional with Gloria and Gabby in the line of fire? But, it's critical for you to monitor your emotions and keep them in check, or you could make serious errors in judgment and screw up the entire operation."

"I know, Eddie. Of course, you're right. This is one operation where I'm losing perspective and not staying focused on the primary objective. It's hard not to let my emotions kick in. I'll never forgive myself if anything happens to either of them."

"All the more reason to control your emotions and stay logical, rational, and focused on the desired results. And the end result is not vengeance or taking out Stevens. Your goal, first and foremost, is to get Gloria back safely. Everything after that is just gravy."

I chuckled softly. "I knew there was more than one reason I keep you around, my friend. You're always a calming voice in stormy situations."

"Hey, and don't ever forget it, buddy." Eddie broke out in his trademark laugh, which included a soft snort.

"Anyway, I called to let you know Gabby has arranged a lunch date for tomorrow with an old school buddy of hers. It'll be good for her to get out to relax and decompress a little after all she's been through."

"Good to know. I'll be discreet and keep tabs on her, just to be sure. And no doubt you'll be eavesdropping on her the whole time, right?"

"Well, probably not the whole time. I'll be focusing on finding that son-of-a-bitch Stevens and where he took Gloria."

"What did we just talk about? Take a deep breath and refocus that energy on the real mission."

I took a deep, cleansing breath. "Okay, coach. I've got it. Talk to you later, buddy."

I hung up the phone. A sense of relief swept over me, knowing that Gabby was returning to her normal life. Now I had to focus on my primary goal—finding Gloria and getting her back safely. And as Eddie said, anything after that would be gravy. I had to admit, I was looking forward to drowning that asshole Stevens in a boatload of gravy when I caught up with him.

CHAPTER

29

My chat with Eddie gave me a renewed sense of purpose and focus, so I turned my attention back to my current situation. Stevens had gotten away and taken Gloria with him. Jimmy and I were sitting helplessly in a beaten-down old Jeep that wouldn't start. Altogether, not the best of circumstances.

Jimmy broke my train of thought and tried to lighten my mood. "Sounds like everything's good back on the home front, at least."

"Yeah, Eddie's got things well in hand up there. Now, if I could just get this piece of shit going."

I turned the ignition key again. The engine sputtered several times, then coughed into life as a black plume of smoke belched from the exhaust.

"There you go. Let the good times roll," Jimmy said. "Let's get after Stevens and get your wife back."

They had over fifteen minutes of a head start, and I didn't know where he was going.

"I don't think catching up to him is in the cards. He's long gone. We'll have to find another way to track him down. Right now, I want to check the cabin and see what all the gunfire was about before they fled the scene. He may have left some clues about where he's taken her."

Oddly, no one had come out of the cabin after Stevens and Gloria left. I put the Jeep in gear and cautiously pulled down the driveway. This time I left the motor running. There was no way I wanted to risk being stuck out here with a broken-down vehicle as night closed around us.

We approached the cabin's open door from both sides with our pistols held at the ready. It was dead quiet inside. Too quiet. Where were Martinez and his men? This could get tricky since you never know what you'll find lurking in the silence on the other side of a door.

With our guns ready, we stood on either side of the door. I cautiously poked my head around the doorjamb and looked inside. The place looked like a scene from Hell. I stepped through the doorway and walked around the perimeter on the right side of the main room. Jimmy followed with his pistol in front of him and moved around the left side. Three bodies were slumped over a small kitchen table. Pools of blood spread across the table and dripped onto the floorboards. Each man had been shot in the head at close range. All three men were unarmed. I looked around the kitchen area and found two rifles and a pistol on the counter. Clearly, they were not expecting an ambush by Stevens. The last thing they expected was him to kill them in cold blood. Why would they, since they worked for him?

Jimmy moved toward one of two doors on the back wall. He opened the door, looked inside, and said, "Clear."

I moved to the second door and swung it open. "Clear."

The room had no windows. The only things in the room were a single cot with a thin mattress pushed up against the far wall and a food tray on the floor beside the bed. My initial scan of the room suggested this was where they held Gloria hostage. I moved in for a closer look. Hopefully, Gloria left some clues about who her captors were. I knew Gloria, and she would find a way to leave a clue if she had a chance. I pulled the mattress off the bed. Some faint scratches on the wall drew my attention. I tapped the flashlight app on my phone and moved closer.

Barely visible and carved into the wall with crude lettering was one word—BILLY.

"That son-of-a-bitch wasn't as careful as he thought," I said, drawing Jimmy's attention to the lettering.

"That wife of yours is pretty sharp," he said.

"She's the best agent I ever worked with. I'll have to fill you in on that some other time. We need to find that son-of-a-bitch and get her back before he harms her. Hopefully, she plays along with whatever game he's playing and doesn't let him know she's onto him."

"I may be out of line here, boss, but I don't think he'll hurt her. Did you see how he hugged her before they got in the car? And from the short sound bite I picked up, he's got a real thing for her. Besides, if he wanted to hurt her, why didn't he do it when he killed the others?"

Jimmy made a lot of sense. I knew firsthand how obsessed Stevens was with Gloria. I'd seen it with my own eyes. But what was his game plan? If he wasn't going to hurt her, what was he thinking would happen in the long run? Did he think she would fall in love with him for rescuing her? I had complete faith she wouldn't succumb to Stockholm Syndrome, where hostages sometimes fall for their captors. She's too well-trained and seasoned for that to happen. My guess was that Gloria would play along and wait for him to let his guard down. Then she would strike.

I said, "No, you're not out of line at all. I need to consider all avenues of thought on this. Stevens was obsessed with her when we first met him at the consulate. He's quite a piece of work and not well-balanced. If you ask me, his wrapper is a little too tight. And it seems like he's got a cocaine habit as well. So, I wouldn't put it past him if he's going for the white knight syndrome. You know, where the self-proclaimed hero rescues the fair maiden from the evil guys, and he expects her to fall in love with him, and they live happily ever after. That sort of fairy tale shit."

"You're probably right. The guy seems a bit weird, and regularly doing cocaine is likely to make him unstable. Probably comes with the territory of being stuck in a dead-end job in an out-of-the-way country like Colombia. Oh wait, am I describing him or me?" Jimmy said and laughed.

He sure had a way of lightening the mood, regardless of how bleak things looked.

I smiled at him and said, "I'm assuming you don't have a cocaine habit like him... so you must be talking about Stevens."

We stepped back into the main room and surveyed the carnage.

Jimmy let out a low whistle. "Man, he's a stone-cold killer."

"You've got that right. And, after the bombing of the condo, I've got first-hand experience of what he'll do to get rid of anyone blocking him from getting what he wants."

I stepped outside and scanned the yard. Nothing but dense jungle on all sides.

"What's that? It sounds like the ringtone of a phone," I said.

It wasn't so much a ringtone as faint salsa music, and it came from inside the cabin.

I followed the sound to where it was coming from. The music grew louder as I neared the kitchen table and the three corpses.

I reached into a dead guy's jacket and pulled out his cell phone. It rang one more time, then went silent.

Jimmy said, "I guess he missed the call."

I chuckled at his twisted sense of humor. With his perfect timing to lighten tense situations, he could have been a stand-up comic.

"I wonder who this guy was and who was calling him?"

"I may be able to help with that," Jimmy said, reaching for the phone.

He tapped on the screen. "Damn, fingerprint security. Hmm, probably his index finger." He lifted the guy's lifeless hand and rolled his index finger over the oval fingerprint sensor. The phone switched screens. "Got it. The guy at least didn't want anyone getting access to his personal information. Smart... but he's still dead. So not too smart." He handed the phone back to me.

"How do I find out who he was?" I asked.

"Probably the fastest way would be to open his Facebook account. That will take you straight to his news feed. At the top, there should be a photo of the guy. Click on the photo, and it will take you to his main page."

I opened the app and followed Jimmy's instructions. Sure enough, there it was. I bent over, looked at the dead guy's face, and then back at the screen. "Our friend here is none other than Martinez. Apparently, after his call earlier today, Stevens must have seen him as more of a liability than an asset. I assume by taking him and the other guys out, he didn't want any loose ends."

I wiped the phone clean of fingerprints and tucked it back into Martinez's pocket.

I was glad I had left the Jeep running. There was no way I wanted to be stranded at the scene of a triple murder.

"I don't suppose you have an address for Stevens in your laptop?" I asked as I put the vehicle in gear.

Jimmy flipped open his laptop, tapped the keyboard, and looked up. "Unfortunately, Stevens hasn't been on our radar as a suspect, so I have nothing on him in the system."

"Damn it. Now we'll have to wait for another opportunity to track him down, and time is not working in our favor."

CHAPTER

30

All night I beat myself up for letting Stevens get away and losing Gloria again. And this morning, the boring work of waiting continued as we took our usual parking spot overlooking the consulate. The minutes and hours slowly ticked by as I waited and hoped he would make a move soon and lead us to where he'd taken Gloria. I felt helpless under the current situation. All I could do was try to stay calm and ready for when the time came for action. To pass the time, I played solitaire on my phone. Jimmy took a different approach and seemed comfortable napping in the seat beside me. It was also a quiet day for Stevens, which made waiting even more challenging. His phone rang once, and that was over an hour ago. The person on the other end wanted help finding a nice hotel. So, of course, Stevens referred him to his friend's place—the Hotel Costa Azul. I assumed Stevens received a kickback for every referral he sent to his friend's hotel. Quite a racket he had going for himself.

It was a good thing I decided to look up from my phone when I did. Stevens had just stepped out of the consulate.

"Hey Jimmy, wake up. He's leaving the building and coming this way."

Stevens was halfway across the front courtyard and heading straight for us.

Jimmy sat up and rubbed his eyes. "Yeah, that's him, alright. And it looks like he's in a hurry. I wonder where he's headed? It's too early to knock off for the day."

As Stevens disappeared below the half-wall of the parking garage, I said, "Get down."

I slid low into the seat below the windows. Stevens rounded the corner and walked straight to his Mercedes, parked in its usual spot at the end of the row. The car alarm chirped as the doors unlocked. I poked my head up to see what he was doing. He stopped beside his car, turned, and quickly looked around. Then he pulled something out of his pocket before climbing into the driver's seat. He lowered his window but didn't start the car. It looked like he was fidgeting with something on the seat beside him. A few seconds later, he leaned over sideways. Then sat upright again, rubbed his nose, and sniffed.

"What the hell is he doing? Is he doing coke again?" I asked.

Jimmy put his headphones on and pointed the small dish antenna toward Stevens' car. "Let's see what we can pick up."

Stevens bent over again. Then sat up and rubbed his nose. He repeated this movement several times.

Jimmy said, "It sure sounds like he's snorting cocaine. I'd say this guy's got a pretty bad habit."

Without warning, Stevens fired up his car, and with the squeal of tires on smooth concrete, he sped down the ramp toward the exit.

"Damn, that's loud," Jimmy said, yanking the headphones off his ears. "I wasn't expecting the screeching tires."

I started the Jeep. Thankfully, this time it fired up on the first try. "Did you hear anything other than the snorting and sniffing?"

Jimmy pulled on the seatbelt and clipped himself in. "He kept repeating, no loose ends, no loose ends. It sounded like he was pissed off about something and coming unglued. What a weird and strung-out little guy."

"He may be weird and strung out on cocaine, but don't forget, he's also a cold-blooded killer. And that combination makes him unpredictable and extremely dangerous."

I paid the parking fee and pulled the Jeep onto the street a block behind the Mercedes.

Mid-day traffic was heavy in the downtown area, and keeping him in my line of sight was more difficult than I expected. I almost lost him twice as I weaved in and out of the slow-moving vehicles. A few times, I braked hard to avoid pedestrians who stepped off the sidewalks as they rushed across the street. But I stayed with him.

"Where do you think he's headed?" Jimmy asked.

"If he's worried about loose ends, he could be going to where he's holding Gloria," I said.

"Could be. He's definitely stressed about something."

My phone pinged, but I ignored it and left it in my pocket. I couldn't take the chance of hitting someone and losing the bastard. I figured it must be Gabby's phone since Jimmy's phone didn't ping to announce one of the other bugs had been activated. Stevens stopped at a red light, four cars ahead of us. While I waited for the light to change, I pulled out my phone and tapped the screen. Nothing happened. The screen was black and unresponsive. The battery had died. There was no way for me to listen in on Gabby or communicate with Eddie. I would have to wait until I returned to Jimmy's place to recharge the phone.

Traffic started moving again, and Stevens turned out of the downtown core. Like yesterday, he was heading toward the bridge across the Rio Magdalena. Could he be going back to the cabin where he had killed Martinez and his men? But why?

It was like Jimmy was reading my mind. "Do you think he's going to clean up the mess he made with Martinez?"

"It's either that or he's heading to where he has Gloria. Wherever he's going this time, I won't let him get away."

Our questions were answered when Stevens turned off the highway and took the narrow dirt road into the jungle toward the cabin.

I turned onto the dirt road. Even though the Mercedes was nowhere to be seen, I knew exactly where he was headed and didn't need to keep my eyes on him to get there.

I slowed the Jeep and looked down the narrow driveway. The Mercedes was parked in front of the cabin. Stevens stood outside, leaning against the car. He poured some coke on the back of his hand, held it to his nose, and snorted it. The guy had a serious drug problem. No wonder he was coming unwound with each passing minute. As I rolled past, I caught sight of something else tucked under the low-hanging palm fronds at the bottom of the driveway. A pale blue van.

"What the hell? The guy who tried to kill us at the safe house is also here. Jimmy, can you listen in on them and see what's going on?"

"I'll need to get an opening with a clear line of sight on them for the antenna to pick up any conversation."

I pulled off the road and parked under the low-hanging foliage. Jimmy slipped on the headphones and slid into the bushes between the road and the cabin while I followed with my Glock held ready for action.

I stretched out on my stomach on the musty, damp ground beside Jimmy and waited. We had a direct line of sight from our position to Stevens and the cabin. The driver of the van was nowhere in sight. I figured he must be inside with the dead men.

Stevens paced back and forth, clutching his head. Then he stopped, looked up at the cabin, wrung his hands together, then went inside.

"What's going on?" I whispered.

Jimmy held the antenna aimed at the door and turned to me. "Some guy named Sanchez just called Stevens into the cabin. Sounds like the guy's really pissed. Stevens is acting like he doesn't know what happened in there."

"That slimy bastard. I guess he'll play out this innocent charade as long as he can."

Stevens and the man known as Sanchez stepped outside. They walked to the blue van, and Sanchez opened the back door. He handed Stevens a shovel. Then, with a machete in his hand, Sanchez led Stevens to the edge of the jungle. They were close enough now for me to hear fragments of what they were saying.

Sanchez took charge. "Go inside and bring the men out. I will clear an area to bury them."

Stevens put the shovel down and went back to the cabin with his shoulders hunched forward, looking like a whipped puppy.

Sanchez watched as Stevens disappeared inside, then pulled a cell phone from his pocket and tapped the screen. "I have bad news, boss. Martinez is dead." He waited for a response from whoever he had called.

"Yes, senor. Martinez and his men are all dead."

Another pause.

"That's right, all of them are dead. And Senor Stevens is using a lot of cocaine. How do you want me to handle this?"

Sanchez listened to the brief reply. "I understand. I will take care of it." He tapped his phone and put it back in his pocket.

Stevens backed out of the cabin, dragging one of the dead men by the wrists.

"Give me a hand with the others," Stevens said as he dropped the first body at the forest's edge.

Sanchez grunted and followed Stevens back inside. A few seconds passed before they emerged, each dragging a body. Sanchez used the machete to slash a path through the jungle undergrowth, then they pulled the three bodies a short distance into the forest.

Stevens came out into the clearing and took the shovel back to where they had taken the bodies.

I nudged Jimmy's elbow. "I've seen enough. Let's get out of here before they finish," I said, crawling back toward the Jeep.

Jimmy climbed in beside me. "Looks like Stevens and Sanchez are getting rid of the evidence. But who was Sanchez talking with on the phone?"

"Whoever it was, he referred to the person as boss. My guess is it was someone higher up the cartel food chain. I'd like to know what he told Sanchez to do next."

Jimmy packed the headphones and listening device into the duffle bag. "I was thinking the same thing. He called the boss as soon as Stevens was out of sight and couldn't hear him. Maybe Stevens is getting played by someone else."

"I think you're right. I thought Stevens had hired Sanchez to put the hit on Gabby and me. But maybe those orders came from higher in the organization."

I fired up the Jeep, and we rolled back to the main road. It would be too risky to hang around and try to follow Stevens again, especially with Sanchez there. Besides, I needed to get back to Jimmy's place and recharge my phone to find out why it had pinged earlier.

CHAPTER
31

We arrived at Jimmy's place in the late afternoon. I was dying inside from being unable to contact or listen in on Gabby. She had her lunch date with Marcos Rodriguez this afternoon while I was out tracking Stevens.

I plugged in my phone and watched with dismay as a small hourglass spun around, but the screen didn't light up. This thing was really dead. There was nothing I could do except wait until it took a charge.

Then an idea came to me. "Hey, Jimmy. Can you fire up the laptop so I can check who pinged my phone earlier?"

"Sure, no problem." He flipped the screen up and pushed the power button. "You want a beer while it's booting up?" he said from the open fridge, holding a cold beer in my direction.

After spending all afternoon in the old Jeep and crawling around in the jungle, I had to admit that a cold beer would help quench my deep thirst. "Sounds terrific, thanks."

"Here you go, boss." Jimmy handed me a beer, then sat at the kitchen table. When the laptop was ready, he tapped the keyboard to pull up the surveillance program.

"Can you look for the most recent file for Gabby? I'm sure her phone pinged mine when we followed Stevens to the cabin."

Jimmy navigated through a few screens and double-clicked on a file. The file loaded into the bar graph of the surveillance program and played.

I smiled when I heard the familiar voices.

"Hello?" It was Eddie answering his cell phone.

"Hey, Uncle Eddie, it's Gabby. How are you doing?"

I love hearing her voice. So sweet and innocent, with a sing-song tone that always lifts my spirits.

"Oh, hi, Gabby. What's up?" Eddie said.

"I'm heading out to have lunch with an old college buddy and wanted to let you know just in case you dropped by the house."

"Sure, not a problem. Thanks for the heads-up. Who are you going with? Do your parents know him? Where are you going for lunch, and when do you expect to be home?"

"Wow, Uncle Eddie, now you sound like my dad." She giggled and said, "I told Dad about the date yesterday. His name is Marcos Rodriguez. It's nothing serious. He's just a friend I haven't seen since college."

"Sounds like fun." Eddie made an exaggerated yawning sound.

"Oh, come on, the guy used to be a lot of fun back in the day, so he should be alright. Besides, doing something boring would be a nice change after my Colombian experiences. So this will be a good start to getting my life back to normal."

"Yeah, I guess you're right. Okay, have a good time, and call me if you need anything."

"For sure. Bye for now."

Their lines cut off, and the file stopped playing.

Jimmy looked up at me. "What's so funny?"

I shrugged and held my hands up in front of me. "What do you mean?"

"You have this big goofy grin on your face and a faraway look in your eyes. If I didn't know she was your daughter, I'd think you were in love or something."

"Very perceptive of you, Jimmy. I am in love. I love that kid more than anything, and I'm really proud of her drive to reclaim a normal life after everything she went through down here. It's as though nothing phases her for too long."

"You're a lucky man, Jake. Gabby sounds like a great gal. Maybe someday, under different circumstances, I'll get to meet her."

"For sure. Hey, I've been wondering about something. Can your program record the ambient sounds near her phone the way my app does?"

"Unfortunately, no. The program only tracks and records actual phone conversations. The app on your phone operates differently. It uses the microphone even if it isn't used with another caller."

"I was afraid of that."

I checked the charge on the phone—ten percent. At least there was enough to start it up and hopefully activate the surveillance app. I pushed the start button and waited. As it finished booting up, an error message showed on the screen—*Data limit reached*.

"Damn it."

"What's the matter?" Jimmy asked.

"I'm out of data, so I won't have access to Gabby's phone."

"That's the problem with those pre-paid burner phones. They usually come with a low amount of data and minutes. They're not the same as a regular phone plan, where you have an ongoing contract. So you either have to buy more minutes and data or get a new phone."

"I knew that. But I thought there'd be enough for a while longer."

I dialed Eddie's number. Unfortunately, instead of connecting to his phone, a recorded message came on the line telling me I didn't have enough phone minutes to make the call.

"Damn it. I feel so helpless and stranded without a phone. Is there someplace I can get more data and minutes? I don't want to get a different phone since this one is already set up with the surveillance app and programmed into your system."

Jimmy checked his watch. "Come on. There's an electronics shop around the corner. If we hurry, we can get there before they close."

I followed him as he took the stairs two at a time down to the exit of his building. About half a block away was a small electronics shop. The door and windows were covered with posters advertising cell phones and data plans. As we approached, the shop owner stepped outside and locked the door. We were too late. The guy was closing up for the day.

Jimmy called out in Spanish and rapidly told the man our story. Unfortunately, the conversation was too fast and too Spanish for me to follow what they were saying. But I gathered from how Jimmy kept pointing to the phone in my hand that he was explaining my urgent need to upgrade my minutes and data.

The shop owner looked at me, then at the phone in my hand while Jimmy laid it on pretty thick. A wide smile spread across the man's deeply wrinkled face, and his warm, brown eyes sparkled. He combed his fingers through his wavy, gray hair and nodded. His grin pushed his cheeks up his face drawing intense laugh lines around his eyes. Jimmy's pleading had the desired effect. Apparently, I was about to make his day.

"Yes, yes. Please come in." He said as he unlocked the door and held it open for us.

The guy either had a kind heart, or he needed the sale. It was probably a little of both. With Jimmy as my interpreter, I told him I wanted the most extensive package of phone minutes and gigabytes of data available for a pre-paid phone. I didn't think the guy could smile any more than he already was. But his lips peeled back, exposing a set of pearly-white teeth at the prospect of the sale. It took him less than five minutes to load my phone with the minutes and data.

"Mucho gracias, senor," I said, thanking him profusely. I'm not sure he fully appreciated how desperate I was to get my phone up and running. Or whether it was just the wad of pesos I handed him. But I had made his day, and he kept smiling as he led us to the door. At this point, I really didn't care about the cost. I had what I needed, and we headed out onto the sidewalk.

"See you later, senor," the shop owner said, closing the door behind me.

Back on the street, I dialed Gabby. I really wanted to hear her voice.

She picked up right away. "Hello. Is that you, Dad?"

"Wow. Good guess, Gabs."

"It's not really a guess. I don't get many calls from unlisted numbers. For a covert agent, you're not being very discreet."

"And you're showing some astute analytical skills. Maybe someday you'd make a good agent. But listen, I only have a few minutes of charge left on my phone. So I wanted to check in and see how you're doing?"

"I'm feeling fantastic. The headaches are gone, and the arm doesn't hurt anymore. But the itching under the cast is driving me nuts. Enough about me, though. Did you find Mom and get her back yet?"

I sighed heavily. "Not yet. I almost had her. We came close to getting her back, though. Stevens was holding her hostage in a shack out in the jungle. As we closed in to take him out, he took off in his car with your mom, and I lost him. But don't worry, I'll find her. He's not going to harm her." I had no way of confirming that last statement, but I wasn't about to give Gabby anything to worry about.

"Good. I don't like that guy. And with his obsessive crush on Mom, you're probably right about him not hurting her."

"Listen, I have to go soon before my phone dies again. Tell me about your big date with your friend from college?"

"I think it went pretty well. Marcos has a pretty exciting job as an immigration attorney for South and Central American immigrants. And get this, he has a big clientele out of Colombia, of all places. He's a nice guy, and I think you and Mom will like him. So we've arranged to get together tomorrow night for drinks. And I have to say, it's fun to go out again and not worry about the cartel trying to kill me."

"All right, Gabs, I gotta go. Sounds like you're having fun. Just keep Uncle Eddie in the loop about your activities, and I'll be in touch soon."

"Jeez, Dad, you and Uncle Eddie are like brooding hens, always hovering around trying to protect me. I'm safe up here. So just focus on getting Mom—"

The phone line dropped and went silent. I looked at the screen. It was dark and unresponsive again. Shit. Time to get it fully charged.

As Jimmy and I walked toward his place, I reflected on what a great kid Gabby is. She was calm, self-aware, and completely unphased by her near-death experiences only a few days ago. Like her mom, she was proving to be bold, strong, and focused, even when the shit hit the fan around her.

And, of course, she was right. I needed to put all my efforts into finding Gloria.

CHAPTER

32

The next day was shaping up to be the same as the previous days. We sat in our usual spot across from the consulate and waited for any activity on Stevens' phone. Once in the morning, he came across to his car to do a few lines of cocaine. The guy really had a bad habit that he needed to feed. Finally, at 11:15, somebody called Stevens' line, causing my phone and Jimmy's to ping simultaneously. I adjusted my earpiece for a better fit and listened for Stevens to answer.

His voice came through the earbuds, and after his usual introduction, a male voice abruptly stated, "Never mind all that nonsense. I need to talk to you."

Stevens' voice shifted from his standard helpful tone to a solemn, focused whisper. "Why are you calling on this number? You know how risky it is phoning me at work."

"I don't give a shit about that. Angel is furious about what's going on down there. I need to know you've taken care of business at your end," the man said.

The man didn't have an accent, so I figured he wasn't one of Stevens' men here in Colombia. From how he addressed Stevens, I assumed he was his boss or someone with authority over him. And there was something familiar about this new guy's voice. But

I couldn't place it. I looked over at Jimmy, who had opened the laptop and brought the screen to life.

Stevens whispered, "Yes, of course. Everything is going smoothly and without a hitch since I had our... problems taken care of."

"Are you telling me that Jake Stone, his wife, and his daughter are all dead?"

If I wasn't at full attention before, I was now. Hearing your name mentioned in the same sentence as being dead will do that to you. I focused on their conversation like a laser. As I listened, I noticed something else. It was too distant and soft to make out. Could it be another voice in the background?

Stevens responded confidently, "Yes... yes, that's what I told you before. There is nothing to worry about from those three. The woman died in the boating accident, and the other two in the explosion at the safe house. Trust me, Martinez and Sanchez made sure of it."

The phone went silent as the speaker on the other end paused before continuing.

"Trust you? That is becoming increasingly difficult, Stevens. If they are all dead, as you say, then maybe you can explain to us why I had lunch with their daughter yesterday?"

That's why his voice was familiar. This was the same guy I overheard talking with Gabby when she set up the lunch date. Damn it. She was walking into danger and didn't know it. My mind raced as I tried to stay focused on the phone conversation.

Stevens gasped and paused. "What? That... isn't possible. Sanchez reported that Stone and the daughter both died in the explosion. There must be some mistake—"

"No. There is no mistake on our end. But it appears to us that you are not being truthful with us or that you have serious deficiencies in your ability to carry out your duties. Either way, you are proving to be more of a liability to us than you may be worth."

Stevens' voice wavered as he rushed to find excuses for his failures. "But... but sir, it was Martinez who made a mess of the scuba diving situation. He should have stayed on the surface and verified they were all dead before leaving. And then Sanchez should have remained at the safe house to ensure Stone and his daughter were dead. You can't blame me for their mistakes."

"Who's in charge down there, Stevens? I take it as a sign of incompetence and personal weakness when those in charge blame others for their own errors and failures. We expect a commitment from you to carry out our orders ruthlessly and faithfully. After so many years with us, I thought you understood that. I shouldn't have to remind you of the damages Stone, and his family caused to our operations. After the killing of Patrón and Dominguez, then destroying our production facility, they have created major production and delivery problems for us."

"Yes, yes. I understand and do my best to carry out your orders."

"Good. We will give you one last chance to correct this situation. Find Stone and kill him. We will require proof that he is dead this time, and you will also provide proof that his wife is dead. I will take care of the daughter up here. When we have confirmation all three of them are dead, we can restore our operations to normal. Are these instructions clear, Stevens?"

My heart skipped a beat when he said he would take care of Gabby up there. I had to find a way to stop him from getting to her.

"Yes, I understand, and I'll get on it right away," Stevens said softly.

"And Stevens, Martinez, isn't answering his phone. Have him call me as soon as possible."

"Yes, I will call him immediately and have him phone you, sir."

"Good, no more screw-ups. I don't want to come down there and clean up your mess."

"No sir, I mean there will be—"

The phone suddenly went silent when the man on the other end hung up.

"Ah… goodbye, sir," Steven said limply into dead air.

I looked at Jimmy, then at my watch. Gabby's date with Rodriguez was several hours from now. So there was still time to warn her and get her to break off the date. "That son of a bitch is going to kill her, Jimmy."

"Can your buddy Eddie do anything up there to protect her?" Jimmy asked.

I was already speed-dialing Gabby.

Shit. Her phone went straight to voicemail.

I spoke quickly and left a message I hoped she would get before her date. "Gabby, I need you to cancel your date with your friend, Marcos. He isn't who he says he is, and you are in great danger. I want you to call Uncle Eddie and have him come and stay with you until I get back home. Please, Gabs, I need you to do this for me."

I hung up and stared at the blank screen. If that son of a bitch hurts Gabby, I'll tear his heart out and stomp on it in front of him.

I turned my attention back to the laptop and Jimmy.

"Are you okay, Jake?" Jimmy said, placing a hand on my shoulder.

"Yeah, I'll be okay. I'll check in with Eddie in a few minutes and get him to stay close to Gabby."

I turned my attention back to the conversation between Stevens and Rodriguez. "It's clear the cartel leadership no longer believes Stevens is a good and faithful soldier for them. What do you think?"

"It sounds like that to me. I'm also wondering if Rodriguez is the guy Sanchez called yesterday to tell him Martinez and his men were dead. That would make sense, as Rodriguez is clearly Stevens' boss. But who is the 'us and we' he kept referring to? And who is Angel?" Jimmy asked.

"If Sanchez did call Rodriguez and told him Martinez was dead, then Rodriguez also knows Stevens is lying to him. That would mean they're setting Stevens up, which won't be good for him. We know Rodriguez is up in Washington, so I'm guessing Angel is Rodriguez's boss. That would make sense, as Stevens is just a low-level middleman in Colombia. But I think I heard something else during the conversation. It sounded like there was someone else talking in the background. Of course, it might have been background noise in Steven's office. Or it could be the person Rodriguez referred to as Angel. Is there any way to isolate that sound and enhance it?"

"Sure. We have the technology," Jimmy said, tapping on the keyboard. "But aren't you concerned about Stevens coming after you now that he knows you're still alive?"

"He may know I'm alive, but he doesn't know where I am, and that's gonna cause him a lot of stress. Right now, I'm more concerned about Gabby."

"And don't forget, Rodriguez ordered Stevens to provide proof of death for you and your wife. So even though he may have other plans for her, he has no choice but to kill her now," Jimmy said.

Multiple scenarios raced through my mind—none positive—as I punched in Eddie's phone number.

CHAPTER

33

Eddie's cell phone rang over and over. As I waited for him to pick up, I reflected on recent events. It was clear that Stevens had ordered Sanchez to kill Gabby and me at the safe house. When he murdered Martinez and his men, he showed he could be a cold-blooded killer when necessary. So he wasn't just the spineless, loser drug addict I thought he was. And that worried me. Especially now, after he had received new orders to kill Gloria. I had underestimated him for the last time. But at the moment, I had to refocus and turn my attention to keeping Gabby safe from Stevens' boss, Marcos Rodriguez. And she was almost 2000 miles away.

Eddie finally answered, huffing and gasping for breath into the phone. "H… hello?"

"Eddie, it's me, Jake. Are you okay? You sound out of breath."

"Oh, hi… Jake. Yeah… I'm fine. I was… on the treadmill… trying to stay in game shape," he panted into the phone.

"Let me talk while you catch your breath. I know for sure that Stevens has Gloria, and we just missed getting her back. So we'll take care of things on our end. But there's a new development up there. The guy Gabby had lunch with yesterday is a member of the cartel, and he's Stevens' boss. I don't have much information about him except his name is Marcos Rodriguez. Gabby said he's an immigration lawyer with ties to South America. But more importantly, Gabby is meeting him again for drinks tonight. And Eddie, Stevens had previously told him that Gabby and I were dead. So Rodriguez knows that's not true since he had lunch with her yesterday. He told Stevens that he would kill Gabby himself. I tried to warn her, but her phone went straight to voicemail. So I left a message hoping she'll get it in time to stop her from going out with this guy."

"What do you want me to do?" Eddie's voice and breathing had returned to normal. He was still in pretty good shape for an old guy.

"I need you to stay close to Gabby and keep an eye on her. But if you can, convince her to not go out with Rodriguez tonight. I also want to get ears on this Rodriguez guy. Is it possible to get bugs in his office and car?"

"For sure. Anything's possible. I'll take care of that right away. Since we don't know much about him, I'll stick close to Gabby and keep her in my sight. Then, when I get an opening, I'll plant the bugs and let you know so you can activate them."

"Good. I'll be tracking her using the phone app the best I can. But the situation here is pretty fluid, and I could get pulled away when things heat up."

"Sounds like a plan. If you think the situation is escalating and getting dangerous with Gabby, call me, and I'll be close enough to her to step in and intervene. I'll also call my contacts with the DEA and FBI and do a background check to find out more about him. If he's a cartel leader, there has to be a money trail showing large sums of cash coming into his bank accounts. So it shouldn't be too hard to find some dirt on the guy."

"Perfect. And Eddie, be careful. That guy is dangerous. There's no doubt he was behind the attempts to murder the three of us down here. We also believe there's at least one other person involved up there, and maybe more. Unfortunately, all we have is the name Angel. Probably an alias, but we'll keep digging. Maybe we'll get lucky once we get ears on Rodriguez. It's pretty clear he's one of the heads of the drug cartel, and this Angel person is pulling his strings."

"Got it. Stay in touch so I can keep you updated."

Jimmy cut in. "Can you ask him for the model number and specs for the bugs he'll use, so I can tie them into our system to track Rodriguez?"

"Hang on, Eddie. I'm going to put Jimmy on with you. He's the agent I'm working with down here. He needs information about the bugging devices you'll use."

I handed Jimmy my phone.

"Hello, Eddie? Yeah, this is Jimmy."

A pause while Eddie responded.

"No, fantastic. Yeah, he's a pretty sharp guy… for someone his age." Jimmy looked at me and smiled.

Another pause.

"I need the make and model numbers of the devices you'll be using so I can look up the specs. I've got this cool program that automatically taps into the listening devices so we can listen from down here."

Jimmy scratched some letters and numbers on a piece of paper. "So basically, you're using the standard company-issued bugs. And the one in his car will be set to pick up ambient sounds even when the phone isn't activated? Great, that's all I need. Thanks, Eddie. Nice talking with you. Here's Jake."

Jimmy handed me the phone. "Everything's all good then, Eddie?"

"No problem. We're good to go. Give me until later tonight to install the bugs, and you'll be online. Oh, and by the way, your buddy Jimmy sounds like a pretty sharp guy. So stick close to him when the action gets going. Remember, you're not as young as you were back in your glory days."

"I hear you. Bye for now." I hung up and felt a wave of relief sweep through my body. With Eddie keeping an eye on Gabby up north and soon to have surveillance bugs planted on Rodriguez, I felt more confident than I was a few minutes ago. But something still bothered me.

"Jimmy, can you pull up the file from the Stevens and Rodriguez call? I want to check what the background noise was."

"No problem. It's already loaded." He reached into a cooler and handed me a cold beer. "Here's to wrapping this up quickly and safely."

"I'll drink to that." I took a long, slow gulp.

Jimmy double-clicked on the audio file. I leaned over so I could look at the screen as well.

"At some point during the call, I heard a sound in the background. I could have sworn it was someone else talking. Maybe it was the person Rodriguez referred to as Angel."

"I had the same thought. Let me run the track from the start. So we can narrow it down."

The audio track of the phone call played through while we listened intently.

"There. Did you hear that?" I said when we came to the moment in the call where I had heard the other voice.

Jimmy tapped on the keyboard, backed the track up, then hit play. There was definitely a voice in the background, but faint and distant. "Let me reduce the foreground sounds and enhance the background." He backed the audio track up again, adjusted some controls on the screen, and hit play.

That did the trick. The other voice came through clearly, leaving us scratching our heads.

A high-pitched whistle followed by, "Auk. Angry Angel. Angry Gabriel. Good boy, Coca. Good boy, Coca. Kill Stone. Angry Angel. Auk." Followed by another whistle.

Jimmy frowned, and his forehead wrinkled as he shrugged, "What the hell is that? Sounds like a bloody parrot."

"A parrot? What is this guy, a pirate or something?"

Jimmy shrugged. "Pirate or drug smuggler? Pretty much the same thing, right?"

"It said, Angry Angel. Angry Gabriel. Sounds to me like Angel and Gabriel could be the same person."

"Man, you're good. I take back that comment about you being good for an old guy. You're just damn good." Jimmy said, clinking our beers together.

If Angel is Rodriguez's boss up in D.C., then how high does this cartel reach, and who's the top dog?

Movement in my peripheral vision caused me to look up from the laptop. Stevens had left the building and was rushing across the front courtyard.

"It's Stevens," I said.

Instead of crossing the street and coming to his car as I expected, he turned and headed away from the consulate building. "Wait. He's not coming this way."

I got out of the Jeep and peered through the opening in the wall of the parking structure. "He's heading down the street. Where the hell is he going?"

Jimmy joined me at the wall in front of the Jeep. "Maybe he's going to get some lunch? Listen, why don't you follow him, and I'll drive back to the apartment. I want to get a tracking device to attach to his car. That way, we won't lose him again."

"Good plan, but you couldn't have thought of that earlier?"

"Hey, I didn't know this piece of shit vehicle you're driving would give us so much trouble. But better late than never. Just wear your Panama hat and sunglasses, and hope he doesn't make you. I'll be back in about half an hour."

I tossed him the keys and headed for the exit. Jimmy rolled by as I hit the sidewalk and turned toward his apartment. Stevens was half a block ahead of me on the other side of the tree-lined street. I kept pace with him and used the lunchtime crowd to cover my movements. Whenever Stevens stopped, I stopped and looked like

I was window shopping. He paused outside two restaurants and checked the menus by the doors. He entered the second one and took a seat by the window.

From what I could make out, he was having a liquid lunch. The server brought him three shots of something. Probably hard liquor. After his conversation with Rodriguez, it was no wonder he needed something to calm his nerves. I took a position behind a tree and waited while periodically glancing his way. The last thing I needed was to be too obvious or stand out like a stalker. But there was no way I was letting him out of my sight. Not with him having orders to kill Gloria.

After about half an hour, he gulped down the third shot and exited the restaurant. I curled back behind the trunk of the tree. Stevens stood on the sidewalk holding his hand to his forehead, shielding his eyes from the sun. He scanned up and down the street, then walked back the way he had come. I let him get ahead of me, then followed. As I approached the front of the parking garage, Stevens re-entered the consulate. I lingered around the corner near the entrance ramp to make sure he wasn't coming back out.

While I waited, Jimmy turned into the garage and drove up to the second level. As he disappeared inside, a van exited and turned away from me. Not just any van. It was the rusted-out, pale blue van from outside the safe house and the cabin where Martinez was murdered. Sanchez was driving. I would recognize him and that van anywhere.

He didn't look in my direction, so I was pretty sure he hadn't seen me.

What the hell was he doing in there? I was about to find out. But first, I needed to check in with Jimmy.

CHAPTER

34

I headed up the ramp to the second level, where Jimmy parked the Jeep in the usual spot.

As I approached, he stepped out of the vehicle and asked, "Was that who I think it was?"

"If you're thinking it was Sanchez, then you're right. But the question is, what was he doing here?"

Jimmy tossed me the keys. "I was wondering the same thing."

"Did you get the tracking device you were looking for?"

Jimmy held up a tiny black box and handed it to me. "I took the one off the fish van. Since no one has stolen it yet, I thought it would be safe for a few days without it."

I turned the device over in my hand, examining it. It was about the size of a matchbox. "Great. We won't lose him again with this attached to his car."

"It's a pretty slick little device with great range and long battery life. Once it's in place, I'll track him using the map app on my phone. So now, wherever he goes, we'll see his location on the map. What did you find out about where Stevens went?"

I handed him the tracking device, leaned against the front of the Jeep, and stared out at the consulate. Heat waves rose off the cement courtyard as people came and went from the building.

"You were right. Just a lunch break. A liquid lunch, from what I could see. After his talk with Rodriguez, I guess he needed something to calm his nerves."

Jimmy hopped up and sat beside me on the hood of the Jeep. "I get that. If I was strung out on coke like he is and had a psycho-killer boss, I'd be drinking heavily too."

I turned his way. "What's our next step?"

Jimmy tossed the tracking device in the air and caught it. "Time to install this little beauty. I don't know why I didn't think of using one before."

"Don't beat yourself up over it. I should have asked about using one of those a long time ago. If I had, I'd probably have Gloria back by now."

"Hey, don't worry about it. I'm the tech expert on this mission, and it didn't occur to me either. Besides, with everything going on here and back home, you have a pretty good excuse for being distracted."

I know Jimmy was trying to be supportive, and a good teammate, but losing focus was a fast track to a coffin in our line of work.

"Thanks, Jimmy. I appreciate the cheerleading, but being distracted could get me or someone I love killed."

He hopped down off the hood and turned toward the Mercedes. "I'll be right back. Let me know if you see Stevens or Sanchez coming."

As he walked toward Stevens' silver Mercedes, I wondered where I would be if I hadn't made contact with Jimmy. Such a great guy and a talented agent. I also wondered whether he and Gabby would hit it off under different circumstances. They were about the same age. No sooner than those thoughts went through my head, my mind screamed—Stop It! This isn't the *Dating Game*! Enough with the match-making bullshit, and stay focused on the task at hand.

The consulate courtyard was quiet, with no one in sight. I turned back to check on Jimmy as he slid under the driver's side of Stevens' car. He was only under there for a couple of seconds, then slid out and waved for me to come over. What the heck does he want now?

I checked the front entrance to the consulate again, then moved quickly to the Mercedes and knelt beside him. "What do you want? I should be watching for Stevens."

"I thought you might like to see this," he said as he slid back under the edge of the car.

I sighed at the thought of not only being hot and sweaty in the Jeep all day, but now I'd be adding grease and dirt to my clothes as well. I rolled onto my back and shimmied under the car beside him. "What's so import—"

The reason became obvious, and my voice stopped in mid-sentence. Mounted under the driver's side was a block of C-4 explosives the size of a cigarette package. Taped to the C-4 was a small detonator with an antenna and a flashing red LED light. Fuck, the car was rigged with a remotely activated bomb, and my face was less than a foot away from it.

I cautiously slid out from under the car and ran for cover behind a heavy cement pillar supporting the parking structure. Jimmy joined me a few seconds later.

I glanced at the car and then at Jimmy. "What the hell, man? I've never had my face that close to a bomb before."

Jimmy smiled. "At least now we know what Sanchez was doing here. I'm guessing Rodriguez has already put a hit out on our guy, Stevens."

"Makes sense, especially since the cartel already thinks he's a liability. But we must prevent them from killing him before finding where he's holding Gloria."

"There's only one way to make sure he doesn't get blown up first, and that's disarming the bomb," Jimmy said as he walked back to the car.

"Wait. What are you going to do?" I said, grab to hold him back.

"Obviously, one of us has to disarm that thing, an supposed to be the explosives expert—"

I shook my head. "Do you have some sort of death wish, or are you just crazy?"

"Neither. I've armed and disarmed hundreds of those things. Well, maybe not hundreds. But it should be a piece of cake. There are only so many ways to rig one of these, and this one looks pretty basic. Stay behind the pillar, and I'll be right back."

Jimmy was not only talented and funny but also had crazy mad skills and was brave as hell. He's the complete package for a deep cover agent in the field. I watched from a safe distance as he slid under the car. A few minutes later, he reemerged with the detonator in one hand and the cube of C-4 explosives in the other.

"There you go. The bomb's disarmed, and I've attached our tracking device in its place. So now, Sanchez won't be able to blow him up before we find your wife. I'm kinda thinking you might want the pleasure of taking Stevens out yourself."

Did I include perceptive in the growing list of Jimmy's admirable traits? It was like he could read my mind.

I patted him on the shoulder and said, "We better get back to the Jeep, so we're not caught standing around if Stevens shows up for his mid-afternoon snort of coke."

True to form, later that afternoon, Stevens made another trip to his car for a quick fix. During the rest of the day, his phone was activated twice by tourists looking for recommendations to local attractions. I guess they thought the consulate was a tourist information booth or something.

We continued to wait for Stevens to emerge from the building at the end of his shift. I tried to call Gabby a couple more times. But, as before, she didn't answer. Had Rodriguez already gotten to her? I took several deep breaths to calm my fears and called Eddie. He was parked down the street from our house and reported that

Gabby was still safe inside. And no one had appeared in the area near the house. He suggested that Gabby was probably preparing for her date and not checking her phone. I hoped he was right, but it frustrated me that she would turn her phone off or not answer it during this critical period.

At 16:45, Stevens left the building and headed toward his car. This was it. Go time.

Time to track him to where he held Gloria and finish this thing.

CHAPTER

35

Jimmy and I slouched down in our seats as Stevens walked past the Jeep. He beeped the locks, got in his car, and did a few lines of coke before leaving. I put the Jeep in gear and followed him at a safe distance so he wouldn't spot us tailing him. Even with the tracking device on his car, I didn't want to lose sight of him. But I had another concern. This time, I had to watch out for Sanchez in his van. He would need to stay close to Stevens' car, so he could trigger the bomb. Of course, there was no way for him to know we had disarmed it, rendering his plan useless.

Rush-hour traffic clogged the city streets, and like every other day, no one seemed to be rushing anywhere. My patience was wearing thin as the frustration of the snarled afternoon traffic got the better of me. I needed something to get my mind off the situation as I wove the Jeep through the maddeningly slow traffic.

I pulled my phone from my pocket and double-clicked on the surveillance app connecting me with the microphone on Gabby's phone.

The next voice I heard was hers.

"I understand what you're saying, Uncle Eddie, but it doesn't change my mind. And yes, I listened to Dad's warning on my voicemail about Rodriguez being in the drug cartel. It just makes me more determined to help take him down."

Eddie pleaded with her, "Gabby, be reasonable. Your dad asked me to keep a close eye on you and make sure Rodriguez didn't hurt you. He's not who you think he is. He's really dangerous, and I don't know what he'll do if he gets you alone where I can't stop him in time."

"I hear you and appreciate that. I really do. But this is something I have to do for myself. I can't just sit around waiting for him to come after me. Especially since he's responsible for trying to kill Dad and me down in Colombia."

I'd heard enough. Gabby was brave, and her resolve was admirable, but even if she pretended to act tough, she wasn't a trained agent. She had no idea how bad it could get when dealing with guys as ruthless as Rodriguez. I tapped the app and closed the program. The surrounding traffic had ground to a halt. Stevens' vehicle was four car lengths ahead. So I punched in Gabby's number and hoped she would answer this time.

She picked up right away. "Hello. Is that you, Dad?"

"Yes, and we need to talk. There is no way I can allow you to go on your date with Rodriguez tonight. Eddie's right. It's too dangerous."

"Let me stop you right there. How the hell did you know I was talking to Uncle Eddie about this?"

Oh, oh. I'd blown it. Up to this point, I thought I had been pretty discrete about my surveillance. But, in retrospect, even though the timing of this call wasn't the best, I had no choice. I had to intervene.

"Ah… that doesn't matter right now. What matters—"

Gabby cut me off. "Bullshit. You and Eddie must have some sort of spying device near me, or you wouldn't be calling at just the right times and always know what I'm doing. Tell me the truth, Dad. Have you been spying on me since I got home?"

I took a deep breath, exhaled slowly, and realized that only the truth would work here. Telling her the truth about what Gloria and I did during our careers with the agency worked last time. Would telling her the straight truth work again? I was about to find out. Besides, I had no choice. I had blown it by calling her, and she'd know if I was lying.

I took another deep breath. "Yes. I had Eddie install a bugging device on your phone so I could—"

"What the fuck, Dad. Do you realize how invasive that is and how you've violated my privacy?"

"I do, Gabs. But let me explain. With me down here trying to find your mom, I couldn't just let you be on your own, especially with the drug cartel trying to kill us. And hey, it's something a dad does to protect his loved ones. Trust me, I'll have Eddie remove the device as soon as this is all over. Can you live with that for a few more days?"

"Absolutely not. This is totally unacceptable. And you're saying Uncle Eddie has been involved and listening in on me too?"

Crap. I had blown it again and outed Eddie. I felt terrible for him. I was miles away on the other end of the phone while he would take her wrath full frontal.

"No, the device doesn't work like that. It only connects with my phone."

"Like that's supposed to make it okay?"

"Look, Gabs, without this small invasion of your privacy, I wouldn't have recognized Rodriguez's voice during our surveillance of Stevens' phone calls. Besides, it's helped us learn more about who's pulling the strings in the cartel and ordered our murders."

The line went quiet for a few seconds as Gabby paused. "Okay. I get it. This is what you used to do as an agent during your career. But if Eddie's involved, then he's—"

"Yes, Uncle Eddie is also an agent, and he's the only person other than your mom who I trust to take care of you and prevent anyone from harming you. And Gabby, he's very good at what he does."

"Uncle Eddie, you're a sneaky old fart," Gabby's tone changed to be less combative.

"Hey, I gotta do what I gotta do," Eddie said in the background.

I hoped my explanation was getting through to her and she would cancel her date with Rodriguez, but I soon discovered that would not be the case.

"So, are we good? Will you call off your date with Rodriguez?"

"Not a chance. I'm going all-in on this mission, and as Uncle Eddie said, I gotta do what I gotta do. Now, what can I do to help?"

"But Gabby, it's too risky, and you're not trained for this type of operation."

My pleas fell on deaf ears.

"Then train me, damn it. I've got a couple of hours. Look, I'm not expecting to go through a full boot camp. Just give me a few tips and the basics for how to handle things. Like, maybe we can get Eddie plugged into my phone as well, so he can jump in if things go sideways. Or he can get me a gun."

God, she is getting more like her mom every day.

I realized I had little to no hope of stopping her from doing what she wanted to do, so I folded. "Okay, put your phone on speaker so all three of us can talk. But there won't be any guns. We'll leave that to the experts, like Eddie."

Eddie spoke up. "Sorry about this, Jake. Gabby's just too smart to keep her in the dark for too long."

"I hear that, Eddie. But, truth be told, she's been running mental circles around me since she was about six years old."

"And don't you two ever forget it," Gabby chimed in. "Okay, what's the plan?"

In front of me, the traffic thinned as we moved toward the city's edge. From what I could tell, Stevens was heading into the hills along the coast. I quickly checked the mirrors and saw no sign of Sanchez behind us. We were still good.

Returning my attention to the phone, I said, "Let's start with you telling us what you and Rodriguez have planned for your date. That'll give us a starting point for how we proceed."

Gabby explained that Rodriguez was going to pick her up at seven o'clock. They planned to go to a bar near our house for drinks and to catch up. Nothing heavy, and they would be in a public location with lots of people around them. So there was no way he would risk killing her in public.

"Okay, Gabby, that's great. Eddie, can you follow them and find an opportunity to plant a bug in his car?"

"Absolutely. Once he's inside the bar with Gabby, I'll break into his car and plant the bug," Eddie said.

"Gabs, I'll monitor your date through your phone. You'll need to keep it on the table in front of you so I can hear your conversation through the microphone. And Gabs, under no circumstances are you to confront this guy or let him think you suspect him of anything. If I sense trouble, I'll phone you. You'll say it's an urgent call and make an excuse to leave the table so we can talk. Then, I'll give you instructions on what to do next. Everyone got it?"

Eddie said, "Sounds like a plan. If necessary, I'll set off his car alarm as a diversion to get Rodriguez out of the bar and away from the table."

"Good idea, Eddie. Let's keep that as a backup option," I said. "How does this sound to you, Gabs? Are you okay with the plan?"

"Yeah, It sounds easy enough. There were a few nights in college when I had to shake off some creep at a bar, so I shouldn't have any problem with this."

"Good. Then we're all set. And Gabs, if you feel uncomfortable, make an excuse to leave the table and get out of there. I want you to play it safe tonight and not try to be a hero. Eddie will be outside, ready to help. Okay?"

"Don't worry, Dad. This is going to be a piece of cake. Bye for now."

Eddie called out before we disconnected, "Don't worry, Jake. We've got this."

"Okay, I gotta go. Bye for now," I said, disconnecting the call.

Yeah, it all seemed straightforward enough. But regardless of how confident Gabby sounded, I was still uncomfortable being thousands of miles away.

CHAPTER

36

I should have been reassured now that we had a plan up in D.C., but I couldn't shake the feeling I had thrust Gabby into a life-and-death situation. Even with Eddie on the case, there were too many unknowns and variables. But what could I do? Gabby was determined to go all in and do whatever she could to help end the cartel's threats on our lives. And once she put her mind to something, there was no stopping her.

Jimmy drew my attention back to the here and now. "Hey, sounds like you guys have a pretty good plan worked out."

"I hope so. There wasn't much I could do since she was going on the date regardless of how hard I tried to convince her not to."

"Look, the way I see it, Eddie is a pretty skilled guy. There's no way he'll let anything happen to her. Besides, that daughter of yours sounds a lot like you. She's got moxie, for sure. And as she said, kids these days can do a lot of growing up in college and learn evasive maneuvers to shake off unwanted advances from drunken creeps."

"I know you're both right. But she's my little girl and always will be, no matter how old she is."

"I mean, I don't have kids yet, but I get it. A dad's first and most important job is to love and protect his kids. Okay, are we done with that for a while? Let's get back to Stevens and our next steps before we arrive at wherever he's leading us."

Jimmy was right. There were still two hours before Gabby would head out on her date. I needed to be present with my focus right here in front of me. With every passing kilometer, we came closer to our final rendezvous with Stevens, and I needed to be ready.

Up ahead, Stevens pulled out of traffic and parked in a small parking lot.

"What the hell is he doing?" I said as Stevens got out of his car.

"Maybe he's grabbing a few supplies to take home."

Stevens entered the tiny convenience store with a large blue and white sign over it. I pulled to the side of the road and stopped half a block from the parking lot. A few minutes later, Stevens returned to his car carrying a bag. He pulled back onto the street and continued to drive toward the coastal hills.

"Hey Jimmy, how's the tracking device working?"

"I've got a strong signal here. Why do you ask?"

"I'm concerned about him spotting us as the traffic thins out. So I think I'll hang back and wait until he's got a good head start before following him."

"That shouldn't be a problem. This thing has an excellent range. As long as he stays with his vehicle, the signal will lead us right to him."

I leaned back and closed my eyes to reflect on our potential next steps. My first inclination was to find Stevens' hideout and go in with guns blazing to rescue Gloria. But on second thought, that probably wasn't the best idea since I didn't know where he was keeping her or if he was going to that location. So any detailed planning would have to wait until we arrived at our destination. Even if that meant just winging it and seeing where the action takes us. After all, that worked for me back at the El Presidente Resort a few days earlier. Of course, that wasn't the best way to approach the situation then, but it was my only option at the time, and it worked. Who knows, maybe lightning will strike twice, and we'll be successful in improvising again.

Jimmy jolted me out of my thoughts. "Hey, I think that's your blue-van guy."

I opened my eyes as the pale blue Ford Econoline van rolled past us and headed in the same direction Stevens had taken moments earlier.

"Sanchez, you son-of-a-bitch." I slammed the Jeep into gear and pulled out. If Sanchez gets to Stevens before we do, he will not only kill him, but he will kill Gloria as well. And I wouldn't let that happen. "Buckle up, big guy. We're heading into battle, whether we're prepared or not."

I kept the Jeep well behind and out of sight of Sanchez's van as we headed up into the coastal hills. As daylight faded, the reduced visibility of dusk would cloak our advance. I kept my headlights turned off to further mask our presence on the road behind Sanchez.

Jimmy monitored his phone as the red dot representing Stevens' car wound along the road several kilometers ahead. "Okay, it looks like Stevens has pulled off the road and stopped. He may be at his house or making another quick stop along the way."

I took a quick glance at Jimmy's phone. The red dot had stopped moving, and the blue dot representing our vehicle was closing the distance to it. "How far ahead do you figure he is?"

"Hard to tell. I'd say we're a couple of kilometers away. Maybe ten minutes."

As my excitement level grew at the prospect of confronting Stevens, I fought the urge to increase my speed. If I went too fast, I risked getting made by Sanchez, who was somewhere up ahead. It didn't take long to close the gap between us and Stevens' vehicle.

As we rounded a sharp curve, Jimmy said, "It should be just up ahead on the left side of the road. Yeah, right there. That's where he pulled off the road and stopped." He pointed toward a narrow driveway slashed through the thick jungle foliage.

I slowed the Jeep and looked down the long driveway. Stevens' Mercedes was parked in front of a massive villa surrounded by dense jungle. There was no sign of Sanchez or his van. Maybe he missed the turnoff.

I let out a long whistle. "Wow. This guy is making some pretty big bucks from the illegal drug trade. Now I get why he can afford that high-end car on his low-end salary."

"No doubt. These guys make a boatload of cash, and none of it's legal, so the government never gets its share. Well, at least they don't get any through taxes. But who knows, there's probably more than a few crooked politicians and bureaucrats getting paid to turn a blind eye to the cartel's operations."

"I'm going to go a little farther up the road, then turn back and park in the bushes. We can go in using the jungle as cover," I said, pulling past the driveway.

I drove around another curve, turned the Jeep around, and guided it off the edge of the road. With darkness closing around us, the vehicle would be hidden under some low-hanging palm branches from anyone traveling along this stretch of road. I figured any drivers coming around the sharp curve at night would be focused on the road and not gawking into the bushes on either side.

Jimmy reached into the backseat and handed me a set of night vision goggles. "These should come in handy. I'll bring the parabolic listening device in case we get close enough to pick up conversations. Have you got enough ammo?"

I dropped the magazine clip out of the Glock, checked it was full, and reinserted it. "I could use a couple of extra clips just in case we get into a firefight."

Jimmy handed me two more full clips. Then, he assembled his sniper rifle, attached the night scope and sound suppressor, and said, "Anything else before we go?"

I looked at my watch—20:15. Gabby would be out on her date by now. "I need to check in on Gabby to make sure she's okay."

"Okay, but you better make it quick. Our window of not being seen could be a short one. And we still don't know if this is where he's keeping your wife or where Sanchez is."

"This will only take a minute." I tapped the icon on my phone, connecting my earpiece to Gabby's phone. A rush of loud bar sounds flooded in. A cacophony of background music, clinking glasses, and multiple voices assaulted my ears. Then I heard Gabby's voice.

"When did you decide to get into the immigration business, Marcos?"

"I did some traveling down in South America right after college. That's when I got the idea I could help people get their papers to come to the States. So I figured I could do something good with my degree and help people at the same time. But enough about me. Tell me about your trip to Colombia?" Rodriguez said.

"Well, there's nothing much to tell. It was mostly just the same old tourist stuff. Quite an adventure, though."

Someone at their table must have taken a drink and put their glass down with a thump. Their conversation came through clearly enough for me to follow along. Gabby's phone was apparently on the table, as I had instructed her to do. They carried on with the small talk for a while. Rodriguez kept fishing for details about her time in Colombia. But Gabby deftly danced around his queries and wouldn't give him a straight answer.

Jimmy slapped my arm and ducked down. I instinctively did the same. I looked up as the pale blue van drove past and slowed as it approached Stevens' driveway. Sanchez pulled off the road and stopped. He left the van a moment later, crouched over, and vanished down the driveway. If he'd seen our vehicle, he thought nothing of it. It looked like he was doing some recognizance of his own.

I peered out of the windshield. "What the hell is he doing?"

"Stay here and take care of business with Gabby and Rodriguez. I'll be right back." Jimmy reached into the backseat and picked up the block of C-4 and the detonator.

I instinctively recoiled away from the explosives. "What are you going to do with that?"

"I just had a thought of how I could put it to good use. This will only take a minute."

He stepped out of the Jeep and disappeared into the jungle. The next time I saw him, he emerged from the bushes beside Sanchez's van and gave me a thumbs up.

I didn't have time to worry about whatever he was up to. I had to trust he knew what he was doing.

CHAPTER

37

With Jimmy out in the darkness doing God knows what, I turned my attention back to Gabby's date and listened in on their conversation.

Through the background sounds of the busy bar, Rodriguez said, "Tell me about your scuba diving adventure."

"Scuba diving? Did I say I went diving? No, I didn't do any diving this time. Although, I spent a lot of time at the pool working on my tan," Gabby said, pivoting the conversation away from his inquiry.

Rodriguez was either incredibly devious, stupid, or both. But one thing was certain, he underestimated Gabby's character and smarts. From what I heard, she was seeing right through his attempts to steer the conversation to gather information from her. What a kid. But she still had to be really careful with this guy.

With Gabby having the situation well under control, I let her continue to play with the guy for a while longer and see where things went. I dialed Eddie, who picked up right away.

"Is that you, Jake?" he whispered into my earpiece.

"Yeah. How's it going on your end?"

"Just about to break into his car and plant the bug. Give me a second while I slip the slim-jim in and give the lock a pop." I heard a soft scraping sound, then a click. "There, I'm in. These high-end BMWs open up as easily as a used Chevy. Go ahead, keep talking. I have my earbuds in so I can work hands-free while we talk."

"It sounds like Gabby's handling Rodriguez, all right. He's fishing around, trying to find out what she did in Colombia. I'll keep you on the line and go back to monitoring her if that's okay?"

"Sounds good. I think the bug will work fine under the dash. At least we'll hear his side of any calls he makes or receives. And if he uses the speakerphone in the dash, we'll pick up both sides of the conversation. But yeah, go ahead and listen in on them. I'll be right here if you need me."

Gabby and Rodriguez's conversation continued, and he was getting bolder with his questions. "How did your parents enjoy the beauty of Colombia? Are they still down there?"

"My parents? They weren't there with me. Why would you think that, Marcos? I'm a big girl now. I do all my traveling on my own these days," Gabby said and laughed off his question.

"I just assumed they would have been there with you. I wasn't suggesting you need them to travel with you and take care of you or anything. How did you break your arm again?" he said, shifting to another line of questioning.

"Oh, that. Didn't I tell you about that at lunch yesterday? Well, it's a long story. But let's just say I tripped at the hostel where I was staying and landed wrong. Got a pretty hard clunk on the head, too. And before you ask, yes, alcohol may have been involved." Gabby said, then giggled.

"Are you okay now?"

"Yeah, I'm fine. I still have some lingering headaches once in a while. The doctor gave me some strong pain meds. I don't take them all the time. Just when the pain gets worse."

From the tone of Rodriguez's voice, it seemed he was only superficially engaged in the conversation. His thoughts were elsewhere as he called for another round of drinks, "Waitress, two more, please?"

A few minutes passed with more of the same casual chatting. Then, shortly after the fresh round of drinks arrived, he tried circling back into previously covered topics.

"I hear there's some fantastic scuba diving off the Barranquilla coast. Are you sure you didn't go out at least once?"

"Now Marcos, if I didn't know better, I'd think you were trying to trick me or something. I told you I didn't go diving, and where is Barranquilla? I spent most of my time around Bogota, with one brief trip to Cartagena, which was cut off early because of my fall."

"Oh, sorry, I forgot. Yes, of course, you said you didn't go scuba diving. Maybe you'll do some diving next time you go to Colombia. I hear it really is fabulous out there in the Caribbean."

I'd had enough. This guy was trying too hard to trick her and get her to trip up. I figured the more drinks he bought her, the more likely she would get caught in a lie.

I dialed Gabby's number.

Gabby interrupted their conversation and said, "Oh, I better get this. A good friend of mine is having boyfriend problems. Give me a few minutes, and I'll be right back."

"Sure, no problem. As long as this isn't one of those safety calls to bail you out of a bad date," Rodriguez said and chuckled uncomfortably.

"Don't be silly. I'm having a wonderful time. Just hold on for one minute."

Gabby answered her phone. "Hello, Susan.... No, it's fine. I told you to call me anytime. I'm just out on a date. Can you give me a second, and I'll go somewhere quieter?"

I spoke fast. "Gabs, I don't like where this guy is trying to take the conversation. It's obvious he knows you're lying about the details of your trip, and he's trying to trick you into making a mistake. I think it's time to shut it down and get you out of there."

"Okay, I'm over by the washrooms where he can't hear me. Has Eddie planted the bug yet?"

"Last I heard, he was working on it. He should be—"

She cut me off. "Hold on a second. What the hell? The sleazy shithead just put something in my drink."

"Gabby, I want you out of there now. No more pissing around with this guy. He's incredibly dangerous."

"That asshole is trying to roofie me. What a prick."

"Hang on while I call Eddie and tell him to create a diversion so you can get the hell out of there."

"How will I know what the diversion is?"

"I'll get him to trigger Rodriguez's car alarm. That should send him running. Then, when you hear it and Rodriguez goes outside, I want you out of there. Understood?"

"All right. Look, I have to get back to the table. I'll make my move when the alarm goes off." She hung up.

I brought Eddie back on the line. "Eddie, the shit's hitting the fan in there. Rodriguez is onto her. I need you to trigger his car alarm as a diversion to get him outside and away from her."

"On it."

A few seconds later, the undulating shriek of a siren came through my earpiece.

A minute after that, a voice came over the loudspeaker in the bar. "Will the owner of a black BMW M8 please go to the parking lot? Something has set off your car alarm."

"Jeez, that sounds like my car. I'll be right back," Rodriguez said.

A couple of seconds later, Gabby called the waitress over. "This isn't the wine I ordered. I wanted the merlot. Please get me a fresh glass and quick before my boyfriend comes back. He gets furious when the orders get mixed up."

What the hell is she doing? I told her to get the hell out of there. As if reading my mind, she whispered into her phone. "Sorry, Dad. I thought it would look too obvious if he came back and I'd vanished. For good or bad, I have to play this out. And don't worry, we've still got Eddie outside."

The waitress rushed the replacement order and dropped off the new drink. "I'm terribly sorry for the mistake."

Gabby said, "No problem. It's easy to get the red wines mixed up. Thank you for changing it so quickly."

The car alarm silenced, and Rodriguez returned to the table a few minutes later.

"Is your car all right?" Gabby asked innocently.

"Yeah, it was probably just someone bumping into it while getting into their car. But it all looks fine and should be okay now."

"Well, that's good. Hey, here's to getting together with old friends. Salute."

Good God, she's toasting him now. The sound of clinking glasses chimed through her phone.

"Salute. To old friends," he said.

Their conversation continued where they had left off. Until several minutes passed, and Gabby started slurring her words. It was subtle at first, but then her speech became increasingly sloppy and unfocused.

"Are you feeling okay, Gabby?"

"Yesh. I'm feeling jush fine. Although, I'm a little lightheaded. It's probably the pain meds not mixing with the wine so well. Do you think you could drive me home now?"

"Absolutely. Here, take my arm. Whoa, not so fast. You don't want to fall and bang your head again."

"I'm sorry, Marcos. I guess I shouldn't have taken my pain meds before going out tonight. Can we have a do-over another time?"

"Of course. Let's get you home, and we'll talk about that tomorrow."

I didn't know what her game was. She told me she hadn't taken any pain meds for the last two days. So she must be pretending his roofie was kicking in. But why?

I redialed Eddie. "Get ready. They're on their way out. She's asked him to take her home. Stay close to her, Eddie. This is probably when he'll try to kill her."

I hung up and didn't wait for him to respond. At that moment, Jimmy opened the door and slid into the passenger seat beside me.

"How's it going up in D.C.?" he asked.

"Things are moving pretty fast, so I have to keep listening for a while. What were you doing over at Sanchez van?"

"He was sneaking up toward the house. So I figured I would play the role of an Amazon delivery guy and make a special delivery of the same package he sent to Stevens. I think he'll get a real bang out of it."

"Has anyone ever said you have a twisted sense of humor? But I like the irony of your plan."

CHAPTER

38

Gabby's faint slurs and the rustling sounds from her phone suggested she had put her phone in her purse or pocket. That made it almost impossible to hear everything going on up there.

I turned to Jimmy. "Eddie has the bug in place in Rodriguez's car. Can you activate it so I can hear what's going on?"

"Sure, that's not a problem, but I think we need to get moving before Sanchez takes out Stevens and Gloria."

I was torn. Jimmy was right. My head told me I needed to re-engage with our mission here and get on with rescuing Gloria. But my heart pulled me back to Gabby's situation. I couldn't let her walk into a life-and-death situation with Rodriguez, even with Eddie nearby and ready to act.

"Just a couple more minutes, then we'll go."

Jimmy nodded and grabbed the laptop from the floor of the backseat. He flipped it open and tapped the keyboard. A new horizontal bar loaded onto the screen. In the left side column, he typed *Rodriguez's car* to distinguish it from the other bugs. "Okay. All set. We should have ears in his car now." He clicked an icon, and the soft purring of a car engine filtered through my earpiece.

Rodriguez's voice came through clearly. "Just relax, Gabby. I'll get you home and take care of you in a few minutes."

"Thanksh, Marcosh. I'm sorry about thish. It mush be the pain meds I've been taking for my headaches. You're sush a good friend." Gabby was playing the drugged victim to a tee. Her college acting classes were finally paying off.

Jimmy tapped my arm and pointed through the windshield. Sanchez returned to his van and climbed inside.

I nodded. I'd run out of time and had to act now. "Okay. Let's leave the bug recording and get moving. It's time to end this."

Jimmy closed the laptop and put it in the backseat. "What's our plan?"

I looked out at Sanchez's van and then turned my head to the jungle foliage beside the Jeep. "We move through the underbrush and set up at the edge of the clearing around the house. Once we're in position, I'll find a way inside and take out Stevens. If Sanchez gets too close, you take him out."

"Sounds simple enough. Don't worry, boss. I've got your back on this one. Oh, and I asked a buddy at the air force base to arrange for a drone to track our location using my cell phone's GPS. It'll give us some eyes in the sky and pick up the heat signatures of anyone inside and where they're located."

"You never cease to amaze me. One more thing," I said as I tapped the app, turning off the incoming sounds from Gabby's phone. "Can you turn off the sound of Rodriguez's bug coming into my earpiece? I want to stay focused while we move forward."

Jimmy re-opened the laptop and tapped a key. The sound from inside Rodriguez's car went silent. I gave him the thumbs up, even as my anxiety level spiked at not hearing what was happening with Gabby.

I nudged Jimmy's arm and pointed up ahead. Sanchez was moving his van. He left the headlights off as he pulled down the driveway and slow-rolled the van out of sight.

"Where the hell is he going?"

Jimmy shrugged. "Looks to me like he wants to get closer to the house but doesn't want to be seen. Either that or he's about to make his move on Stevens."

"Then, times up. We need to go." I double-checked my Glock. It was fully loaded, the safety was off, and it was ready to go. I slipped the night vision goggles on my forehead and stepped out of the vehicle. Jimmy joined me at the jungle's edge. He had the long-barrelled sniper rifle slung over his shoulder, the parabolic antenna in his hand, and a broad smile across his face. He was enjoying the opportunity to get into some action, and I was about to find out how good he was.

All around us, the area was alive with the riotous chirping of cicadas. A veritable concert of thrumming and clicking sounds from their eternal mating ritual. As we pushed the thick bushes apart and entered the jungle, the sounds abruptly went silent, with an almost deafening effect. In the absence of the cicada sounds, the annoying buzz of mosquitos took over. I swatted at a particularly annoying one that landed on my neck for a suck of blood. God, I hate mosquitos. It's not so much the mosquitoes themselves I dislike, but the itchy welts they leave. All my life, I've been a tasty treat for them.

I grabbed a handful of damp dirt and rubbed it into the skin of my neck and face. Hopefully, that would camouflage me for our assault on the villa and help hide me from the blood-thirsty creatures buzzing around my head. I lowered the night vision goggles over my eyes, and the surrounding area lit up in pale greens.

I moved like a predator through the underbrush, placing every step carefully so I didn't make any noise. The last thing I needed was to announce my presence to either Sanchez or Stevens. The clearing came into view up ahead through the underbrush. The space between the edge of the jungle and the building created a moat-like barrier. It would be almost impossible to get across the opening without being seen.

I lowered onto my stomach and belly crawled toward the foliage's edge. The smell of warm, decaying vegetation and damp soil always brings back childhood memories of playing in the forest as a kid. There's something primordial about getting flat against the ground and inhaling nature's rich, earthy aromas. As I wriggled forward, something broad and tube-shaped glistened in front of me. I reached out to touch it, but Jimmy grabbed my arm and shook his head.

What I thought was a carelessly discarded and harmless old inner tube slowly slithered away from me. Jimmy was right. This was not the time to make friends with a giant anaconda. I took a deep breath and slid backward, away from the monster snake, as it vanished into the thick undergrowth.

As my heart rate returned to normal, we took our position at the edge of the clearing. The overhanging palms and jungle plants provided us with enough cover that anyone looking in our direction wouldn't see us. In addition, the pale light of the waning moon rising from the jungle behind us cast long shadows from the forest, further cloaking us from view. From our vantage point, I had a direct line of sight to the front of the villa less than twenty yards away. The two-story building rose above the forest against the indigo night sky.

Jimmy held his phone in front of me and pointed to several heat signatures on the screen. By the looks of things, there were two people on the roof and two more inside the villa. I assumed the two inside were Stevens and Gloria, and the other two on the roof were guards.

Jimmy moved his rifle off his shoulder and flipped down the support legs to steady it. He pointed toward the two guards on the roof. One on either end of the building. Then he removed his goggles, adjusted the scope on the rifle, and took aim. A moment later, a quiet popping sound emitted from the gun's sound suppressor. The guard on the right side of the roof dropped out of view. He shifted the rifle to the left and adjusted his aim. A second soft pop. The other guard dropped. Jimmy was right when he told me he was a crack shot. He was damn good. Two shots, two direct hits.

With the guard taken out, the way was now clear for me to advance to the villa, except for Sanchez, still somewhere up the driveway. But I had to take the chance and hope he wouldn't see me. Or if he did, he wouldn't act against me and prematurely disclose his position.

"I'm on my way," I whispered. "I'll head for the near side of the car and use it as cover. Let me know if you see or hear anyone coming."

Jimmy gave me a thumbs-up. "Ten-four, boss. I've got your back. Can you hear me okay in the earpiece?"

"Loud and clear," I whispered.

I slithered clear of the underbrush like my friend, the anaconda. After a quick check of the area, I crouched low and ran across the clearing. I squatted in the shadows behind the car and poked my head over the fender. No one was visible outside the villa or in any of the windows. I held my position for a few seconds to confirm no one had seen me move into position. So far, so good. No alarms sounded. Then I looked back toward Jimmy and saw no trace of him. The foliage and shadows completely hid him, but I knew he was there, watching and looking out for me. I glanced toward the blue van parked near the bottom of the driveway. Through the night-vision goggles, I could see Sanchez sitting behind the steering wheel, talking on his cell phone. Who the hell is he talking to in the middle of a stakeout? No matter. At least he was distracted for the moment and hopefully hadn't seen me make my move to the car.

I lowered myself into a sitting position, leaning against the side of the Mercedes, and removed the phone from my pocket. I double-tapped the surveillance app.

Jimmy's voice cut in. "What are you doing, boss? It's kind of a bad time to call in a pizza order, don't you think?"

Funny guy.

"I'll just take a few seconds to check on Gabby, then get back on the mission," I whispered.

Jimmy's sigh was all the response I needed to know he was right. But I had to find out if Gabby got home safely.

CHAPTER

39

I remained in position behind the Mercedes, with the shadows shrouding me from anyone looking out of the villa. Stevens' residence loomed on the other side of the car, with several downstairs windows lit up. Sanchez sat in his van about 30 yards away near the bottom of the driveway. Somewhere along the edge of the jungle, Jimmy lay waiting and ready to cover me.

Gabby must have moved her phone out of her purse. Smart kid. She continued slurring her words as if she was under the influence of the roofie Rodriguez had slipped into her wine. Obviously, he wasn't aware that she had switched out the contaminated drink with a fresh one. And apparently, her ruse was working as she pretended to be drugged.

"Ish really okay, Marcos. I'll be fine."

Rodriguez chimed in, "I won't have it, Gabby. I'm not leaving until I know you're safely inside. Now come along. Let's get you in the house."

They must be parked outside our house, and he was trying to get her inside, where they would be alone.

"But I don't need your help. I'm a big girl and can do thish on my own."

"I said, let's go," Rodriguez said in a more demanding tone.

"Hey, you're hurting me. Let go of me, Marcos."

This is getting out of control. Where the hell is Eddie?

Rodriguez continued to press. "Come along quietly, and I'll take good care of you. This will all be over in a minute."

Eddie's voice suddenly burst into my earpiece. "Hey, do you need any help?"

Thank God, Eddie. Now make quick work of this dirtbag.

"No. We're fine." Rodriguez snapped, "I don't need any help."

"I wasn't talking to you. I was talking to my niece. Are you okay, Gabby?" Eddie asked.

"Oh, hi, Uncle Eddie. I'm so glad to see you," Gabby said.

"Thanks, buddy. I'll take it from here," Eddie said.

"Marcos, thish is my Uncle Eddie. He's staying with me until my mom and dad come home from their trip. Isn't that right, Uncle Eddie?"

"That's right. But it sounds like you've had too much to drink, young lady. Let's get you inside and into bed. How the hell could you let her drink so much?"

Rodriguez said, "She only had two drinks. She said it's probably her pain medication that's causing this reaction."

"That's right, and don't you forget it, buddy. Hahaha." Gabby was having a lot of fun at Rodriguez's expense now.

"Look, Gabby, call me tomorrow. We can set up another date when you're not on pain meds. All right?"

"Okay, shee you, Marcos."

"Come along, Gabby. Let's get you inside," Eddie said.

A car door slammed, followed by an engine revving and squealing tires as the car sped away. Rodriguez was not happy that his plan had failed.

My heart soared when I heard the front door click closed. Thankfully, Gabby was home and safe from the deadly clutches of Rodriguez.

"What the hell were you thinking, Gabby? You know you never mix alcohol and pain meds, especially when dealing with someone as deadly as that guy." Eddie said.

Gabby's sober voice returned. "It's okay, Uncle Eddie. I was faking it. I haven't taken any pain meds for two or three days. He slipped something into my drink, so I wanted him to think his drug was working on me. When you set off his car alarm, I switched out the drinks. After he returned from checking on his car, I finished what he thought was the drink with the roofie in it."

"Wow. You really are a chip off your mom's block. But, even so, that was pretty risky. He could have taken you somewhere other than home to kill you. And if I had lost you…. Gabby, you have to be more careful around that guy."

"I get it. But I needed to trick him into thinking he had drugged me and that I didn't suspect him of his role with the cartel. He was getting too pushy and asking too many questions about my trip to Colombia. It was pretty obvious that he was trying to find out what I know about what's going on down there."

"What did you tell him?"

"I denied everything. I said that mom and dad went somewhere else and not to Colombia. And I told him I hadn't gone scuba diving."

"That son of a bitch asked you about the scuba diving incident?"

"Yeah, and he came at it several times after I told him I hadn't gone diving. So it was pretty clear he was fishing to find out where mom and dad are."

"Look, I'm going to stay here for the night in case he tries to come back. Let's talk more in the morning."

That's when the conversation took a sudden turn sideways.

"Eddie, how do you install a bugging device?" Gabby asked.

"Why?" Eddie asked.

I thought that was a logical response to her question. But her answer caught me completely off guard.

"Because I plan to plant a bug in his office."

"Oh no, you're not. Your dad would never let you do that, and neither will I. It's far too risky. What if you get caught?"

Gabby's voice grew louder. I assumed she must have moved the phone close to her face. "Are you listening, Dad? If you are, then you know what I mean to do. We need to get a bug into his office to gather more evidence against him and the cartel. And I'm the only one who can do that. You're probably unable to call right now, so if you are listening, suck it up and know that this will happen."

Damn. I felt impotent and unable to step in and confront her. In my current position, hiding behind Stevens' car and getting ready to storm his villa, I couldn't exactly call her on the phone and have it out with her. My frustration was getting the best of me.

Eddie tried to reason with her to calm things down. "Look, Gabby, it's been a long day, and there's no way we can get a bug into his office tonight. So, let's sleep on it and revisit the topic in the morning."

Gabby's voice returned to normal. I assumed she had lowered the phone from her face. "You won't change my mind, Uncle Eddie. I will have the kind of access to his office that you don't have. First, I'll call him tomorrow morning and apologize for making a complete ass out of myself tonight. Then, when I set up another date, I'll arrange to meet him at his office. Once I'm there, I'll plant the bug. So it would help if you taught me how to do that."

"Good God, I hope your dad isn't listening to this. He's going to kill me."

You're right about that, Eddie. If you go along with her plan, you're a dead man walking when I get my hands on you. Then on sober reflection, it occurred to me that Gabby had a good point. She would have easy and credible access to Rodriguez's office, which Eddie didn't. If he could train her quickly enough, she just might pull it off. But that would have to wait until tomorrow.

Feeling reassured that Gabby was safely home with Eddie, I turned my full attention to my mission here in Colombia. I turned the app off, put my phone away, and refocused.

CHAPTER

40

A quick scan of the surrounding area confirmed that Sanchez was still in his van near the bottom of the driveway. He was now sitting up, leaning over the steering wheel, and staring directly at me. For sure, he'd made me. Well, that couldn't be helped. It would have been virtually impossible for him to miss me as I crossed the clearing to the Mercedes. After all, if I had him in my direct line of sight, he would also have a clear view of me. But what Sanchez couldn't know was that I had an ace in the hole. Or, more accurately, I had Jimmy watching my back and ready to him out if he moved toward me or became a threat. I poked my head over the car's fender and studied the villa's front. There was no movement or activity behind the windows on the ground floor. It was time for me to find a way inside.

I hand-signaled in Jimmy's direction that I intended to advance to the front door. His voice whispered in my earpiece as I rose to make my move.

"Wait. Don't go yet. The two heat signatures inside the villa are on the move. And I'm picking up chatter inside. They're talking. Well, more like arguing. Yeah, definitely arguing. A woman is yelling now. Stevens is pleading with her to stay with him so he can protect her. But the woman's not buying it. She just called him a lying, pathetic drug addict."

That sounded like something Gloria would say. She was tough enough to not shy away from a prick like Stevens and confront him even in the face of danger. The situation was shaping up to be even better than I had hoped. Stevens had already shown signs of coming unglued because of the pressures from his cartel bosses and his cocaine addiction. Now Gloria was turning on him. Her badgering and calling him out would increase the stress he was dealing with. I hoped to catch him off guard as I entered the scene, and I held an advantage since there was no way he could suspect I was waiting for him just outside his front door.

I shifted my position to the front edge of the car.

Jimmy whispered, "Get down. They're moving toward the door. I think they're coming out."

I ducked low behind the fender and removed my night-vision goggles just before the door burst open, flooding the area in a blaze of white light.

Gloria rushed through the doorway. But Stevens grabbed her arm and tried to pull her back into the house.

"Get away from me, Bill. I've had enough of your lies and deceptions. I need you to take me to the airport right now." Gloria said, shaking her arm loose from his grip.

"But baby, be reasonable. It's getting late. I'll take you to the airport tomorrow. So just come back inside, and we can talk about it calmly," Stevens pleaded.

Baby? Wow, is this guy delusional or what?

"What the hell are you talking about? I'm not now, nor will I ever be, your baby," Gloria yelled as she backed away from him.

Stevens' voice grew louder and more demanding. "Get back in the house, Gloria. I mean it, or else."

"Or else, what? You slimy, good-for-nothing reptile."

Wow! She was really pissed. Thank God it wasn't me she was lashing into. When she gets this angry, it's like a hurricane approaching, and it's always best to run for cover and stay out of her way until the storm has passed.

Stevens pulled a pistol from behind his back. He grabbed her by the collar and waved the gun in her face. "Or else... or else. Just get inside, Gloria. I don't want to use this, but I will if I have to."

Gloria tried to pull away. "Fuck you, asshole. You don't have the guts to use that thing."

Stevens held her firmly and wrenched her back toward the house. The situation was rapidly spiraling out of control. He was coming unglued and unstable, which is a dangerous and unpredictable emotional state where he might do anything. And this seemed like the perfect time to throw a curveball at him and up the pressure even more. So I aimed my pistol in his direction and rose from behind the car.

"Drop the gun, Stevens!"

He spun his head around and jammed the barrel under Gloria's chin. "Where... where did you come from?"

"I said, drop the gun!" I snapped the Glock's slide back, loading a bullet into the chamber. "Do it now! I won't tell you again!"

He shifted sideways, wrapping Gloria in a headlock with his left arm as he positioned her in front of him as a shield. His pistol hand shook noticeably, suggesting he was less stable and not as confident as he was letting on. With his gun pointing at Gloria's chin, anything could happen at any moment. I needed to neutralize him as a threat as quickly as possible.

Jimmy said into my earpiece, "I don't have a clean shot with Gloria in the way."

I took two slow steps sideways along the edge of the car, keeping it between Stevens and me. I rested my arms against the car roof, steadied my pistol with both hands, and took aim. Like Jimmy, I didn't have a clear shot. With Gloria in front of him, tight against his body, all I could see was part of his face as he peeked around her head. I hoped he would try to take a shot at me, giving

Gloria a chance to break free of his grip. Of course, I also hoped he was a terrible shot.

His eyes flared as he yelled, "Get… get away from the car, Stone."

We were in a stand-off, and neither of us wanted to give an inch. So it was time to clarify his options and what was at stake for him.

"I don't think so, Stevens. Let Gloria go. There's no way you can get away with this. You know as well as I do that this has to end here. And it ends one of two ways. The first way, you surrender and live. The second way, you die right here."

"Why? Tell me why it has to end here?" He yelled like a child having a tantrum.

"Oh, I almost forgot. There's a third way this can end. The cartel cleans house and takes you out. You've become a liability to them. It's only a matter of time before they kill you."

That seemed to rock him a little. At first, he seemed stunned, as if I had knocked the wind out of him with a body blow to his guts. Then, ever so slightly, he lowered his gun away from Gloria's chin and pushed her toward the car while holding her close in front of him.

"No, you're wrong. The cartel needs me. I'm too important to them. They'd never do anything to get rid of me." Stevens moved another step closer to the driver's side of the car.

Obviously, he hadn't received the memo from Rodriguez and didn't know that Sanchez had orders to kill him. He was completely delusional or so caught up in his self-importance that he didn't get it. I'd hit a nerve, and it was time to keep poking at it.

"I don't think you fully understand how precarious your situation is, Stevens. I have evidence that Rodriguez has told Sanchez to take you out."

"How do you know about Rodriguez and Sanchez?" He shook his head violently as if to clear his mind. "How could you possibly know that?"

"We've been monitoring your phone calls for quite a while. So even if you take me out, the U.S. Government will be all over your ass. Now, for the last time, lower your weapon and let Gloria go."

He shoved her closer to the car. "Get in, Gloria. We're getting out of here. Back away from the car, Stone, or I'll shoot her."

Gloria looked me in the eyes and held my gaze. Her face expressed confidence and strength. She knew the risks, and she also trusted I had a plan. I hoped my eyes conveyed the same message to her even though I didn't really have a plan. My gut was telling me I was running out of options and time, and I wasn't about to show any signs of weakness or doubt. Instead, I wanted to create as much doubt in Stevens' mind as possible and look for an opening for a clean shot.

As Stevens and Gloria got closer to the car, a massive flash of white light flooded the clearing, followed immediately by a sound wave that rocked me backward and shook the car. With Stevens, Gloria, and me all close to the car, Sanchez used that moment to deliver the package he had mounted under the Mercedes. Unfortunately for him, he was sitting directly above it when he pressed the detonator. Flames and shattered parts of the van blew upward and out into the jungle as the vehicle exploded into a fiery ball and disintegrated.

As Stevens turned toward the van, he pulled his gun hand away from Gloria and used it to shield his eyes from the flash of the explosion. Gloria jumped into action. She broke free from his headlock, pulled herself out of his grasp, punched him in the head, and ducked out of the way.

This was the chance I was waiting for, and I didn't waste it. I pumped three slugs into Stevens' chest. The impact of the shots knocked him backward off his feet. Before he knew what hit him, he lay dead on the driveway.

"Daddy's home, asshole!" I said, taking a page from Gloria's dramatic entrance back at the cocaine fields.

Gloria popped up on the other side of the car and smiled. "What the hell took you so long, Stone?"

I ran around the front of the car, pulled her into my arms, and hugged her. "Hey, he was pretty elusive. Even for a... what did you call him? A lying, pathetic drug addict?"

She stood on her toes and gave me a long kiss. God, it felt good to hold her again.

"Even so, did you have to drag out the hostage rescue scene that long? I thought I'd have to take him down myself."

"Come on, Gloria. Save the critique for later. Let's get the hell out of here." I whistled and waved for Jimmy to come out of hiding.

He emerged out of the shadows and strolled towards us. His sniper's rifle was slung over his shoulder, and the other paraphernalia was hanging from his belt. After a quick round of introductions, I jumped into the Mercedes. Damn, no keys. I got out, rolled Stevens' lifeless body over, and fished the car keys from his pants pocket. After a quick stop at the Jeep to collect the rest of our gear, we headed back toward Barranquilla.

Gloria looked at me from the passenger side of the front seat. "Where's Gabby? You didn't let anything happen to her, did you? You know my promise still holds. The authorities will never find your body if you let anything happen to her."

Before I could answer, Jimmy laughed from the back seat. "You were right about her, Jake. She really is an incredible woman."

"And I never forget that, Jimmy. Gabby's safe at home with Eddie. I'll fill you in during the flight home."

Gloria slid over and leaned against me. "Is there any way you can get a shower and clean up before we go? No offense, but you stink. And there's no way I'm sitting beside you smelling like this for the next six and a half hours."

I raised my arm and sniffed my armpits. Whew! She wasn't wrong. A hot shower and a change of clothes were in order.

Jimmy's laughter from the back seat was contagious.

As we approached Barranquilla's outskirts, I quickly called Eddie and asked him to arrange a rapid airlift home.

Eddie called back with our extraction details as I steered the Mercedes to the curb in front of Jimmy's place. It was wheels up at 04:15 aboard a U.S. Air Force troop transport. He had us on a direct flight to D.C. from the same place Gabby flew out of at the Barranquilla airport.

CHAPTER

41

With several hours to burn before our flight home, I turned my attention to getting cleaned up and ready to go. Gloria called Eddie back and got a full update from him about Gabby's situation. Thankfully, I was in the shower, so she couldn't confront me about Gabby's intention to plant a bug in Rodriguez's office. Poor old Eddie would take the worst of her wrath. Thankfully, he convinced her that I was doing everything in my power to protect her. Clean-shaven and showered, I felt like a new man. Unfortunately, clean clothes were not an option since Jimmy stood several inches taller than me.

I entered the front room and caught them in full-throated laughter.

"What's so funny?" I said, taking a seat beside Gloria and cracking open a beer.

Gloria put her hand over her mouth and snickered. "Jimmy was just filling me in on some of the more… memorable moments you guys had over the past few days."

"And I suppose those are all about me?" I said, then took a long gulp of beer.

Jimmy's face turned serious. "Not all of them, boss. Well yeah, most of them."

"Like what?"

Gloria looked at Jimmy. "Make the face he made when he saw the bomb under Stevens' car. That was priceless."

Jimmy distorted his face as his eyes expanded, showing wide white rings around the irises. His mouth dropped open with his chin hitting his chest.

"Very funny. You guys are friggin' hilarious." I crossed my arms and legs defiantly.

Gloria pouted and, with a soft snort, burst out laughing again. "And there's another one of Jake's classic faces. He gets that frustrated little boy look when he's embarrassed."

"Look, it's not like I see a live bomb every day, and never that close to my face. So go ahead and have fun. But I'd like to see how you'd react in the same situation, Gloria."

"Oh, I would handle it differently, for sure," she said as she mocked my facial expression again.

"Like how?"

"Well, to start with, I'd draw on my professional training and skills. Then I'd have to change my underwear after shitting myself," Gloria said and burst out laughing again.

That got us all laughing. There was something cathartic and healing that came with our full-throated laughter. It seemed like forever since I had a good belly laugh, and I had to admit, Gloria was right. I was lucky I didn't shit myself on the spot when I saw the bomb up close and personal. But in hindsight, seeing the humor in the whole situation helped me to relax.

I looked over at Jimmy and clinked my beer bottle against his. "All I can say is, thank God for Jimmy. He was a rock and handled it beautifully."

"Thanks, boss. You must have been so scared you didn't smell the crap in my shorts. But, hey, that isn't something anybody sees too often. Especially when you know there's a guy somewhere out there waiting to detonate the thing."

"Exactly," I said. "Well, all I can say is, at least Sanchez got a big bang out of it in the end."

Another round of laughter felt good and released more pent-up tensions from the past couple of weeks.

Jimmy handed me my phone. "I've loaded a copy of the recording we got from inside Rodriguez's car after he dropped Gabby off at home. So you and Gloria can listen to it on the flight back to Washington."

"Thanks, man. I really appreciate everything you've done for my family and me this past week. I don't know what I would have done without you."

"No problem. I'm sure you'd do the same for me in a similar situation."

Gloria headed to the bathroom to freshen up. "I gotta get out of here. All this male bonding, love fest is getting a little too much." Her laughter continued even after the bathroom door closed behind her.

It felt good to hear her laughing again. Even with so much uncertainty at home, my heart filled with joy, knowing the love of my life was back with me.

Jimmy changed the subject, bringing my focus back to our next steps. "I hope you don't mind, but while you were in the shower, I called a buddy at the air force base. She'll meet you at the airport and escort you through to the transport. Her name is Private Amelia Lopez."

"Hey, I met her when I dropped Gabby off for her flight home. She's a good-looking woman. Anything going on with you two?"

"No, she's happily married with two young kids. Amelia and her husband, Joseph, are great people. Besides, I'm still waiting for the right one to come along."

"When you're ready for the right one, she'll show up. It's the way of the universe. First, you prepare yourself to be open to receive, then set your intention, and after that, the universe delivers."

"Wow. A skilled agent and philosopher-king as well. You really are a man of many talents, boss. But enough philosophizing for now. Gloria gave me your sizes, so I asked Lopez to round up some clothes for you. Hopefully, she'll come up with something suitable to replace what you're wearing.

I leaned over and fist-bumped him. "Thanks, Jimmy. You really are a godsend, and I mean it. If there's ever anything I can do to return the favor, you have to do is ask."

"Don't worry about it. I should thank you. The last few days on this mission were the most fun I've had in ages. After being buried in deep cover for so long, it was great to break out and get into some action. Hopefully, we'll be able to get together on another mission in the future."

"I'd like that. But, even though I'm retired, anything can happen in life. So, let's hope an opportunity comes up for us to kick some ass again."

Gloria came back into the room. "Oh, for the love of…. Why don't you two get a room? We should get going if you guys are just about finished with the bromance."

I slapped my knees and stood. "Right, let's get going then. Eddie's arranged for our flight home. We have a change of clothes waiting for us at the airport, and we have some audio to listen to during the flight. So I'd say we've got everything covered." I tossed Jimmy the keys to Stevens' Mercedes. "You drive. I want to get reacquainted with my girl."

I put my hand on Gloria's hip, pulled her close, leaned over, and kissed her.

"Maybe you two should get a room," Jimmy said.

Gloria playfully pushed me away. "That won't be necessary. I think we can wait until we get home. And Jake, there's only going to be one of us in the back seat going to the airport." Her lower lip rolled outward as she mimicked my pouty face again and laughed.

Man, I love this woman. Her laughter is like music from Heaven.

The drive up to the air force base went smoothly. In Barranquilla, the traffic after midnight was light and almost nonexistent, at least until we got closer to the main terminal of the Ernesto Cortissoz International Airport.

Private Lopez was waiting for us in front of the departure terminal. She shifted to stand at attention as we got out of the car and approached her. The duffle bag at her feet presumably had a change of clothes for Gloria and me.

Jimmy quickly introduced us. I reminded Private Lopez that we had met several days ago when Gabby left for home. She remembered me and graciously led Gloria and me over to the airport's secured U.S. Air Force section. Jimmy stayed behind, always watching my back.

Just before we disappeared into the hangar to prepare for our flight, I turned and waved. He gave me a salute and got into the Mercedes. I was going to miss him. And not just his outstanding skills but also his interesting sense of humor and companionship.

I hoped I would see him again soon. But for now, it was time to get home and put a stop to any further threats to my family from the cartel up in Washington.

CHAPTER

42

Once inside the U.S. Air Force hanger, Private Lopez handed me the duffle bag. "I requisitioned a change of clothes for each of you based on the sizes Jimmy gave me. Hopefully, they fit, and you find them suitable for your trip back home."

Gloria took the bag from me and said, "I'm sure they'll be fine. Thank you, Private."

I waved my hand toward my dirt-smeared shirt and pants. "I'm sure they'll be perfect and be a major upgrade to what I have on. Especially since these desperately need a good cleaning or incinerating."

Private Lopez cracked a broad smile. "There's a changing area just over there that you can use." She pointed toward a set of doors leading to a coed locker room for pilots and crew members.

Private Lopez had chosen well, as the military jumpsuits fit perfectly. Although they were military-issued camouflage fatigues, they would be fine until we got home and into our clothes.

We didn't have long to wait for our flight. As expected, the Boeing C-17 Globemaster transport flight took off right on time, at 04:15. There's a lot of truth to what people say about military precision—they reviewed every step in the planning for the flight and double-checked everything down to the smallest detail. As the aircraft rose off the runway, I thought about how commercial airlines could benefit from the disciplined approach and standards our air force used. Of course, military flights aren't subjected to the vagaries and challenges of multiple incoming and outgoing flights at overloaded airports. Or the endless security screenings and lineups the public is forced to endure. At any rate, I couldn't complain. Our flight home was courtesy of the US government, and you can't beat a free ride.

The cavernous inside of the aircraft was virtually empty. Besides Gloria and me, only a couple dozen young men and women were on board. They were on their way stateside after their tour of duty in Colombia. Our estimated time of arrival in D.C. was 09:30. With any luck, we would avoid most of the morning rush hour traffic and get home in time to stop Gabby from meeting Rodriguez for lunch.

The seating wasn't as comfortable as the first-class seats in a commercial airline or the plush leather armchairs of a private jet. But the price and convenience of this flight were worth any minor discomfort I felt sitting in the perimeter jump seats. In addition, the sound-reducing headphones they gave us when we boarded dampened the thunderous noise inside the aircraft.

Once the aircraft leveled off and established its cruising speed, I offered Gloria one of Jimmy's communication earpieces.

She pulled the headphone off her left ear, inserted the slim earpiece, then returned the headphone over her ear. "Can you hear me?" she said, looking up at me.

"Loud and clear, babe. Okay, I'm going to run the recording we made from Rodriguez's car while Gabby was on her date with him. I don't know what's on it, but let's run it and see. Hopefully, there's something we can use against him and the cartel."

Gloria nodded and gave me a thumbs-up.

I tapped the screen on my phone to play the recording.

A low hum came through the earpiece. I adjusted the volume to drown out the background groaning of the aircraft engines.

After a few seconds, Rodriguez's voice came through. "Damn that meddling son-of-a-bitch. I almost had her. Shit, shit, shit."

A loud thumping sound mixed with his voice. Was he hitting the steering wheel? He was clearly frustrated that his plan to kill Gabby was interrupted by Eddie.

It was a good thing Eddie arrived when he did, or we would be going home for a funeral.

Gloria tapped my arm. "Is that Rodriguez?"

I nodded and paused the recording. "Yes, that's him. The prick had spiked Gabby's drink in the bar. She saw him do it while she was away from the table, talking with me on the phone. I had Eddie create a diversion by tripping his car alarm. When Rodriguez went outside to check on his car, she had the presence of mind to switch drinks. I had instructed her to get the hell out of there, but she faked being doped up instead. Then she told him she was having a reaction to the alcohol and the pain meds she had supposedly taken earlier. It was a risky but good ruse since he thought the roofie he put in her drink was causing her dopiness. Eddie intervened when Rodriguez tried to get Gabby into the house to be alone with her. I have no doubt he planned to kill her when they got inside. He'd most likely make it look like an accident or something."

"Thank God for Eddie, then," Gloria said.

"My thoughts exactly."

I tapped PLAY and restarted the recording.

The soft purring sound of the car engine continued in the background. After another minute or two, the car's hand-free speakerphone rang.

"Hello?" Rodriguez said.

A woman's voice replied, "Do you have me on speakerphone?"

"Yes, I do, Gabriel. I'm driving. But I'm alone. What can I—?"

"Damn it, Rodriguez. How many times do I have to tell you never to use my real name?"

"Ah… I'm sorry, Angel. I've had a stressful day. It won't happen again."

"It better not. We have enough trouble with Stevens and the Stone family down in Colombia. I don't want to think we have another problem with you."

"No, everything is good, and I understand fully."

There was a noticeable nervousness in his tone. This confirmed my earlier assumption when we listened in on Rodriguez's call to Stevens that whoever Angel Gabriel was, she was one of his bosses in the drug cartel.

Angel continued, "Good. Now, what's the status in Colombia? Has Sanchez killed Jake Stone and his wife yet?"

Gloria and I looked at each other. Once again, the term *killed* used along with my name in the same sentence focussed my mind with razor-sharp clarity.

"I have everything under control. So there's no need for you to worry about it," Rodriguez said.

The woman named Angel raised her voice, noticeably pissed off and losing patience with him. "I didn't ask you if things were under control. It's a simple question, Rodriguez. Which is it? Are they dead or not? And while we're at it, what the hell are you doing about Stevens? He's been a liability for too long and needs to be taken out immediately."

"Understood, Angel. Sanchez is taking care of Stevens tonight. As for Stone and his wife, Sanchez is tracking them and will eliminate them soon. After tonight, they will no longer be a threat to our operations."

"He better get it done tonight. After the mess they made with Patrón and Dominguez, I want no more screw-ups. Is that clear enough for you?"

"Yes, Ma'am."

"And Rodriguez, I don't need to remind you of what's at stake if this all goes sideways. So get it done and clean up the mess down there. And I mean, get it done tonight."

The car phone buzzed and went silent as Angel hung up.

The thumping sound returned. "Fuck, fuck, fuck," Rodriguez said.

Again, I assumed he was hitting the steering wheel in frustration.

So, that was the person known as Angel Gabriel. The same person Rodriguez's parrot talked about during the previous recording on Stevens' phone. Whoever Gabriel was, she was clearly Rodriguez's cartel boss. I was quickly coming around to thinking Gabby was right. We need to get a bug in his office to gather more information about him and others involved with the cartel. Although, I wasn't ready to agree to let her do the job of planting the bug. We had to find another way into his office that wouldn't put Gabby in danger.

The recording continued, accompanied by the soft drone of the engine and road noise.

"Call Sanchez," Rodriguez said. The car phone automatically dialed, followed by the rumbling of a phone ringing at the other end.

"Hola, boss," Sanchez said as he answered.

"Sanchez, I just got off the phone with Angel. She's furious that the Stones and Stevens are still alive. You need to kill Stevens and the woman tonight. Then track down Jake Stone and eliminate him as well. And, Sanchez, you need to do it quickly before they cause any more trouble for our operations. Is that understood?"

"Yes, boss. I'm outside Senor Stevens' villa right now. I delivered the package under his car, as we discussed earlier. It is only a matter of time before he will receive it."

"We don't have time to wait anymore. You must finish the job tonight, no matter what it takes. Just make sure all three of them die tonight."

"I understand. Wait, someone is sneaking up to the house."

"Who is it?"

"It looks like Senor Stone. Yes, it is definitely Stone. He must be here to rescue his wife."

"Good, now we have them all in the same place. Do your job, Sanchez, and finish this now."

"Yes, Senor. Stone appears to be waiting for something. I'll wait until he goes inside, so I don't alert Stevens' guards. Then I will go in and take care of all of them."

"I don't care what you have to do. Just get it done tonight. Listen, I have to go. Call me when it's finished."

"Wait, senor. Stevens just came outside, and he has the woman with him. They are arguing. He just pulled a gun on her. Let me put the phone down so I can get a better look."

Apparently, Sanchez had been on the phone with Rodriguez the whole time I was outside of Stevens' villa. So when I had seen him on the phone in his van earlier, he must have been providing Rodriguez with a play-by-play of the action.

Sanchez continued, "I think I can take them all out with the package. Stevens is moving the woman and himself toward the car. Stone is on the other side of the car, pointing his gun at Stevens. When they get a little closer, I'll be able to take them all out with the bomb."

Sanchez switched from play-by-play to talking to himself. "That's it, Senor Stevens. Just a little closer, and I will—"

The phone call went silent.

"Sanchez, are you there? What the fuck?" Rodriguez said as a dial tone sounded through the car speakerphone.

"Dial Sanchez," he instructed the car phone again.

Sanchez's phone rang over and over. But there was no one there to answer, nor was there a phone to be answered.

"God damn it, Sanchez. What the hell is going on down there?" The last sounds on the recording were the car engine shutting off, the car door closing, and the beep of the alarm as the doors locked.

I turned to Gloria. "That's pretty much how it all went down. Sanchez didn't realize the car bomb was directly underneath his seat when he pushed the detonator. So his timing was perfect for me to take out Stevens."

"We need to talk with Gabby and Eddie and shut down this insane idea she has of planting a bug at Rodriguez's office," Gloria said. "These people are homicidal maniacs."

"I agree." I dialed Eddie's phone number. Nothing happened. I looked at the screen. There were no signal bars at the top. "There's no signal. We must be over international waters and out of the Colombian service range."

If that was the case, I had my doubts the phone would work when we landed, either. I checked my watch—05:53. We still had several hours before arrival in D.C., and then, who knows how long it would take to get through traffic and reach Gabby in time to stop her?

CHAPTER

43

The massive Boeing C-17 Globemaster made good time for an aircraft that massive. It always amazes me that something so huge can actually fly and stay in the air. We touched down at Andrews Air Force base just after 09:30. The heavy thump of the wheels hitting the tarmac jolted me out of my slumber. Gloria sat beside me, holding my cell phone over her head, searching for a signal.

"Hey. Good morning, gorgeous. Did you get some sleep?" I asked, stretching out my arms and shoulders.

My lower back hurt like hell, and my legs were numb from sitting in the cramped position on the uncomfortable jump seat.

She handed me the phone. "Not as much as you did. But I got a couple of hours. You were right about this phone. No signal. I'd say it's time to get some new gear that actually connects to the phone systems in the States."

"I was afraid of that. Maybe we can use a landline in the terminal to reach Gabby and convince her not to meet with Rodriguez today. She has to drop this insane idea of planting a bug in his office."

The big bird taxied to a stop, and the back-end doors slowly opened. Our co-pilot climbed down from the cockpit and escorted us down the rear ramp with the other returning military personnel.

At the bottom of the ramp, a young air cadet met us and escorted us into the terminal. As the door of the arrivals area closed behind us, muffling the sounds of aircraft outside, he turned and said, "I bet you're glad to be back home stateside?"

I glanced at his name tag. "You don't know the half of it, Private Daniels. Can you take us somewhere quiet with a phone? I need to make an urgent call."

"Absolutely, sir. Please follow me."

Andrews Air Force base was a gathering point for returning and departing military personnel. There was a constant flow of incoming and outgoing troops moving through the crowded terminal. It did my heart good to see couples embracing each other as returning personnel reunited with their loved ones. It's never fun being away from your family for extended stretches of active duty, and the joy they felt being back together was palpable. We wove our way through clusters of families with young children clambering to be the first to hug their mom or dad. I felt an ache in my heart as I considered being reunited with Gabby again.

Daniels opened the door to a small office. "You'll have privacy in here, sir. Just hit nine to get an outside line. Then, when you're ready, I'll arrange for a taxi to take you wherever you're headed this morning."

"Thank you, Private. I appreciate that."

Gloria and I entered the office and closed the door behind us. The room fell deafeningly silent as soundproofing in the walls and door abruptly cut off the bustling noise of the terminal. I dialed Gabby's number. Her phone rang once and went straight to voicemail.

"Damn it, Gabby. Where are you?" I said impatiently into the phone.

"What's wrong, Jake?" Gloria asked.

I glanced up at the large round face of the clock on the wall—09:45. She should still be at home. It's too early for her to be meeting Rodriguez for lunch. "Her phone went straight to voicemail. I'll try again. Maybe she was talking with someone."

I dialed her number, and again it went straight to voicemail. So this time, I left a message.

"Gabby, it's Dad. Your mom and I just landed at Andrews Air Force base. We should be home in less than an hour. But Gabby, please stay there so we can talk about your decision to meet with Rodriguez. To be clear, your mom and I think it's a terrible idea and too risky. So just stay there, and we'll be home soon."

Gloria held out her hand for the phone. "Listen, Gabby. Please listen to your dad. He's right. This idea of going to Rodriguez's office to plant a bug is reckless and too dangerous. So stay put at home until we can get there. I love you, sweetie. See you soon."

Gloria handed me the phone, and I hung up. Her face showed me that she was as worried as I was. Deep creases stretched across her forehead, with her lips pushed together in a tight, straight line.

"What are you thinking?" I asked.

"I don't think she's home. And if it was me, I'd turn my phone off so no one could talk me out of going to see Rodriguez."

Gloria was right. Gabby had become more and more like Gloria the deeper she got involved with the cartel. I had watched her boldness and confidence grow as the events in Colombia unfolded. And that worried me. The thought of her facing off against a vicious killer without the experience and proper skills scared the hell out of me.

I called Eddie's phone. The ringtone repeated over and over in my ear.

Come on, Eddie, pick up.

After several rings, his voicemail kicked in.

Once his generic greeting ended, followed by the beep, I left him a short message. "Eddie, where the hell are you and Gabby? She's not answering her phone, and we need to stop her from doing something crazy. We're leaving Andrews Air Force base in a couple of minutes, but we don't have a working cell phone, so keep her there until we get home."

I ended the call and looked at Gloria. Her face hadn't changed. She still displayed the concerned expression from earlier. "Come on, Jake, stop pissing around. We need to get going."

She was the first out the door. Private Daniels led the way to the exit and flagged a cab for us. As the taxi pulled up, he stood at attention and saluted us. I returned the salute, then shook his hand. "Thank you, Private, you've been a great help."

"Not a problem, sir and ma'am. Have a great day."

Private Daniels' last words echoed in my ears as the taxi pulled into traffic. *'Have a great day.'* All I could think was, from your lips to God's ears.

Even with the bulk of the morning rush hour traffic over, the snarled, slow-moving chaos on the Beltway blocked our progress. It took over an hour to get to the other side of the city and out into the suburbs. The taxi hadn't come to a complete before Gloria hopped out and ran to our front door. I paid the driver with my credit card and looked at the empty driveway. Eddie's SUV was nowhere in sight. Nor was Gabby's car. That could only mean one thing. Gabby wasn't home, and Eddie was out there trying to stop her from planting the bug at Rodriguez's office. The thin sliver of hope I had held onto since leaving the airport slipped away, leaving a hollow pit of despair in my gut.

Gloria called out as I entered the house, "Gabby, are you home?"

No answer. Gloria went upstairs to check the bedrooms while I walked through the downstairs rooms, looking for a clue about where Gabby might have gone. I found a note on the kitchen counter with a smartphone beside it.

Jake,

Gabby left before I got up this morning. I'm afraid she's on her way to meet Rodriguez. I'm heading there now. The DEA and FBI are coming in on this. Mastermind appointed me as the lead agent in charge. I'll be in the Command Centre organizing a raid on Rodriguez's office. His address is below. I set the phone up with the same surveillance app you used in Colombia to monitor Gabby's phone. She took the bugging device with her. Don't worry. We'll get her back safely.

Eddie

I put the note down and yelled, "Gloria!"

She put her hand on my arm, and the unexpected contact almost made me jump out of my skin.

"I'm right here," she said from behind me.

"For the love of… don't sneak up on me like that. You almost gave me a heart attack. Here, read this. Seems we're too late. Gabby's already gone."

"No shit, Sherlock. What was your first clue?"

"Hey, come on, Gloria. Don't get snarky with me. This isn't my fault."

"I know. I'm just frustrated. But give me enough time, and I'll find a way to make it your fault. Let's get going."

I thought I saw a hint of a smile on her face or at least a slight twinkle in her eyes. But it wasn't enough to wipe away the intense resolve she had on display. She had her game face on. An expression I had seen many times during our careers, and it meant she was completely focused and all business.

I checked the time, then the address at the bottom of the note. "As long as the traffic cooperates, I think we can get there in less than half an hour."

I grabbed the car keys off the hook in the laundry room and hit the garage door opener. Then, while the door clunked and groaned, sliding up the guide rails, we jumped into the car, and I fired it up.

I clicked the start button on the phone and handed it to Gloria. As the screen flashed into service, I said, "When it's finished booting up, I'll walk you through how to operate the surveillance app to monitor what's going on around Gabby."

She tapped on the phone and navigated through the screens. "Just drive. I'll figure it out."

Gloria has a much better grasp of technology than I ever had, so I stuck to what I'm good at—driving—and let her handle the technical stuff.

CHAPTER

44

I punched the accelerator and swerved past a slow-moving pickup truck. If Gabby was on her way to plant a bug in Rodriguez's office, we needed to get there as fast as possible to stop her. And the clock was ticking. My eyes swept from the rearview mirror to the side mirrors and back to the road ahead. The last thing I needed was a cop to pull us over for speeding.

I handed Eddie's note to Gloria. "Can you enter Rodriguez's address into the nav system?"

She entered the address, and a mechanical female voice came on, offering suggestions for the fastest route to our destination. I was right on course and making excellent time.

Gloria tried Gabby's number, and her phone went straight to voicemail again. She was determined to follow through on her plan right to the end, regardless of the personal risks. Our one ace in the hole was the surveillance app that activated her phone's microphone.

Gloria tapped the app, and the clicking of leather-soled shoes on a hard surface came through the phone's speaker, followed by Gabby's voice.

"Mom and Dad, I hope you're listening. I have to tell you why I'm doing this. I shut off my phone, so you can't call and try to talk me out of planting the bugging device in Rodriguez's office. After what this asshole tried to do to us in Colombia and to me last night, I decided I had to do this. Whether you believe I should be involved or not, I already am and have been since day one."

It sounded like a door squeaked and swished closed with a click. The background behind Gabby's voice took on a hollow, echoing quality. She must have gone into an enclosed space. Her footsteps grew louder as they echoed off the walls of the enclosure. Her breathing became more labored. Could she be walking up an interior staircase? If so, that meant she was already at Rodriguez's building and heading to his office. I stepped harder on the gas and shot forward through the traffic.

Gabby continued, "The cartel tried to kill me on four separate occasions. Five, if you included last night. They kidnapped you, Mom, and they tried to kill Dad at least four times as well. We won't be safe until we stop these people. My intention is to do whatever I can to bring them down. I know what you are thinking, Dad. And you're right, I'm not trained for this kind of work. But I'll find a way."

I shook my head and grimaced. How could I have let her get this involved? The expression on Gloria's face had not changed since we left the house. She listened intently to Gabby while I refocused on the surrounding traffic.

"Anyway, I'm almost there," Gabby said. "I want you to know how much I love you both. If anything happens to me, make sure you get this son-of-a-bitch and take him out."

I wanted to scream as my frustration boiled over. If anything happens to Gabby, the people who hurt her will pay the ultimate price. Even if it was the last thing I did, I'd unleash vengeance on everyone involved.

Another clicking sound came over the phone, followed by a swish. She must have opened a door. The hollow, echoing background noise changed to the soft rhythmic tapping of her shoes on what I imagined was a polished hallway surface. A few seconds later, a loud scraping came across the speaker, followed by muted sounds. Had she put her phone in her purse?

I checked the map on the nav system screen. We were close now. I needed to take the next exit, so I cut wildly across several lanes of traffic to the angry honking of shocked drivers and pulled off the main road. At the bottom of the exit ramp, I merged right and cut through the narrow streets. Fortunately, the street lights were in our favor, but frustration flooded back in as the slow-moving traffic blocked my progress. Finally, three blocks from the exit, the voice on the nav system told me to take a left turn and announced our destination was on the left side of the street.

I turned the corner and pulled over in front of a 1920s-era four-story brownstone building. Thick thermal-efficient blue-green glass windows with chrome accents modernized the front façade. A sign on the front wall near the door indicated it was a professional building, not a condo residence. According to Eddie's note, Rodriguez's office was on the fourth floor. I pulled away from the curb and slowly drove past the building, so we could assess our entry options.

The Command Centre was parked around the corner at the end of the block. From there, it was out of view from Rodriguez's building. The large, unmarked cube van appeared capable of housing several computers, high-tech monitoring, and communications devices. I pulled over and parked. From the outside, the Command Centre van looked like a significant upgrade over Jimmy's ancient fish van in Barranquilla. But I had no doubt that both vans had similar high-tech equipment and capabilities.

"Gloria, can I have the phone for a second? I need to call Eddie and let him know we're here."

She handed me the phone, and I dialed his number.

Eddie answered immediately. "Hello?"

"Eddie, It's Jake. We're parked behind the Command Centre. Can you give us access?"

"I'll be right out." His phone clicked off.

A moment later, the back door of the cube van opened. Eddie poked his head out. Gloria and I got out of our car and approached.

He climbed down and hugged Gloria. "I am so glad you got out of Colombia safe and unharmed." He turned to me and shook my hand. "Good to have you back home. Come on inside."

He led us into the van. Two techs sat in front of a panel of large-screen monitors and keyboards. Near the door, two armed personnel in bulletproof vests and battle gear waited for the go signal. One with DEA letters stenciled across the front and back of his vest. The other with FBI across her vest.

Other than the armed personnel, the inside of the Command Centre appeared similar to Jimmy's set-up. Although, this one had more gadgets. It was also in pristine condition and even had the new vehicle smell.

Eddie did a quick round of introductions. "Jake and Gloria, these are Special Agents Carter, and Williams of the DEA and FBI, respectively. They'll lead the assault teams when I give the order to go." Then, he turned to the agents. "These are my closest friends and the parents of the woman inside the building with the bugging device. They're both retired agents and fully capable of engaging with our target."

I shook their hands, and Gloria did the same.

"What's the status in there, Eddie?" I said, glancing at the monitor screens as if I understood what I was looking at. I almost fell over when I recognized the images on one monitor. Across the screen were several horizontal bar graphs. They were the same pattern as the ones on Jimmy's monitor and laptop that we used to track the bug on Stevens' phone.

Without missing a beat, I pointed to the screen. "Who are we listening to here?"

"The top one is the bug in Rodriguez's car. The second one is the bug Gabby has with her," Eddie said.

I looked closer at both graphs. The top one was motionless. Obviously, there was no activity in the area near his car. The other one showed small spikes.

"We activated the bug Gabby is carrying a while ago and heard her telling you what she is doing and why. That's one hell of a brave girl you two have there," Eddie said, looking at Gloria and me.

"You mean *we* have," I said, pointing at him. "Gabby is as much a product of your involvement in her life as ours. So, you better not let anything happen to her, or we'll both be answering to Gloria." I tried to smile, but it just wouldn't happen.

It was as if Gloria hadn't heard us. She focused on the bar graph and held the phone to her ear, trying to hear what was going on with Gabby. "When you two are finished goofing around, can we get the volume turned up on the bug?"

"For sure," Eddie said. He tapped one of the tech agents on the shoulder and signaled for him to turn up the volume on the speakers so we could all hear what he was listening to through his headphones.

Rodriguez's voice came across the speakers in the van. "I'm so glad you called this morning. I was quite concerned about you last night."

I wanted to confront the guy. And call him out for the lying piece of shit he is. The only thing he was concerned about was that he hadn't killed her last night.

Gabby responded as if she was unaware of his murderous intentions. "As I said this morning, I felt awful about the screw-up with my meds. That never happens to me. But I promise I haven't taken anything today. So, I should be good for lunch. Although this time, I'll stay away from alcohol. That is if you still want to take me out again."

"Of course. It's not a problem. We all make mistakes. I'm just glad you're feeling better today."

A loud flirty whistle came over the speakers, followed by a high-pitched, almost mechanical voice. "Auk. Gabriel. Gabriel is angry. Angry Angel. Auk." Then another loud, high-pitched whistle.

It was the voice of the parrot that I had heard when Rodriguez called Stevens to order the murder of Gloria and me.

Gabby's voice came over the speakers again. "Oh, what a beautiful bird. What's its name?"

"That's Coca. He's an Amazon parrot from Colombia," Rodriguez said.

"He is such a pretty boy. I love its colors. With the bright green feathers and the reds and blues on his face, it looks like he's wearing theatrical makeup. Hello, Coca. You're such a pretty boy."

Coca mimicked Gabby's words. "Auk. Pretty boy, Coca. Good boy, Coca. Auk."

"Wow. He can really talk. Have you had him long? Apparently, they can live up to 40 years or more."

"I've had him for a couple of years. I just hope he doesn't outlive me. If something happened to me, I don't know who would take care of him."

"Yeah, that would kind of suck for both of you if you were dead, and he's left all alone with such a long lifespan."

Where the hell is she going with this? A moment later, my tension level shot up to new heights.

A cell phone rang in the background. "Hello? Yes, one second. I have to take this private call, Gabby. I'll be right back."

"No problem, take your time," Gabby said.

A door clicked, followed by Gabby whispering. "If you guys are listening, I am putting the bug under his desk now. There, it's done. He's gone into the next room. When he gets back, I'll make an excuse to leave."

I sighed deeply and put my arm around Gloria's shoulders. "Good. Now she can get the hell out of there."

My renewed hope of getting her safely out of there evaporated a few seconds later.

CHAPTER
45

Inside the Command Centre, another graph bar lit up, and a line spiked on the screen when Rodriguez answered his cell phone. I cast a confused look at Eddie.

As if reading my mind, he said, "We got a warrant to tap his phones, including his cell. But, unfortunately, it came through after Gabby had left home this morning, so I couldn't tell her to call off her actions."

"Sir, we have incoming audio from his cell phone," said the tech guy monitoring the screens.

Eddie moved closer. "Turn it up."

I looked over Eddie's shoulder to get a better view of the monitors.

The tech guy adjusted the volume, and Rodriguez's voice came out of the speakers loud and clear as he said, "What is it? I'm busy at the moment."

"Don't use that tone with me, Rodriguez. I'll call you anytime I want. Now shut up and listen."

It was the woman known only as Angel Gabriel.

"Yes, ma'am," Rodriguez said, instantly cowed by the dominant voice of his superior.

"The Archangels have information that Jake and Gloria Stone are still alive and have returned to the United States. What do you have to say about that?"

"That... that isn't possible. Sanchez killed them both and Stevens last night. There must be some mistake."

"No. There's no mistake. The information we have is accurate and has been verified by a reliable source. It appears the only mistake is you, Rodriguez. Several times, we ordered you to carry out the hits on those two and their daughter, and you have failed us every time."

"But—"

"No buts, Rodriguez. We also understand the daughter is still alive, contrary to your promises that you would eliminate her. Isn't that true?"

"Yes, Angel, but... that couldn't be helped. Her uncle intervened and blocked me from completing the job."

"Once again, you fail to grasp the magnitude of your incompetence. As long as those three are alive, the Archangels are at significant risk of being exposed, jeopardizing all of us and our entire operation. Am I making myself clear, Rodriguez?"

"Yes, Angel. I understand, and I will deal with the girl today. I won't fail this time, and I'll take care of her parents tonight. You have my word."

"Your word no longer carries any weight or credibility with us. So we now require proof they're dead. And Rodriguez, you won't get another chance if you fail us again."

The speaker went silent as Angel hung up.

I swallowed hard as a lump formed in my throat. My pulse quickened, causing a pounding in my ears that drowned out all sounds around me.

"Jake, snap out of it." Gloria's voice shattered the fog I had fallen into.

I shook my head to clear my thoughts. Gloria's eyes pleaded with me as a sense of fear and panic descended on us. I wrapped my arms around her and held her tight. "Don't worry, I won't let him hurt her."

I hoped my words sounded more confident than I felt. It was time to intervene and get Gabby away from Rodriguez before he killed her.

Eddie put his hands on our shoulders to comfort us. "He's not going to do anything to hurt her in his office. The last thing he wants is a dead body to dispose of up there. I know that's not what you want to hear right now, but we'll take him out when they leave the building."

I searched Eddie's eyes for reassurance. Where emotions and doubt clouded Gloria's and my eyes, Eddie's projected confidence and focused resolve. He was in charge and had this under control. After knowing him for a lifetime and working on many missions with him, I knew he was right. My confidence level slowly returned, knowing he was in charge of this operation and wouldn't let us down.

The swishing sound of a door opening in the background came over the speakers. The new bug Gabby planted in Rodriguez's office was active and transmitting.

Rodriguez had re-entered the office. "That was a client who needed some immigration advice for a family member. So what do you say we get out of here and have lunch? There's a nice Italian place around the corner that does a great pizza."

"Marcos, I'm actually feeling a real nasty headache coming on. It must be from the concussion I got down in Colombia. Would you mind if we reschedule for another day?"

"I'm sure you'll be fine once you get a little food in you. So come on, let's go."

"Maybe you're right," Gabby said. "But I was wondering why you named the parrot Coca? Isn't that the plant cocaine comes from?"

Her questions threw me for a loop. Where is she going with this? For God's sake, Gabby, just let it go and get the hell out of there.

"Auk. Cocaine, money, money, money. Big shipment. Auk." Coca said.

"Shut up, Coca. Bad bird," Rodriguez snapped.

"Auk. Bad Coca. Coca, bad bird. Shut up, Coca. Auk."

"What's he talking about, Marcos? I thought these birds only mimic what others say?"

"I don't know where he would have heard that sort of thing. Probably on the radio or television."

Coca whistled. "Auk. Bug under the desk. Put the bug under the desk. Are you guys listening? Auk."

"What? What have you done, Gabby?"

"Nothing. I don't know what he's talking about," Gabby said.

"Auk. Under the desk. Bug under the desk. Are you listening?" Coca repeated.

The damned bird had blown her cover and ratted her out.

I turned to Eddie. "We've gotta go right now. Rodriguez is onto her."

Eddie had already jumped into action and moved to the van's rear door. "Carter, Williams, assemble your teams. We're going in on my mark." He handed Gloria and me bulletproof vests with DEA emblazoned across the front and back. "Put these on. The last thing we need is civilian casualties."

Through their communications headsets, Carter and Williams instructed their team members to get into position at the front and rear entrances to the building. They were to wait for the go signal from Eddie.

I moved toward the door, but Eddie put his hand on my chest, stopping my forward movement. "You and Gloria need to stay behind us on this operation and let me and my team handle things," he said.

"But Eddie, that's Gabby in there," I said.

His eyes drilled into me with a mixture of confidence and compassion. "Exactly. You and Gloria are both too close to this one. It's too personal."

Gloria stepped in front of me and confronted Eddie. "And it isn't personal to you? You've known Gabby her whole life."

"And that's why I asked for this command. Look, the only reason you two are here at all is because of our shared love for Gabby. So I'm asking you to let me and my team handle this. You'll be right there when we take the bastard out. And I promise I won't let him harm her."

I put my hand on Gloria's shoulder and turned her to me. "It'll be okay, Gloria. I trust Eddie to handle this. Let's back him up and get going. Arguing is only wasting valuable seconds."

I could tell from the expression on Gloria's face that she wasn't satisfied with taking a back seat, but she nodded in agreement. She knew Eddie was right.

The tech guy said, "Sir, you need to hear this."

We all turned back and listened.

Over the speakers, Rodriguez said, "Then what is this? A bug? Who are you working for, Gabby?"

"I don't know what you're talking about. Get away from me, Marcos. Let me go. You're hurting me."

Coca whistled. "Auk. Dead. I want them dead. Kill them all, or else. Auk."

"Shut up, Coca," Rodriguez yelled. "Bad bird."

"Auk. Bad Coca. Coca, bad bird. Shut up, Coca. Auk."

Things were getting intense in Rodriguez's office, and we needed to get up there to defuse the situation.

"Give me two sets of inner ear coms," Eddie said to the tech guy. Then, he turned to me and said, "I want you both to listen to the feed from the office and our operational commands so we're all in sync as we move out."

The tech guy reached into a drawer and handed us the earpieces. They were the same kind Jimmy and I used down in

Colombia. I inserted it in my ear and immediately heard Gabby and Rodriguez's voices arguing.

A moment later, the voices went silent. He must have destroyed the bug. Now we only had the surveillance coming from her phone app to rely on. And if he found that, we would lose all sound from inside with no way of knowing what was going on up there.

The lump returned to my throat; this time, I was choking on it as I followed Eddie out of the Command Center.

CHAPTER

46

The climb up to the fourth floor seemed to take hours. In front of us, four DEA agents armed with semi-automatic rifles moved cautiously forward. My heart pounded in my chest as I faced a wall of bulletproof vests blocking me from running up the stairs. A fifth agent in front of me carried a handheld battering ram to bust down doors. I checked behind my back and felt the Glock tucked into my belt. As I put my arm around Gloria's waist to keep her close, my hand brushed against something hard—she was also packing a firearm. At least we had options if needed.

In my earpiece, Gabby and Rodriguez continued their argument.

"Let go of my arm, Marcos. You're hurting me," Gabby said.

"Who are you working for? The DEA? The FBI? Who?"

"I'm not working for anybody. You have to believe me. I really don't know what you're talking about."

"That was a bug, and you know it. Tell me who you were planting it for, and how much do they know?"

"Know about what? Your cocaine operations in Colombia and your cartel connections? Or how you tried to kill my family and me several times?"

For the love of God, Gabby, just stop already. It sounded like she was trying to make him more upset than he was already.

Rodriguez's voice intensified and sounded belligerent. "I don't know what you're talking about. There's no cartel or cocaine operation in Colombia that I'm aware of or involved with."

Gabby was steering the conversation and pushing the attack. "Then why does Coca talk about cocaine and killing my parents and me?"

"You don't know what you're talking about, Gabby. Accusations like that can be very dangerous." Rodriguez sounded like he was getting cornered.

He had no idea what an excellent chess player Gabby was— both literally and verbally. She could outmaneuver me in a few deft moves, and I would never see it coming. With her intellect and quick mind, she could talk circles around most people. And Rodriguez was about to meet his match as she maneuvered him into checkmate.

She wasn't buying what he was trying to sell her. "Then why did you try to kill my parents and me while we were in Colombia?"

Rodriguez didn't respond, and after a brief pause, Gabby continued her verbal attack. "That's right, Marcos. You can look innocent and confused, but I know everything about you ordering Stevens to kill my parents and me. And I know how you spiked my drink at the bar last night. You didn't really fall for my acting, did you?"

She had hit a nerve. Or maybe several. Rodriguez was coming unwound. He was no longer in the driver's seat and rapidly losing ground. "Shut up, shut up. I need to think."

"Think about what? How you failed over and over to do what Angel instructed you to do?"

Rodriguez yelled, "How the hell do you know about Angel?"

"I'm a very resourceful person. I also know there is more than one leader in charge of the cartel giving you orders. Who else is involved, Marcos? What are their names? If you come clean, you can make a plea deal with the Feds."

Clearly, her verbal assault was trying to get a confession out of him.

Eddie heard it too. He held his fist up to signal the assault team to hold their position. Then he glanced at me and held my gaze. I nodded slightly in agreement with his unasked question. We would wait and see if Gabby could get him to reveal details of the cartel's operations and those involved. He might let his guard down if he believed it was only him and Gabby talking. As far as he knew, the bug she had planted under his desk was destroyed, and they were no longer being monitored.

The DEA assault agents fanned out on either side of Rodriguez's office door, ready to move at a moment's notice. At the end of the hall, a cluster of five FBI agents stood prepared to engage and flood the office when Eddie gave the orders. By my count, there were ten special agents armed to the teeth. Also, Eddie, Gloria, and I were armed and more than ready to engage. There was no possible way for Rodriguez to get out of there with Gabby. And if he hurt her, I estimated his chances of getting out alive were somewhere between a snowball's chance in Hell and zero. But our task was to intervene before he could harm her. A tall order, considering they were on one side of the door and our assault teams were on the other. A lot could happen in the few seconds it would take to break into the office and acquire our target.

Coca chimed in again, "Auk. Gabriel is angry. Angry Gabriel. Angel Gabriel. Auk."

"Is one of the leaders named Gabriel? What are the names of the other cartel leaders?"

"I said, shut up!" Rodriguez barked.

"No, Marcos. I won't shut up. You at least owe me the truth since you plan to kill me, anyway. So, be a man and tell me who's making you do this. You were never like this in college. What happened to make you go down this road? Come on, Marcos, we've been friends for a long time. Don't you think you owe me an explanation?"

Gabby pushed hard to get him to reflect on their friendship and open up to her. And it was working.

Rodriguez sighed loudly. "It started in my last semester at college. They approached me and offered to fast-track my career." He sounded defeated and tired. All his lies and deceit were finally catching up with him.

Gabby's voice softened as she tried to console him and get him to say more. "Who, Marcos? Who offered to fast-track your career, and at what cost to yourself?"

"They call themselves the Archangels. That's all I know. They use the names of the Archangels to mask their real identities. You don't know how persuasive they can be. Or how deadly. They made me an offer, and once I took it, there was no way to get out when I realized what they wanted from me. They provided the financing and arranged for my license to establish my immigration law practice. At first, they would send me clients who wanted to immigrate to the United States."

Rodriguez paused. Maybe he was rethinking what he was saying and would stop talking and move back to the attack. But Gabby kept coercing him to keep talking.

"But then it all changed. Didn't it?" Gabby had adopted a casual, friendly tone, and Rodriguez was being drawn into her trap without realizing it.

"Yes. After a while, they insisted I make arrangements for unspecified shipments into the United States from Colombia. They introduced me to Stevens at the consulate in Barranquilla. He was the perfect cover for their operation. A low-level bureaucrat with an overblown sense of importance who was easy to manipulate and use for their operation."

"You mean for the drug cartel operations?"

Rodriguez sounded relieved to be finally getting his secrets out in the open. "Yes. Eventually, they put me in charge of the day-to-day operation of coordinating the drug shipments. At that point, I couldn't see a way out. The money was incredible, and the Archangels kept pushing for more and more shipments."

Gabby had him. He was revealing details of the cartel that would be useful to track the rest of the leadership group. But he still hadn't given up any names. Just a few more well-placed questions by Gabby, and he would give them up, too. Then everything changed suddenly as another player re-entered the conversation.

A high-pitched whistle rang out, followed by, "Auk. Big shipments. Cocaine, money, money. Archangels are angry. Kill the Stones. Auk."

Coca's comments seemed to shake Rodriguez out of a mental fog, and he quickly returned to his senses.

He aggressively went back to the attack. "That's enough, Gabby! Are you wearing a wire? Is somebody listening to us?"

Gabby's ruse to get him talking and to get a confession out of him had worked for a while. But that was now over. Rodriguez had come back to his senses and suspected she had tricked him. I looked at Eddie, and he nodded his head in silent acknowledgment. We were thinking the same thing. It was time to stop this and make our move.

Gabby continued to reason with him. "No, I'm not wearing a wire, and nobody's listening. You already destroyed the bug. Now you're just sounding paranoid."

"So, you admit it. You planted the bug."

"Let go of me. That hurts."

"Not until you tell me who you're working for."

Gabby's voice rose sharply. "Is that a gun? What are you going to do with that? You can't shoot me here, in your office. Other people will hear the gun go off and call the police."

As if things weren't intense before, now they suddenly turned life-threatening. Eddie held up three fingers. All the agents fixed their eyes on his hand as he started the countdown. It felt like an eternity as one finger folded into his fist, then the next. As the third finger dropped, I held my breath and pulled the Glock from behind my back.

Everything moved at the speed of light from there. The agent with the battering ram slammed it into the door. As the door exploded from its hinges and crashed to the floor, four agents flooded through the opening with their rifles in front of them. Gloria and I followed Eddie inside.

Even with years of training and field experience, nothing could have prepared me for what was in front of me. My heart pounded as adrenaline coursed through me. Nothing can be worse for a parent than when you come face to face with a madman holding a gun to your daughter's head. And this madman had limited options and a history of killing.

CHAPTER
47

When the door shattered, I glimpsed a man shifting his position with the speed of a rattlesnake striking its prey. It took several heartbeats for me to realize I had stopped breathing. All my attention focused on the terrifying scene on the other side of the room. Rodriguez held Gabby in a tight headlock with his left arm wrapped around her neck. In his other hand, he pressed the muzzle of a pistol against the side of her head. He held her against his body, using her as a shield to protect him from being shot. All the DEA and FBI agents fanned out on both sides of the doorway. Each had their weapons aimed at him.

I quickly assessed the situation and found Gabby's eyes. Our eyes locked together, and she held my gaze. Her expression showed no fear, only a calm confidence utterly inconsistent with the situation.

I lowered my weapon. There was no shot that didn't include a chance of hitting Gabby.

Eddie stepped between two agents and said, "Drop your weapon, Rodriguez. And let her go."

Rodriguez scanned the room. Ten agents with their semi-automatic weapons aimed at him. Eddie had his handgun trained on him as well, while Gloria and I held our pistols by our sides.

With a four-story drop, there was nowhere for him to go. The only way out was through the door that we just broke down. And there was no chance of him getting past the armed agents blocking his path.

"I think not," Rodriguez said. "I plan on walking out of here with her, and I'll kill her if anyone tries to stop me. So, lower your weapons and back away from the door."

Eddie confidently pressed his point. "You leaving this room with the girl is not an option, Rodriguez. And the longer this standoff continues, the less likely it is we'll take you alive. So I say again, drop the gun and let her go."

My pulse continued to race, and my breathing became shallow again. The outcomes of this type of stand-off were always unpredictable. They could only go one of two ways. Either the hostage is released, and the gunman surrenders peacefully, or the hostage is killed immediately before the gunman gets obliterated by the agents staring him down. Obviously, I wanted the former outcome.

I stepped forward and put my gun on the floor in a gesture to gain his trust. "Rodriguez, please listen to reason."

"Who are you?" he said, turning his gun in my direction.

"I'm her father, Jake Stone. All I want is to get Gabby back safely." I took another cautious step forward.

Coca whistled. "Kill Stone. Get Gabby back safely. Kill them all. Auk."

He pressed his gun against the side of Gabby's head again. "Don't come any closer, any of you. I mean it. I'll kill her."

I moved back two short steps, holding my hands up in a surrender pose, showing him I was unarmed. Gloria took my arm and pulled me close to her.

Eddie renewed his side of the negotiations. "Rodriguez, you must know you have limited options here. And I assure you, none of them includes you getting away. Take a look around. You're outgunned with nowhere to go except out this door. And that's not happening."

Rodriguez's face paled as he scanned the room before locking his eyes on mine. A twisted smirk crossed his face. The kind of expression a psychopath makes just before he does something incredibly evil.

Gloria stepped forward to plead our case. "Come on, son, be reasonable—"

"It's you that have few options! Now drop your weapons and move aside, or I'll kill the bitch!" Rodriguez yelled and waved his gun at Gloria.

He should never have used the term bitch when referring to Gabby. The look in her eyes changed the moment he said it. Something snapped inside her. She struck the instant he moved his gun away from her head.

Her right arm was a blur as her cast flew upward, slamming hard against his face. A sickening crack of breaking bone rang through the room. In the shock of the unexpected attack, Rodriguez released his headlock hold on her and clutched at his face. Gabby pivoted and launched her knee upward into his groin, grabbed him by the shirt, and threw him over her hip. His gun clattered to the floor as he lay sprawled on his back, groaning in agony.

It all happened in a heartbeat. One second, Rodriguez held a gun at Gabby's head. The next, he was on his back, with blood gushing from his flattened nose pressed sideways against his cheek. Three agents rushed forward. One kicked the pistol clear of Rodriguez's reach. The other held him against the floor while a third secured his hands behind his back with handcuffs.

Gabby ran into my arms and hugged me until I couldn't breathe. "Hey, not so tight. I gotta breathe, you know."

Gloria pulled Gabby to her and crushed her in a protective momma bear hug.

I joined them and wrapped my arms around both of them. A tear slid down my cheek as the magnitude of what had just happened weighed on me. "Thank God you're safe, Gabs. What the hell were you thinking of making a move like that? He could have shot you."

Gabby looked up into my face and smiled. "Nobody messes with my family. And if they do, they're going to get Stoned." She snickered softly. "And yes, the pun was intentional."

"I bet you've been waiting to use that line for a while?" I said.

"It came to me when the prick called me a bitch. At that moment, I realized I'd had enough of this guy and the cartel."

What a kid. She may be more like her mom in most ways, but her humor was all mine.

With Rodriguez secured, two DEA agents led him from the office.

Eddie came over and hugged Gabby. "You really are a chip off these two old blocks," he said, nodding toward Gloria and me.

"And don't you ever forget it, Uncle Eddie. You know, I sort of like this line of work. I'm thinking a career change is in order. So, I'll be looking for a reference letter from you when I apply to the agency next week."

Eddie didn't bite on her comment about joining the agency. "Come on, let's get you down to the Command Centre and check you over to make sure you're okay," he said as he led the way out of the office.

At the door, Gabby stopped and turned back. "What's going to happen to the bird?"

I turned around and looked at the strikingly beautiful parrot perched quietly in his cage.

Eddie shrugged and said, "He'll probably end up in the zoo until they can find a home for him."

Gabby walked over to Coca's cage and bent close to look at him. "I want to keep him. What do you say? After all, he is the star witness, isn't he? And where would he be safer than in witness protection with us?"

She turned her head and gave me the look. It was the look she had mastered as a little girl to wrap me around her fingers to get what she wanted. And she knew she had me.

Gloria looked at me and shrugged. "I'm okay if you're okay. But I'm not cleaning up after it."

"Sure, he can stay with us until we find a more suitable home for him. But you have to promise to clean his cage every day," I said.

"Deal. Can somebody give me a hand carrying him?" She waved her cast in the air, suddenly feigning the inability to use her arm.

"Auk. Deal. We have a deal. Big drug deal going down. Auk."

Coca would definitely need some reprogramming to change his vocabulary to suit our house's more suburban domestic lifestyle.

CHAPTER

48

I carried Coca and his cage down to the Command Centre. At first, I thought about putting him directly in the backseat of our car. But after careful consideration, the thought of a solar-roasted parrot wasn't appealing to me. Even though roast parrot probably tastes like chicken, I figured I'd give the little guy a break. Eddie had an ambulance standing by in case of casualties during the raid of Rodriguez's office, so Gloria escorted Gabby to have the paramedics check her for any potential injuries.

The paramedics were fawning over Gabby inspecting her cast as I approached with the birdcage.

"What do you want me to do with the bird?" I said, holding the caged creature in front of me.

"Auk. Pretty bird. Pretty boy, Coca. Auk." Coca chimed in, followed by his usual high-pitched whistle.

Gabby poked her finger between the bars of the cage and smiled. "Isn't he to die for? Oh, check that. Bad choice of words. He's just so gorgeous and precious."

"Then I'll leave him with you while the medics check you out. I need to talk with Eddie in the Command Centre."

Gloria held Gabby's hand, providing her with moral support. Even though I had the feeling that it was Gabby providing moral support to Gloria rather than the other way around. They sure are two tough birds. Make that three tough birds with the addition of Coca.

Eddie was finishing his debriefing with Special Agents Carter and Williams when I climbed into the back of the van.

As I entered, he looked toward me, nodded to acknowledge my presence, then finished with the two agents. "All in all, I think the operation went smoothly and according to plan. It's always a good day when we can execute a raid and hostage rescue without injuries or casualties. I'll expect your written reports by tomorrow morning. Again, thank you both, and please express my appreciation to your teams for a job well done."

"Yes sir," they said simultaneously.

As they left the van, Agent Carter stopped and said, "Your daughter acted bravely up there. You should be proud of her, sir."

"Thank you, Agent Carter. I am. She's a pretty resourceful woman who never ceases to surprise me."

With the raid successfully completed and Gabby returned to us unharmed, I could finally take a few minutes to unwind. I removed the bulletproof vest and slid into a chair beside the surveillance monitoring consoles. Leaning back, I inhaled deeply and sighed.

"I hear that," said Eddie, sliding into the chair next to me. "It got pretty intense up there for a minute. But Gabby somehow found the strength and opportunity to turn the tide for us. Do you think she's serious about joining the Agency?"

I sat up and leaned forward with my hands on my knees. "Who knows? It could be the adrenaline rush and the thrill of the moment. You know kids these days. They're always shifting from one thing to the next. But I have to say, she showed some pretty excellent skills for a civilian. So, I wouldn't put it past her. Especially now that she knows what Gloria, me, and you did for a living."

"Hey, I'm still doing it for a living. I've got another fourteen months until retirement. On another note, we've received all the surveillance recordings from your buddy Jimmy in Barranquilla. With those recordings and what we've gathered up here from Rodriguez's car and his cell phone, we should have enough to put him away for a long time."

I shook my head slowly. "I'm not sure any of those will be admissible as evidence."

"Oh, we're all good with that. Mastermind had all the required warrants in place from the FISA court. The agency was tracking the consulate down there for quite a while. She went through the proper channels to stay onside with the Foreign Intelligence Surveillance Act. The agency didn't want any screw-ups on this file. So yeah, we're all good, and we can use all the recordings to prosecute Rodriguez."

"That's great. But there's one other thing. Rodriguez took his orders from a woman named Gabriel with the code name Angel. And there are others in the cartel leadership group we haven't identified yet, including her. She referred to them as the Archangels. If Gabriel is one of the Archangels, as I suspect, then who are the others she referred to on the recordings? We need to get Rodriguez to turn State's evidence and give up those other names. So the job isn't done until we find out who they are and take them down as well?"

"We're already on that. The Internal Revenue folks are working with us and the FBI to scour Rodriguez's accounts for unusual financial activity. I gotta tell you, he was pulling in a lot of cash here in the states from onshore transfers. So we're tracing those transfers to follow the money trail back to their sources. Hopefully, within a day or two, we'll know where the money came from and who owns the source accounts."

"I'm sure glad I'm one of the good guys. I wouldn't want the full weight of the government scouring through my life." I smiled uncomfortably at the thought of out-of-control bureaucracies potentially digging around in people's lives and monitoring their every move without proper oversight.

Eddie shook his head and smiled. "You'd think we'd be used to government surveillance by now, given the work we do."

"There is something else the bird said that's been bothering me. When we were about to rush into Rodriguez's office, the bird squawked something about a big shipment coming in. Any luck figuring out the cartel's smuggling routes and schedules?"

"We're working on that too. Once we gather all the information and files from Rodriguez's and Stevens' offices and homes, we hope to find those details. The search warrants are being issued and executed as we speak."

"Good. If we can shut down the cartel operations and put away the leaders, we'll keep a lot of dangerous drugs off the streets. Let me know if I can help in any way."

Eddie patted my shoulder. "Thanks for the offer and everything you, Gloria, and of course, Gabby, have done so far. But don't forget, you guys are retired, and Gabby isn't an agent, even if she is starting to behave like one. So, let's leave the follow-up to the bureau and agency. You guys should just kick back and let us take it from here."

I knew Eddie meant well, but his comment still stung a little. I guess once you're an agent, you never really get the desire for action out of your blood. Even when you're supposed to be fully retired and back in civilian life.

Eddie cleared his throat quietly and said, "There's something else, Jake, and I hope you don't take this the wrong way. Mastermind has ordered a security detail be put on you guys until we arrest the other key members of the cartel."

That wasn't what I was expecting to hear from him. Of all people, Eddie and Mastermind knew Gloria and my capabilities.

"Is that necessary? You know Gloria and I can take care of ourselves," I said.

"Look, this isn't a commentary on your skills. You know as well as I do that the cartel has a hit order on you and your family. Besides, no one knows better than you how ruthless these people are and how far they'll go to silence any threats to their operations. Once the leadership is locked up, we'll reassess what happens next."

I wasn't about to let Eddie know it, but I had to admit having trained agents looking out for us for a while would provide a welcomed sense of security.

"I suppose you're right. Besides, I don't have much choice in this, do I?"

Eddie smiled and put his hand on my shoulder. "Not really, so your cooperation will be greatly appreciated."

Gloria and Gabby poked their heads into the back of the van, and Gloria said, "You ready to go, Jake? Gabby's all good. No injuries. Just a cracked cast that they replaced. So, we're good to go anytime you are."

"That's good to hear. Yeah, I'm just finishing the debrief with Eddie. I'll be with you in a minute."

Eddie stood and said, "Hey, it's okay, Jake. I can take it from here. They've got me taking the lead on this right up to the point when the Justice Department issues arrest warrants. That's when they'll back me out. Mastermind doesn't want me exposed or revealed as an Agency asset. I'll keep you up-to-date as things progress, for sure."

"I appreciate that, Eddie," I said, shaking his hand.

"Hey, it's the least I can do. After all, you had a huge role in taking out the cartel. And, of course, you have a personal stake in what happens next. So go home and spend some time with your family and have a few beers for me. On second thought, keep some beers on ice, and I'll drop by later."

"You got it, buddy."

Eddie turned to Gabby and said, "If you have a few minutes, I'd like to talk to you alone. I need to debrief with you on what happened today. It won't take long. Jake, could you and Gloria wait outside while Gabby and I talk?"

"No problem." I helped Gabby climb into the Command Centre, then I stepped outside.

As Gloria and I approached the car, she said, "Hold on a second, Jake. Let me open the windows to cool the car down before you put Coca inside."

I laughed, then said, "Oh, come on, Gloria. You know he's from the tropics, where I'm told it can get pretty hot. Do you think he'd be okay if I don't put the air conditioner on?"

"Auk. Come on, Gloria. Pretty hot, Gloria. Pretty hot. Auk."

"You know, I'm starting to like this bird more and more," Gloria said as I placed the birdcage in the backseat.

Gabby finished her debrief with Eddie in less than ten minutes. It was mostly a formality since he had everything recorded from the surveillance bugs and wiretaps.

Gabby climbed into the backseat and leaned close to Coca. "Such a pretty boy, Coca. Okay, I guess we are free to go now."

"Auk. Free to go. Pretty boy, Coca. Pretty hot, Gabby."

Gloria looked over her shoulder into the backseat and laughed. "He may be a pretty boy, but he's also pretty fickle."

CHAPTER

49

Two weeks had passed since the raid on Rodriguez's office and his takedown by Gabby. Life was returning to normal, or as normal as expected under the circumstances. And by circumstances, I mean living with a loud, never-ceasing, chatter-box parrot. Coca reminded me of a two-year-old who constantly asked, *why?* At first, his mimicking everything you said was fun. But that grew old fast. Very fast. In fact, just like with a two-year-old's constant questioning, I had to find a way of tuning him out as background noise. Either that, or I'd have to throw the little bastard in the microwave. And having a cooked parrot on my hands would be difficult to explain to Gabby and Gloria.

Of course, Gabby had fallen head over heels in love with the little creature. And she discouraged me from making any threats or comments like, *'shut the fuck up.'* After raising a child with rapidly developing language skills, I knew you never used foul language around them. You just never knew when the little bugger would throw an f-bomb into a conversation.

At any rate, life in our house had returned to mostly the way things were before our Colombian adventure. We had FBI agents parked down the street, keeping an eye on our house night and day. And with a stroke of luck or out of fear, Rodriguez chose to turn State's evidence and rat out the rest of the cartel. He was being held in protective custody until he testified to the Justice Department. The whole thing had dominated the news cycle with daily updates and the media speculating about what would happen next.

I remained interested in the case, but I also knew these things could take several years to work their way through the court system. Besides, it appeared as though the Justice Department was no closer to finding the identities of Angel or the other Archangels than the day we arrested Rodriguez. Eddie kept us up-to-date on any progress or line of inquiry the agency was exploring. Still, they seemed to be constantly hitting a wall, preventing them from breaking the case open.

The searches of Rodriguez's and Stevens' offices and homes had uncovered information about illegal drug shipping dates and routes. And yesterday, a massive cocaine shipment was seized off the Florida Keys. A Coast Guard cutter loaded with DEA and FBI agents intercepted a small submersible craft as it approached Key West. After threatening to sink the vessel, two Colombian nationals surfaced the craft and surrendered. On board, the agents found 1000 kilos of pure uncut cocaine and one million fentanyl tablets. When cut, the cocaine would have a street value of anywhere from 100 to 200 million dollars. This was a big win for the good guys and an enormous setback for the cartel. Not to mention preventing an untold number of deaths from the fentanyl or the lives destroyed by additions.

With their shipment routes and schedules exposed, blocking future cartel shipments wouldn't take long. Especially with two of their crucial frontline members either dead or in prison.

I followed my nose into the kitchen. Something smelled incredible. Gloria and Gabby were planning a big meal, and Eddie would join us for dinner this evening as usual.

"Wow, something smells great," I said, opening the oven door to check things out in my normal supervising, head-chef capacity.

"Shut that and get out of here, Jake. Supper will be ready in an hour," Gloria said, slapping my arm playfully.

I snuggled up behind her, wrapped my arms around her stomach, nuzzled her neck, and whined, "But I'm so hungry."

She giggled and pushed my hands away. "Then have an apple. Just leave us alone so we can finish in here."

Gabby glared at me as I crunched into a bright red Gala apple. I grabbed two beers from the fridge and went into the den to wait for Eddie to arrive.

Eddie opened the front door and rushed in a few minutes later, huffing and puffing, trying to catch his breath.

"I thought you were getting in shape?" I said as I handed him a beer. "Sounds like you could use more time on your treadmill."

"Are you watching the news?" He said, looking for the television.

"No, why?"

Without answering, he grabbed the remote. The screen glowed and came into focus.

"You won't believe what just happened. Oh, come on. How do you change the channels on this thing?" He handed me the remote control. "Put it on one of those twenty-four-hour news channels."

I punched in a sequence of numbers, and the screen changed to a reporter with the dome of the U.S. Capitol building looming behind.

"What's going on?" I said, adjusting the volume.

"Apparently, Rodriguez committed suicide last night."

"What? How does that happen? He was supposed to be in isolation and under constant watch as the key witness."

"I know. I just received the preliminary findings from the medical examiner. It says he hung himself with the sheets from his bedding." Eddie pulled a folded paper from his jacket pocket and handed it to me.

I quickly scanned the document. It was the last page summary of the findings from the autopsy. Bottom line—Rodriguez hung himself at roughly 03:45 this morning while alone in his cell. There were no witnesses. The report stated the guards had left the area to respond to a loud commotion in the next cell block. When they returned a few minutes later, they found Rodriguez dead in his cell.

"This is unbelievable, Eddie. Do they have any video surveillance of his cell?"

"No. It seems the video link was cut during the time the guards weren't there."

"I don't believe this. It's too convenient. How does the video get cut off at the same time as the guards are called away? And when they return, the state's key witness is dead. It just doesn't add up."

"I know. I can assure you there will be a thorough investigation into this."

"So, with Rodriguez dead, where does that leave the case now? I don't suppose the Justice Department had deposed him and taken his evidence before he died?"

Eddie took a gulp of his beer and settled onto the sofa across from the television. "I'm afraid not. During his plea deal, all he gave them were the code names for the cartel leadership— Archangels Gabriel, Michaels, and Raphael. He was scheduled to meet with the Justice Department tomorrow morning to give his sworn testimony and other details about the cartel's leadership and operations."

I looked up at the screen, then back to Eddie. "Doesn't that seem a bit too convenient and suspicious to you? The timing of his death is perfect for shutting up the only witness who can identify the cartel's leaders."

"I'm with you on that, Jake."

I rechecked the Medical Examiner's summary. A detail I missed on the first look caught my eye. "The M.E. says his hyoid bone was crushed. That's unusual in hanging deaths. But it's very common in strangulations. So I don't think I'm going out on a limb when I say I think someone murdered him to keep him from testifying."

"Let me have another look at that." Eddie took the sheet and read through it. "You're right. I was so stunned I must have skipped right past that detail the first time I read the report."

"Eddie, if the Archangels can get to a witness in protective custody and under constant observation in a maximum-security prison, there's no telling how high up and connected they are."

"Dinner's ready, boys. Come and get it," Gloria said from the door of the den. Then she paused. "What's wrong? You two look like you've just witnessed a murder."

"You could say that," I said, walking out of the den.

"What's wrong, Dad?" Gabby said as Eddie, and I entered the dining room.

I pulled out a chair to sit at the table. "Rodriguez killed himself last night. But I think he was murdered to silence him before he could testify against the rest of the cartel."

"What happens now if the state's key witness is dead?" Gabby asked.

"Without his testimony, it becomes more difficult to identify and prosecute the leaders of the cartel. And that could mean the case falls apart."

"Well, let's eat before it gets cold. There isn't too much we can do about that right now," Gloria said.

As usual, she was right. Our meal was a delicious but somber affair. Not at all like our usual Sunday get-togethers with Eddie. As I was helping to clear the table, Coca screeched and whistled from the living room.

I turned to Gabby and said, "Can you take him some nuts or whatever he eats to keep him quiet?"

She filled a small bowl with nuts and seeds and carried it into the living room, where Coca stood in his cage. From his perch, he had a clear view of the television in the den.

As I put a stack of plates on the kitchen counter, Coca screeched and whistled. "Auk. Angry Angel. Angry Gabriel. Auk."

That got my attention. He hadn't said those words since we brought him home two weeks ago. So why now? Something must have brought back those memories and upset him.

Gabby called from the den, "I think you guys need to see this."

When we arrived in the den, a woman with short, neatly trimmed, silver hair was standing at a podium with the seal of the Senate on it. Two American flags hung behind her. She was listening to a question from a reporter.

"Thank you for the question. We are doing everything in our power to find out what happened last night. Mister Rodriguez was a critical witness for our investigation into alleged drug cartel activities in the United States," she said.

The speaker's voice was vaguely familiar. But I couldn't place it. I must have heard it on the news recently and had thought nothing about it.

Coca again burst out when the woman answered the question. "Auk. Gabriel. Angry Gabriel. Angry Angel. Auk."

I looked at Coca, then back to the screen, then to Eddie. "Who is that, Eddie? I know her voice from somewhere."

"I don't know. There was talk about putting together a Congressional Sub-Committee to investigate cartel activity. But as far as I know, they hadn't appointed a chairperson yet."

"Be quiet, you two. I want to hear what she's saying," Gloria said, turning up the volume.

The woman continued, "This morning, we have struck a Congressional Sub-Committee to look into illegal cartel activities. Unfortunately, at this time, I am unable to give you any more information. But, as the Chairperson of the sub-committee, I will hold regular press conferences to keep the American people informed as our investigations proceed. The illegal and immoral activities of drug cartels in our country will not be tolerated. We will identify those involved and bring them to justice. Thank you."

"Auk. Gabriel. Angry Gabriel, Angry Angel. Auk."

A spokesperson stepped to the podium. "Thank you, Senator Gabriel. As the Senator has said, we will hold regular updates to advise of any new information in the case. There will be no more questions at this time. Thank you all for coming."

CHAPTER

50

I was stunned as Senator Gabriel walked away from the podium and disappeared into the corridors of power. As the weight of evidence fell over me, I concluded the cartel leader, Angel Gabriel, was none other than Senator Gabriel. And she was the Chairperson of the Congressional Sub-Committee investigating cartel activity in the United States. But with the death of the state's key witness, Marcos Rodriguez, the problem was how to prove it.

Gloria turned the television off. "Well, I didn't see that coming, did you?"

"I can't say I would have put that together at all. I mean, I've never heard of Senator Gabriel before today," I said, turning to Eddie, but he had left the den.

I found him in the kitchen.

He was talking rapidly on his cell phone as he relayed instructions to someone on the other end. "That's correct. I want you to pull together all the voice recordings we have of Angel Gabriel. And I want you to run them through the voice recognition software and compare them against today's news conference with Senator Gabriel."

Eddie glanced up at me, then continued. "Yes, that is correct. And if you need more samples of her speaking, pull them from other venues and appearances. I want your preliminary analysis completed within the next hour. Call me on my cell when you have the results."

Eddie hung up and leaned back against the kitchen counter.

"I see you're on the same page as I am. What's your plan going forward?" I said, picking up a chocolate chip cookie.

"If my hunch is correct, we'll match Senator Gabriel's voice signature to that of Angel's from the wiretap recordings with one hundred percent accuracy. Mastermind has agreed to arrange for the appropriate warrants to check her financials and phone records. The warrants will also allow us to search and seize evidence from her office and residences. But she's made it clear she won't get those warrants until I provide her and Attorney General Johnson with proof of her voice matching those on our recordings. They're not prepared to take this action against a US Senator unless the evidence is absolute and undeniable."

"Got it. Is there anything Gloria and I can do to help?"

"I don't think so, Jake. But I'd say having that bird living with you significantly contributed to the cause. Without him recognizing her voice just now, we may never have picked up the lead connecting the Senator with the cartel."

"As much as a pain in the ass Coca is, I have to admit, he's got a pretty good ear for voices, and he's proving to be helpful in this case. He could be the state's primary witness, especially now that Rodriguez is no longer an option."

Even as I said it, I realized how dumb that last statement sounded. I can't remember a time or a case when a talking bird was sworn in under oath to testify in court.

Eddie crunched into a cookie. "I'm not sure the judicial system is ready to admit evidence from a bird just yet. Especially when it comes to the trial of a sitting U.S. Senator."

The next hour passed rapidly as we gathered in the kitchen to clean up after supper. Eddie and I washed and dried the dishes while Gabby and Gloria packaged the leftovers and put them in the fridge.

We were moving back into the den with a couple of cold beers when Eddie's cell phone rang.

"This could be it," he said as he tapped the screen.

He turned his attention to the incoming call. "Are you sure? I mean absolutely one hundred percent positive. There can be no margin for error on this. Yes, send a copy to my phone through my secure email account. You've done a great job. Thank's for this."

Eddie tapped the phone, ending the call. He took a long gulp from his beer.

I held up my hands impatiently. "Well, don't keep us in suspense. Is it a match? Does Senator Gabriel's voice match with Angel Gabriel?"

Eddie looked up as Gloria and Gabby entered the den, then put his beer down and surveyed our expectant faces. "That was my team. They ran a preliminary analysis to compare the wiretap recordings of Angel Gabriel with Senator Gabriel's news conference. And they match one hundred percent. To be certain, the tech guys ran the voice analysis against other recordings of the Senator's voice. And they confirm that Senator Gabriel is the same person we have identified as Angel on our surveillance tapes."

"That's great news. Now what?" I said.

"They're sending me the report in a few minutes. Once I get it—"

Eddie's phone vibrated. "Hang on a second. This should be the report now." He scrolled through some screens and sighed. "The report clearly confirms that there can be no doubt Senator Gabriel is Angel. We have her. My next step is to get together with Mastermind and the Attorney General and have them obtain the search warrants."

I inhaled deeply and let it out slowly. "What a relief. Now on to the detailed evidence gathering to lock this thing down and get a conviction."

Eddie stood and moved toward the door. "I need to leave and review what we have with Mastermind and Attorney General Johnson. But I'll keep you up-to-date as things proceed." Eddie gave Gloria a hug. "Thank you for a wonderful dinner. And with the help of our little friend, Coca, the evening turned out to be one hell of a great reveal party."

"Auk. Little friend, Coca. Good boy. Pretty boy. Auk."

I wanted to smack the bird's cage to get him to shut up but restrained myself, considering what a tremendous asset he was for helping us break the case open. Besides, Gabby and Gloria would probably beat me senseless if I touched or threatened the little chatterbox.

CHAPTER
51

As night closed in on the neighborhood, I considered how intense the next few days were about to get. Eddie had left a couple of hours ago to secure the necessary warrants for the search and seizure of evidence against Senator Gabriel. After the murder of Rodriguez while in protective custody, it was clear the cartel would go to extraordinary lengths to silence any witnesses to protect their operations. Until all of the cartel leadership was behind bars, I felt a sense of relief and security knowing FBI agents were parked just down the street, keeping an eye on us.

Before turning in for the night, I took my usual stroll to the unmarked car to check if Agents Evans and O'Reilly needed anything. Both were in their early thirties and married with young kids at home. So being assigned the night shift was a major inconvenience for them and their families. And I knew from personal experience how difficult it was to be separated from your loved ones. But, hopefully, we would get the cartel leadership locked up soon so we could all return to our normal lives.

They sat up as I approached.

Evans lowered the passenger window and asked, "Is everything okay, Mr. Stone?"

I leaned over and glanced through the window at the two agents.

"Yeah, everything's great. Just shutting it down for the night and heading off to bed. Can I get you guys anything?"

Evans glanced at O'Reilly sitting behind the steering wheel, then back at me. "No, we're good. Our wives made sure we had lots of coffee, so we'll be all right. But thanks for asking."

I patted the top of the roof of the car and said, "Okay then, goodnight."

O'Reilly leaned sideways across the front seat and said, "Goodnight, sir. I know I don't have to tell you this, but check that all the doors and windows are locked and secured."

He was right. He didn't have to remind me since I went through the same routine every night. But it was just one of the little details that I liked about these guys. They were conscientious and dedicated to our safety.

"Will do," I said, then turned and walked back to the house.

I bolted the front door and double-checked the door leading from the kitchen to the backyard. It was already locked. Coca was in his cage and silently watched me as I moved from room to room to check the windows were secured before heading upstairs.

At the top of the stairs, I checked in on Gabby. She was asleep, so I softly closed her door, then entered our bedroom.

Gloria took off her reading glasses and put her book on the bedside table. "Everything okay with the boys outside?" she asked.

"Yeah, they're good. We're all locked up for the night. It's just another night in paradise."

As I turned off the bedside lamp, I climbed into bed and thought about the last couple weeks since Rodriguez's death. Every day and night were the same. There had been no signs of threats to Gabby, Gloria, or me. And as reassuring as it was to have the agents outside keeping an eye on us, it was starting to feel like overkill.

I leaned over and gave Gloria a kiss. "Goodnight, gorgeous."

She reached up, turned off the lamp on her side, and said, "Goodnight, handsome."

* * *

I abruptly woke as Gloria shook my shoulder and whispered, "I think someone's in the house."

I sat up and checked the alarm clock—03:33. The room was dark except for the thin wedge of moonlight piercing the curtains. I strained to listen for any unusual sounds, but all was quiet. Then I heard it. Coca was shuffling in his cage. He usually slept through the night and didn't make any noise, so that got my attention.

"Call Eddie," I said. "He'll notify the agents outside and get them to respond."

Gloria was one step ahead of me. She held her phone to her ear and whispered, "Eddie, I think there's someone in the house." Then she hung up, opened the drawer, and lifted her Glock out.

I took my Glock from the nightstand beside the bed and held it under the covers to muffle the sound as I cycled the slide to load a cartridge into the firing chamber. Then, I crept to the bedroom door and silently cracked it open.

The rest of the house was dark and quiet except for Coca rustling in his cage. Gloria joined me at the door.

"I'll stay with Gabby," she whispered. "But Jake, don't be a hero. Eddie's calling the agents, and they'll handle this."

"Don't worry, it's probably nothing, but I'll check it out and make sure everything's still secure downstairs," I whispered, then slipped out into the hallway.

I silently moved past Gabby's bedroom, peeked over the railing, and scanned the dark void of the main floor below. Behind me, Gloria opened Gabby's door, slipped into her room, and closed the door behind her. I took the stairs slowly and cautiously. When I hit the ground floor, I moved for cover against the wall beside the entrance to the kitchen.

Soft footsteps came from the other side of the living room. I snapped my head around as a dark shape moved in the den. Whoever was in there would have a clear line of sight to my position. I needed to move, or he'd see me when he came out. A cool breeze swept over my feet as I slipped around the corner and into the kitchen. The back door was open. I slid behind the center island and crouched low to conceal myself as a shadowy figure moved past the area I had just vacated. A second person, dressed in dark clothes and a balaclava covering his face, entered the kitchen and went toward the stove.

What the fuck is he doing, and where is the other guy going? But there was no time to think. I had to move around to the other side of the island, or the guy would see me when he got to the stove.

The hissing sound of gas came from the stove as he turned on all the burners and made sure they didn't ignite. He then laid a bag on the floor and pulled something out. From upstairs, two gunshots rang out, followed by a thump.

The guy in the kitchen jumped up, pulled a pistol from his belt, and turned toward the stairs. That was my chance. I raised my gun over the edge of the countertop and took aim.

"Drop your gun, or I'll drop you," I yelled.

The guy spun around and fired. The bullet left the gun's muzzle with a soft pop from the sound suppressor. Thankfully, it went wide and slammed into the wall behind me. I fired two shots, and he dropped to the floor.

I ran over and kicked the gun away from him. He lay on his back, clutching his gut with blood oozing between his fingers. I pulled the balaclava off his face and stared into his eyes.

A movement in the kitchen doorway caught my eye. I aimed at a dark figure but pulled up as Gloria entered and turned on the lights. She went straight to the stove and turned off the gas.

I turned back to the injured hitman and said, "Who sent you?"

The guy's eyes flashed with fear as he slowly bled out.

"Who sent you?" I said again.

With shallow, gasping breaths, he opened his mouth to speak. His voice was weak and raspy. I leaned close to hear.

"Mi... Michaels. Help me..." he wheezed as his barely audible voice trailed off, and a fixed death stare came through his lifeless eyes. He was gone.

"How's Gabby?" I asked as I stood.

Gabby came into the kitchen clutching a bathrobe around her. "I'm fine, Dad. Are you okay?"

"I'm good. What happened to the other guy?" I asked.

Gloria said, "I took him out when he opened Gabby's door."

In the distance, a siren approached.

Eddie burst through the front door a few seconds later and ran to the kitchen. He scanned the scene. "Are you guys all right?"

I nodded and said, "Yeah, we're all good. There's another one upstairs. Where are Evans and O'Reilly?"

Eddie frowned and shook his head. "Both dead in the car. These guys must have snuck up on them and taken them out before coming in here."

I opened the bag the guy in the kitchen brought with him. It was loaded with several blocks of C-4 explosives and detonators. Apparently, they were going to shoot the three of us in our sleep, then cover up the murders by making it look like a gas leak blew up the house.

A few minutes later, the local police entered the house, and Eddie flashed them his credentials and badge. Then, he walked them through what had happened. I took Gabby and Gloria into the den to wait until the cops were finished checking out the crime scenes upstairs and in the kitchen.

As I passed Coca, I gently tapped his cage and said, "Good boy, Coca. You just saved our lives."

He stared back at me and squawked, "Good boy, Coca. Good boy. Auk."

I have to say, after tonight, my opinions of this little guy were changing fast. Even though his constant chattering usually annoys the crap out of me, without him alerting us to the intruders, we'd probably all be dead.

CHAPTER

52

A week passed since the hitmen tried to take us out. Eddie had implemented an increased FBI presence near our house. Until all the cartel leaders were in custody, he wouldn't take any chances with our safety. I fully agreed with him this time and didn't even consider not accepting the extra monitoring. In the meantime, I waited to hear of any breaks in the case. It's been said the wheels of justice move slowly. But at other times, when all the evidence lines up and everything is in place, justice can move like the *Drop of Doom* ride at a carnival—swift, sure, and severe with a satisfying conclusion.

Eddie arrived at our house in time for the weekly news conference when Senator Gabriel would provide an update on the sub-committee investigation into cartel activities. He joined Gloria, Gabby, and me in the den and accepted the cold beer I had waiting for him.

On the TV screen, a vacant podium stood with the seal of the Senate on the front. In the background, two American flags hung at an angle against the dark, polished wood paneling.

Eddie was almost giddy with excitement. "This should be good. In fact, you could say it's going to be must-watch television," he said with a broad smile. Clearly, he had inside information about what would go down that we didn't.

"Are you going to let us in on what's going to happen, Eddie?" I asked.

"You'll have to wait and see. There's no way I'm going to spoil the surprise."

We turned back to the TV as an aide stepped to the podium. "Ladies and gentlemen, Senator Gabriel will now provide a brief update and take a few questions. Senator?" The person stepped away from the podium as Senator Gabriel approached the microphone.

She scanned the reporters in the foreground off-screen, then spoke, "As you know, my sub-committee is looking into the alleged activities of drug cartels in the United States. I must remind everyone that it is early in our investigation. However, at this point in time, we have uncovered no credible evidence of illegal cartel activities. Furthermore, we have found no evidence of wrongdoing in the death of Mister Rodriguez."

Gabby groaned. "Oh, come on. Alleged activities? No credible evidence? This smells like a cover-up."

"Shush," Gloria said. "Let's hear what she has to say."

Gabby was right, though. Senator Gabriel appeared to be misleading everyone about the existence of the drug cartel and that no conspiracy was involved in the death of Rodriguez.

Movement on the edge of the screen and behind the podium caught my eye. A tall, gray-haired gentleman slowly moved into view. Senator Gabriel quickly glanced in his direction.

"Ah, I see Attorney General Johnson has joined us." She cleared her throat and gripped the edges of the podium with both hands while scanning the reporters. "As I was saying, at this point in our proceedings, we have found no credible evidence to suggest an active cartel exists in the United States of America. However, I want to assure the American people that our investigations will continue. We will leave no stone unturned until we get to the bottom of these allegations."

Attorney General Johnson stepped forward to stand beside Senator Gabriel.

The Senator bristled uncomfortably at his interruption of her news conference and the intrusion into her physical space. Obviously, she had not expected the Attorney General to be present or for him to speak to the reporters.

She glared at him and said, "Excuse me, sir. I'm not finished. You'll have an opportunity to make a statement and take questions in a minute."

I looked at Eddie and smiled as I sensed what was coming next.

"Excuse me, Senator, but my announcement can't wait. If you will allow me?" Attorney General Johnson didn't wait for her to answer.

He slid in behind the microphone and cleared his throat. "As of a few minutes ago, the FBI and DEA have coordinated raids on the homes and offices of three high-value suspects associated with the cartel's leadership. The Justice Department, in coordination with Interpol, has conducted parallel investigations with that of the Congressional Sub-Committee. And we have uncovered sufficient evidence to issue arrest warrants for those three individuals. Their financial accounts have been frozen effective immediately, and we have seized their other worldwide assets."

Senator Gabriel's cell phone pinged. She looked at the screen, and her face paled as all color faded from her cheeks. Her confident bearing dissolved as her shoulders slumped.

The Attorney General continued, "Further, the whereabouts of two of the suspects are unknown at this time. We believe they may have fled the country. I have requested Interpol's assistance to locate and bring those individuals to justice. The arrest of the third suspect is imminent." He turned his head to the side where he had entered. "Agents, if you please?"

Two agents stepped up behind the Senator. They were Special Agents Carter and Williams from the raid on Rodriguez's office.

Johnson turned to the Senator. "Senator Gabriel, you are under arrest for conspiracy to commit murder, compelling others to commit murder—"

The explosion of reporters calling out questions drowned out the rest of the charges. Cameras flashed as chaos took over the news conference.

"Oh, snap," said Gabby. "I didn't see that coming."

"Well done, my friend," I said, clinking my beer against Eddie's.

Eddie still had a broad smile on his face. "Thanks. It didn't take long once we dug into her phone records and bank account transactions. For some reason, she kept detailed records of cartel activities with names, dates, and schedules at her office. I'm not sure why she did that. Maybe she was over-confident and figured no one would ever suspect an elected Senator. But we found enough evidence for the Attorney General to lower the boom on her and the other two."

"Well done, Eddie. I guess that puts a wrap on this whole ugly mess," Gloria said.

"I hope so. We still have to track down the other two Archangels, but with any luck, we'll have them in a day or two," Eddie said.

"Auk. Well done, Eddie. Well done. Good boy, Eddie. Auk." Coca said from the living room.

"You can say that again, Coca," I said.

Obviously, encouraging Coca to repeat himself was the wrong thing to say.

"Auk, Well done, Eddie, Well done. Good boy, Eddie. Auk."

CHAPTER

53

A lot of action happened during the three weeks since Senator Gabriel's arrest. The Senator agreed to provide evidence that would implicate the other members of the cartel leadership group. She hoped her cooperation would lead to a reduced sentence. Authorities found a second Archangel, known as Raphael, dead in his Blue Ridge Mountains cabin in West Virginia. Evidence at the scene pointed to suicide by a self-inflicted gunshot wound. The search continued for the third Archangel, known as Charles Michaels. He was the owner of a private import/export company. He was believed to have fled the country and was somewhere in Central America. Although, the Justice Department had no leads about his exact whereabouts.

Gloria, Gabby, and I met with the Attorney General, who presented us with commendation letters signed by the President of the United States. The President, although unable to attend the ceremony, wanted to express his appreciation for our efforts in exposing and bringing down the cartel.

The lazy days of summer had arrived, and barbecue season was in full swing.

Eddie arrived in mid-afternoon with a case of cold beer. Gloria and Gabby had made an assortment of salads, and I was in charge of the barbecue. So today would be a relaxing, stress-free gathering to kick back, drink some beer and eat charred steaks.

We were all out in the backyard enjoying the remains of the day when the doorbell rang.

Eddie moved first and went toward the house. "I'll get it. I hope you don't mind that I've invited a guest to join us this evening. I'll be right back."

A few moments later, Eddie returned with a tall, good-looking man in tow. He was carrying a bottle of red wine and a bouquet of flowers. Something about the man seemed familiar. But I couldn't quite place him. He looked to be in his early thirties and in good shape. His neatly groomed, blonde hair accented his clean-shaven, dark-tanned face and bright white teeth. His smile expanded, and his blue eyes lit up when he saw me.

I stood to welcome Eddie's guest.

"Hey, guys," Eddie said. "I'd like to introduce you to—"

"Jimmy," I said.

I rushed over and vigorously shook his hand. He hugged me and said, "How are you doing, boss? I hear you had a bit of excitement up here without me."

"Wow, Jimmy. You look so... so... civilized. You sure clean up nicely. I almost didn't recognize you. How the hell are you?"

Gloria hugged him and said, "It's so good to see you again, Jimmy. What brings you up this way?"

He handed Gloria the bottle of wine and the flowers. "These are for you. My mom taught me to never come to a party empty-handed."

"That wasn't necessary. But I think I'd like your mom," Gloria said.

Jimmy continued, "Well, life got really boring after the action we got into down there." He nodded toward me. "Thankfully, my deep cover assignment in Colombia ended with the collapse of the cartel. Anyway, I had lots of banked leave coming to me, and Eddie suggested I take some time off and come up this way for a while. So, here I am. I hope you don't mind me crashing your party."

"It's absolutely all right, buddy. You're welcome here anytime. Can I get you a beer?" I said, walking him into the backyard.

Gabby cleared her throat. "Ah, excuse me. Are you forgetting something? I'm standing right here." She had her palms turned up and an annoyed look on her face.

I turned to her and said, "Oh, for heaven's sake. I'm sorry, Gabs." In the excitement, I had forgotten about her. "Jimmy, this is our daughter, Gabby. Gabby, this is Jimmy. He's the agent I worked with in Barranquilla to get Mom back."

Jimmy stepped up to Gabby, smiled that warn confident smile of his, and shook her hand. "It's very nice to finally meet you, Gabby. I've heard a lot about you from your dad."

"And it's nice to meet the man who took care of my dad after he shipped me home."

They both briefly glanced at me and smiled.

Gabby had a twinkle in her eye. "So, Jimmy, you're the guy my dad says has lots of skills and packs a large—"

"Gabby," Gloria said, cutting her off in mock horror.

"What? I was going to say he packs a large gun," Gabby said with a coy smile.

For all his covert undercover experience and sharpshooting prowess, his cheeks still flushed pink under his tan. "Ah, yes... well... sniper rifles are rather large," he said.

"Come on, Jimmy, let's get you a cold one. It looks like you could use it." Gabby took his hand and led him to the cooler, pulled out a bottle, twisted the top off, and handed it to him.

Gloria nudged me in the ribs. "Time to get cooking, Dad. Those steaks aren't going to burn themselves."

The rest of the afternoon was filled with laughter as Jimmy settled right in with us. He and Gabby seemed to click. They spent the rest of the afternoon chatting and laughing together while I tortured the steaks on the grill, and Gloria fussed over the seating arrangements. Eddie laid back on a lounger and sipped beer with his straw hat pulled low over his face.

As the sun moved closer to the top of the side fence, I hauled the dirty dinner dishes into the kitchen. When I returned, I wrapped my arms around Gloria and kissed her.

"Do you think Jimmy and Gabby will hit it off?" I whispered in her ear.

She looked up into my eyes with a broad smile.

"What are you smiling about? You look like that Cheshire cat from *Alice in Wonderland*," I said.

She didn't say anything, just put her arms around my neck and nodded toward the far side of the yard.

I looked up in time to see Gabby and Jimmy as they vanished through the gate leading to the front of the house.

"I'd say the kids are hitting it off just fine." Gloria rose on her toes and gave me a kiss.

I gazed into her eyes. "Do the same rules about protecting our daughter apply to him?"

"Whoa, slow down, big guy. They just met. Let's not get ahead of ourselves. But yes, the same rules will apply. And if anything develops between them, I'll tell him what those rules are and the consequences of letting any harm come to her. However, you realize that won't let you off the hook. Remember, they will never find your bodies." She laughed. "Come on, let's not leave Eddie hanging by himself."

I laughed as we walked hand in hand over to join Eddie.

CHAPTER

54

Four months had passed since the end of the cartel, and the long, lazy days of late summer were wearing thin on me. Gabby and Jimmy hit it off and were well into establishing a relationship. As Gabby had suggested after the successful raid on Rodriguez's office, she applied to the Agency, and they accepted her as a new recruit. She was in her third month of training as a field agent. Coca and I had entered into a quiet appreciation of each other as he continued to grow on me. Life was good, with one exception. I was bored. I needed something to keep me busy, and I needed it in a bad way. After the action and excitement in Barranquilla, retired life was incredibly dull by comparison.

Gloria kept telling me I needed a hobby to keep me busy. I knew she was right. But what should I do? I'm not really into golf. A round or two of golf a year is about all I can manage. And fishing? That doesn't do much for me, especially after the scuba diving incident in Colombia.

Retirement is supposed to be a time to do the things you didn't have time for during your working life. Or so I was told. But for the last four months, every day was the same. Get up. Have a cup of coffee. Look around and try to figure out what to do with the rest of the day.

Then one day, I had this brilliant idea—at least it seemed brilliant to me at the time—while Gloria was off somewhere for the day. I figured I would apply my highly refined organizational skills in the kitchen. Moving stuff around to better organize our kitchen cabinets, so everything was located more logically seemed an appropriate use of my talents. When I finished, everything was more organized than before. At least, I thought so. Everything was right where it should be. It would be way more efficient and require less physical movement to access plates, cups, knives, forks, spices, herbs, pots, and pans. I was ecstatic. I had finally found my calling and a hobby I could work with. Sitting back at the kitchen counter, sipping a beer and marveling at my handiwork, I pondered starting a business organizing kitchens. I didn't know if there was any money in doing that, but that didn't matter. My feelings of accomplishment had restored a sense of purpose in my life.

Those feelings lasted until a few minutes after Gloria returned home. I was in the den when all hell broke loose in the kitchen. I clearly remember her saying, "If you ever touch my cupboards again, there'll be hell to pay."

Well, that was enough for me. Gloria never made empty threats. It was time to find another hobby.

Recently a friend told me about a memoir-writing group she belonged to. She said it would be a fun way to explore my life experiences and write about some of my adventures. So I thought, what the hell? Why not try writing? After all, how hard could it be? I was pretty sure clicking away on a keyboard would be a piece of cake compared to the actual field experiences I could write about. I also figured this would be an excellent opportunity to join a group to learn about writing and how to craft my memoirs. But like many things in life, the reality was very different from what I had imagined.

About a month after joining Tammy's Online Memoir Writing Group, I was ready to kick the computer and pull my hair out.

This writing stuff was way more challenging than anything I had ever done. Tammy and the other members of the group were really supportive, though. They said things like, "Just type one word after another, and pretty soon, you'll have your story out."

Yeah, right? Maybe writing came easily for them. But I must have missed that class in school. After working on my memoir for over a month, I started to think English might be my second or third language and not my primary one. Nothing sounded right. You see, I'm not exactly a great communicator. Sure, I can order meals and drinks in three different languages if I have to. As an example, I'm pretty fluent in British. "I'll have a pint of Guinness. Cheers, mate." Or in American, "I'll have the ribeye steak, medium rare, and a lite beer. Thanks, buddy." Or in Mexican, "Un margarita por favor, no salt. Gracias, amigo."

I realize those aren't three official languages, but you know what I mean. Anyway, this writing thing is a whole different beast. Sitting at the laptop, hour after hour, staring at a blank screen is brutal. My shoulders and neck ached from being hunched over the keyboard. Calluses formed on my index fingers as I methodically hunted and pecked to find the right keys. But, I gotta tell you, spellcheck is a godsend.

Even now, deep into the first draft of my memoir... well, deep into the fourth rewrite of page one, it isn't going quite as smoothly as I thought it would. As a former special agent, I was a man of action and spontaneity. My job had clear guidelines and parameters. Get in, get out, and go home. Or find and secure the asset. And sometimes, find and neutralize the problem. It was never about how to compose something grammatically correct in the English language?

I was well into another afternoon of staring at the blank screen and doing everything except writing when the phone rang.

A few moments later, Gloria came into the den and said, "It's Mastermind. She wants to know if we're available for a brief trip to Peru. I told her I could go but that you were having too much fun writing your memoirs."

Funny girl, that Gloria.

I slammed the laptop closed and put Mastermind on speakerphone.

A trip to Peru on the government's dime was just what I needed. It turns out someone was stealing ancient Incan treasures to help fund the possible insurrection of the Peruvian Government. The Agency believes the looters have links to illegal weapons trafficking. They wanted to get experienced agents on the ground down there to provide some recognizance. The mission would be strictly a tourist-type operation—observe and report—with no actual engagement. Mastermind thought Gloria and I, a retired couple on vacation, would provide the perfect cover.

This would be a simple assignment and the perfect tonic for a soul lost in retirement. But, like writing memoirs, I had no idea how wrong I would be.

Please turn the page for a preview of
Peter B. Dunfield's next novel;

THE JAKE STONE FILES

A COVERT ACTION THRILLER SERIES

STONE-COLD REBELLION

Available November 2023

CHAPTER

1

All hell broke loose just after 02:00 a.m. A massive explosion rocked our taxi as we entered the main square. Flames and smoke blasted from the colonial-style hotel opposite the Government Palace, the official seat of the Peruvian Government. Rock and glass fragments shot out across the grassy park between the two buildings as the fourth floor disintegrated. The vehicle swerved hard, jumped the curb, and screeched to a stop on the sidewalk.

Gloria snapped to attention beside me. "What happened?"

I stared at the devastation. "Our hotel just blew up."

Gloria leaned across the back seat, looked through my window, and uttered words I'm sure no tourist has ever spoken, "Thank God for the delays at the airport."

Our flight arrived in Lima an hour later than scheduled. Then it took us another two hours to get our luggage and clear customs. By all rights, we should have been sound asleep in our fourth-floor room at *The Hotel del a Mision.*

Noticeably shaken, Manuel, our driver, turned in his seat and asked, "Are... are you hurt?"

Above the roar of fire and sirens, I leaned forward and said, "No, we're okay."

"I... I don't think you will be staying there tonight, Senor. Let me take you to another hotel, so we can get away from here before the police arrive and block the roads."

Good idea.

He jammed the vehicle into drive and floored it. The taxi bounced off the sidewalk and over the curb. Then, with tires screeching, he pulled a u-turn and left the square. Behind us, the inferno grew, casting an eerie red glow in the night.

Manuel carefully navigated the cab through clusters of people as they rushed into the street to get a better view of all the excitement. Emergency vehicles with flashing red and blue lights raced toward us as we fled the area. If we had remained at the scene any longer, we would never have gotten out of there. Five minutes later, the taxi pulled up to the entrance of a decent-looking place several blocks from the site of the blast. A few people gathered around the front doors, staring in the direction we had come from.

He turned to us and said, "I think they will have a room for you here. Is this all right, Senor?"

"Yes, thank you, Manuel." I paid him the fare and slipped him an extra twenty bucks as a tip.

Gloria and I grabbed our luggage and pushed through the agitated crowd. Some wore only bathrobes—obviously shaken out of their sleep by the explosion and sirens. As we entered, a night clerk followed us to the front desk. Another group of anxious-looking people stood around the lobby, peeking through the front windows, trying to see what was happening outside. I was relieved when the clerk let us know a room was available, even though we didn't have a reservation.

I tossed my luggage on the bed and pulled the curtains back from the window of our room. In the distance, the orange glow of flames lit the billowing smoke rising in the night sky above the squat stone structures of the downtown core. Flashing lights lit the street, and sirens wailed as firetrucks, ambulances, and police cruisers streamed past. The timing of the blast put my senses on high alert. I shook my head as I tried to process what had happened and how narrowly we'd missed being blown up.

I turned from the window. Gloria had changed into jeans and a dark hoodie. I checked the alarm clock beside the bed. "It's 03:00 a.m. Are you going somewhere?"

"Absolutely. Aren't you curious about what happened back there?"

"Well yeah, for sure. But don't you think it can wait until the morning?"

Gloria glanced at me as she straightened her top. "No. We should get back over there and see what's going on. This could be connected to our mission."

She was right and obviously had the same concerns I was wrestling with.

Our mission was to come to Peru as tourists, discretely monitor, and report to the agency about the situation we found here. The agency believed an anarchist group was plotting an insurrection to bring down the Peruvian Government, an essential ally of the USA. Over the last several weeks, the vigilante splinter group had created mischief at various sites around the country as they increased the frequency of their anti-government protests. Until tonight, those protests were mostly peaceful, with the police and military disbanding the protestors and arresting those who resisted. However, if the explosion was a deliberate attack, it could signal a significant escalation into violence.

Of course, it was still too early to tell if it was a targeted attack or an accident. My bet was on the attack scenario. Were Gloria and I the intended targets? If so, who else other than agency members knew we would be there?

I quickly changed into dark jeans, a baseball cap, and a hoodie. Then we headed for the stairs and down to the street.

The closer we got to the square, the more surreal everything looked. The buildings along the streets were lit with the fire's undulating crimson glow, mixed with the flashing lights of emergency vehicles. Police were busy setting up barricades to prevent pedestrians and vehicle traffic from entering the area. Crowds jostled for positions to get better views behind the police lines. We took an indirect approach, going down a side street to avoid the police. Our route took us behind the massive Cathedral de Lima. The hotel and park came into view as we approached the cathedral's front edge.

It was like a scene from hell. I held the edge of my hoodie over my nose to filter out the acrid stench of smoke curling down from the fourth floor. Crews had set up portable lighting to increase visibility and support the emergency responders. Firefighters and paramedics rushed into the building and escorted injured people onto the street to a mobile critical care unit. A row of black body bags lay on the lawn amongst the shattered glass and stone rubble. Workers labored to load them into a large van before taking them to the morgue for identification and processing.

The reality of the situation wasn't lost on me. As I stared at the body bags, a sense of relief overtook me as Gloria's comment about the airport delays rushed through my mind.

We stayed in the shadows of the cathedral and blended into a small crowd behind a barricade. The consensus of those around us was that the Incan Liberation Army was responsible for the attack. This was the same group the agency suspected of planning to overthrow the Peruvian Government, liberate the Incan people from the oppression of the democratically elected government and restore Peru to pre-colonial rule.

Over the next three hours, we watched the frenzied activity of the emergency crews. As the first light of dawn swept aside the inky black of night above the buildings in the central core of Lima, a new energy settled over the square. The fast-paced coordinated actions of the disaster response slowed. The casualties and body bags were gone, and the fire was extinguished. Residual smoke and steam continued to rise into the early morning sky. Exhausted firefighters sat slumped on the grass in the park as they tried to make sense of what they had just gone through.

As daylight increased, the crowds thinned, and it was time for Gloria and me to leave before we drew unwanted attention. So we slipped back around the cathedral and headed toward our new hotel.

Once we were back in our room, I would contact Mastermind and advise her about what had happened. She would undoubtedly already have some intel from other sources and the media. But more importantly, I had to ask her about the potential of a leak at the agency. If we were the intended targets, then I needed to know who else could be involved and why.

ABOUT THE AUTHOR

Peter B. Dunfield is a retired safety professional. Peter lives in Parksville, British Columbia, on the west coast of Canada. During the winter, he resides in Loreto, Baja California Sur, Mexico, on the Sea of Cortez.

Stone-Cold Vengeance: A Covert Action Thriller is Peter's first book in the series, The Jake Stone Files.

Other novels by Peter include *Pirates' Gold, The Magic Realm, and Jack Through Time* in the Middle-Grade Storyline Adventure Series.

Peter's books are available through online vendors such as https://amazon.com/author/peterbdunfield or his website https://peterbdunfieldauthor.ca

Printed in Great Britain
by Amazon

50628215R00182